I0672687

The Legend of Three I'd Billy

Lost Souls of Paradise, Volume 2

Ian Ritchie Stewart

Published by Ian Ritchie Stewart, 2025.

This is a work of fiction. Similarities to real people, places, or events are entirely coincidental.

THE LEGEND OF THREE I'D BILLY

First edition. November 1, 2025.

Copyright © 2025 Ian Ritchie Stewart.

ISBN: 978-1735302232

Written by Ian Ritchie Stewart.

Table of Contents

Dedicated to Rear Admiral Dr. Bertram S. Brown, for his support, inspiration and friendship. Here's to you, Grand Master. I hope I passed the audition.

This evening, I walked over to the historic seaport, past the turtle cannery, out on the dock behind the Dockmaster's office, and sat in the old rickety green chair that stays hidden behind the ice machine, always waiting to serve my need for a seaside repose. That's where I go to watch the tall ships sail out of the harbor on their nightly sunset celebratory cruises, loaded to the gunnels with vacationing tourists, drunk on a day of margaritas, beer, and cheap wine. That's where I go to watch the funnel clouds begin their stretch toward the surface of the sea, where my sunset begins, and where I go to sort through the constant stream of inspirations that seemingly roll, like waves, across my mind. Tonight, one of those inspirations refused to wash back into the dark abyss from which it came! It's demand, this tale be told! Welcome to "The Legend of Three I'd Billy"!

Ian Ritchie Stewart

1. BREAKFAST AT SCHOONER'S

"Good morning, Dr. Colburn!"

"Oh, good morning, Sandy," Dr Colburn responded, delighted to be greeted so warmly by the morning clerk standing behind the counter, at the Key West Gallion Resort.

"Are you headed over to Schooners for their "Terrific Tuesday" breakfast?" She asked with a smile as she slid her completed stack of nightly reconciliations across the marble countertop and out of her way.

He chuckled with fondness for the way she seemed to always know just how to greet the Gallion's residents and guests with the warmth and sincerity one would expect to receive at such a classy resort. "Now, how did you know I was headed to Schooner's?" He reached to grab a complimentary copy of *The Citizen Newspaper* from the end of the counter, and added, "Not much on the schedule for today, and you know, I do love their dockside breakfasts."

"Well, have a good one, and be careful! The fog's just as thick as it was yesterday! One misstep could land you in the water!" She warned.

"Thanks, Sandy, I will!" He turned and walked through the heavy glass doors, then stepped outside and into the covered breezeway. There was a thickness to the air! It seemed heavier than expected. He hesitated, then pulled his arms closer to his body, as if there was a need to protect himself against invasion from some ghostly force. He walked through the parking garage and over to his fog-engulfed roadster, then stopped to reconsider the risk of driving in such conditions.

Doctor Colburn often walked from his condo, at the Key West Gallion Resort, along the historic harbor, to the Schooners Wharf Bar and Grill. It was an immensely pleasurable and stressless walk! It availed him opportunities for friendly engagement with familiar island faces and memories of his last days of walking the picturesque, historical docks with his beautiful wife, Amelia, on the last evenings before her tragic death.

"You aren't thinking of driving, are you?" Her voice seemed so real to him! He had spent the past two years trying to convince himself that he should not continue expecting to hear it, but he was a haunted man! How could he will against such a powerful expectation when it was fueled by such an intense love, as the one he held for her? He shoved his key fob back in his pocket, turned into the fog, and walked toward the harbor at the end of Front Street.

Visibility was twenty feet or less, as he stepped over the curb and turned toward the wooden dock that led along the Historical Seaport Harbor Walk. He leaned against the stucco wall of the Key West Treasure Shop, and peeked through the window to see if Laney might be setting up for the upcoming day's shoppers. The first cruise-ship passengers disembark their ships at Mallory Square by 9 am, and then start filtering through the island's narrow streets in search of their "perfect" souvenir. Most find satisfaction in the open-air tee-shirt shops that clog the roads and alleys closest to the ships, but the more experienced island-hoppers ignore the tourist traps and make a beeline for the historic district. That's where the real treasures lie hidden! He tapped gently on the glass to get Laney's attention. She looked up from behind the display case and threw a kiss into the air with a wide sweeping swish of her arm and a bright smile on her face. He captured her gesture with his hand, as it popped through the glass, placed his fingertips over his lips, then silently blew its return. She clasped her hands over her heart and waved good day to her friend, then returned to her duties.

"Wow! You really are enjoying this single life thing!" His imagination was predetermined to find her filling in the pauses between his thoughts. It had stopped being bothersome to him long ago! Now, he expected it. "You know very well, she's happily married," he smiled as he fantasized Amelia wrapping her hand around his, while they turned the corner of the A & B Lobster House. A full two years could not erase the memory of the last time they walked this walk together. His memories were her ticket to immortality, and he knew it well.

The fog hung like smoke in the windless, tropical air! A faint and unfamiliar pulsation caught his attention as he walked over to the railing and squinted into the grey abyss that had engulfed the bight. What was this pulsing? It felt like a heartbeat! Maybe some alarm designed to alert boat captains of an unseeable threat hidden by the fog! Closer attention revealed it to be blinking lights! First red, then blue, then red, then blue! Red! Blue! He determined that the lights were, most likely, coming from a police car on the other side of the marina. Apparently, there was some trouble being attended to by the Key West boys in blue. Dr. Colburn was acquainted with many of the officers who worked on the Island's police force, and he had become close friends with Officer Carl Dixon and his wife, Barbara. He turned and resumed his walk toward Schooner's, expecting that whatever the event on the dock might be, would probably make it into the next edition of *The Citizen* newspaper.

"Mornin' Walt! We got room for one more if you wanna join us!" Captain Bob Bowmann and his first mate were getting ready for the day's charter when the doctor's image broke through the fog. *Daddy's Hooker* was a 1999, 50ft Viking Convertible with a 25ft tuna tower, powered by two German-made 1050 Man diesel engines, and a sight to behold when underway. It was the largest charter boat docked in the Key West Bight harbor, and Captain Bob was one of the most experienced charter boat captains this side of Islamorada. That said, his greatest professional ambition had nothing to do with fishing! Nope! His greatest professional ambition would be outliving the humiliation that has haunted him since that afternoon he clipped the last three granite boulders of the breakwater while steering to avoid a collision with one of the Fury's Sunset Party boats loaded with tourists. Hindsight has convinced him that sinking a Fury boat full of drunken tourists might be easier to skirt the blame of, than enduring the shame of causing the harbor to be closed while the dock master and his crew repaired the damage. Dr. Colburn approached the open dock box behind the Hooker and grinned as he looked down at the two men standing on the back of the boat and replied, "Thanks, Bob, but not today. I've got to filet about two dozen reports as soon as I get back from breakfast. Some of us have to actually work ta eat, ya know!"

"Ok, Doc! You're always welcome to join us, anytime you want"! Captain Bob and his mate were shoveling ice into the Hooker's catch box as Dr. Colburn turned, then headed further down the dock toward Schooner's Wharf.

"Hey," Amelia's voice ricocheted through his brain, "there's the lobster boat where that white pelican was hanging out while we ate dinner. Remember?"

He stopped to reflect on that night! Two years earlier, while they dined at The Conch Republic Seafood restaurant, they had watched this same lobster boat being unloaded of its day's harvest. A white pelican stood on a piling, watching the fishermen stacking lobster-filled boxes on the dock. The reflection of the lights dancing across the water made the scene surrealistic! He strolled past the very table where they had sat, and imagined the two of them toasting to their wonderful life. "Yes dear, I remember everything!"

The pulsating lights were less pronounced as the fog began to burn off! Visibility was improving! He crossed the brick-paved promenade that stretched from the Conch Republic Seafood Company restaurant over to the stairs to the dock that runs along the waterfront side of Jimmy Buffett's Key West recording studio, *Shrimpboat Sound*.

JIMMY BUFFETT – KEY WEST HEART CONCERT
The Southernmost City's Favorite Son Performs Surprise Concert for the
2011 *Parrotheads in Paradise* Convention

He had read the news article two days earlier, while sitting on his balcony, enjoying his coffee and listening to the sounds of another beautiful Sunday morning in paradise. "Now, that's what I'd call a tribute," he thought, as he gained on the top stair of the deck and gazed across the display of Buffett-esque memorabilia that had been lovingly laid against the harbor-facing wall of the studio, by the fans that had attended the annual convention.

In August of 1979, Amelia and he had flown out to Denver to see Jimmy play at the Red Rocks Amphitheater. The trip was their first wedding anniversary present, given to them by her older brother Cameron. He, at that time, was the road manager for Jimmy and had attended the show with them. It was the second night of his *Volcano* tour, and after the show, Jimmy signed a T-shirt and a copy of his new album for Amelia. For years, that shirt was the most valuable thing she owned. Now, the memory of her dancing across their Chicago apartment's living room floor, in that tee-shirt, to Jimmy's song *Dreamsicle*, was like falling headfirst off a cliff. This was a hard fall! He hadn't been hit like that in over a year.

Leaning against the railing, he struggled to recover his breath, and slowly scanned through the assemblage of articles that had been lovingly placed on the dock, from one end of the building to the other. Album covers, flip-flops, tennis shoes, salt shakers, license plates, tee shirts, ball caps with shark fins on top, a mug full of guitar picks, candles, photos, flowers, six packs of beer, and at least a dozen bras had been left as solemn tributes to the troubadour of tropicality. He's touched so many souls with his music and stories. This kind of adoration seemed to be well deserved! Walter took a deep breath, gathered his composure, then turned toward his destination.

"Hi, Dr. Colburn! Would you like to sit in the upper level, inside, where the fog won't be so thick?" Jeannie had become familiar with the doctor as one of her breakfast regulars. She lived about a mile offshore, in the mooring field, where several of her neighbors had been helped by the programs that Dr. Colburn oversaw at the Depoo Hospital's Homeless Services outreach center. After six years of living on her 33-foot Neptunian ketch, she knew more about what it took to survive in paradise than anyone you might meet, anywhere!

"Oh, thanks, Jeannie! That would, probably, be a lot more comfortable!" He followed her across the sandy floor, past the bar, and into the heavily fortified dining room. Historically, the building was an icehouse, where the local shrimpers stored their famous Key West pinks, awaiting transport to the processing facilities five miles away, on Stock Island. The building had also been used regularly as overflow storage for the Key West turtling industry! When the turtle kraals (corrals) were filled to capacity, live sea turtles were slid, on their backs, along the dock from the cannery to the ice-house, then stacked upside-down, three deep, inside, until their time for harvesting. Few patrons of Schooner's Wharf Bar were privy to these morsels of antiquity, but Dr. Colburn had an insatiable appetite for history, especially Key West history!

"Who's in the kitchen today?" the doctor asked.

"Oh, it's Marty! He's by himself for breakfast. Calvin's on clean-up!"

"Do you know if he has any cheese grits?" Dr. Colburn asked.

"Oh sure! He always has a pot of grits. He cheeses them to order!"

"Could you ask him for some, with a half-dozen pinks chopped into bits? He fixed them like that last week, and they were spectacular!"

Jeannie laughingly responded, "He used to work at Burger King, and you know what their motto is. He tells it like a joke, 'Have it Your Way, YOU SHEL-FISH THING'," She reached to grab his menu as he responded, "Yeah that's what I love about this place. I always get it my way." As Jeannie took his menu, she asked, "What else can I get you?"

He finished his order with a smile, "wheat toast, turkey bacon, and coffee."

"You bet! We'll get right on it", she said as she turned and headed toward the kitchen.

Minutes later, she returned with his coffee, and he asked, "You wouldn't happen to know what's going on over toward the Turtle Museum, would you?"

Jeannie answered, "Well, we think somebody was hurt on the dinghy dock. The police have been there since sunrise! Calvin rode his bike past the EMS truck, on his way to work, and told me that its back doors were wide open and someone was inside, on a stretcher." She kept talking as she moved from table to table, arranging silverware and checking the condiment levels as she talked, "He said that the EMS guys were standing outside! That means to me that whatever happened can't be very good!" She slid the north-facing heavy door open, wide enough to see if the fog had improved, then continued, "When I motored in this morning, there was a COP on the dinghy dock stopping people from tying up. He directed me over to the Simonton Street pier, and it took half an hour to find it in the fog. I got here a little bit late, but nobody cares."

"And no idea who's involved?" Dr Colburn asked.

"No, not at all! We're all anxious to find out." She slid the door closed, turned toward his table, and continued, "There's only one other dinghy that ever pulls in ahead of me, and that's Marva Andersen's! She brings her daughters, Mya and Delcia, in on weekdays. They ride their bikes to the Montessori School on the other side of the Island. I think that's on United Street! Anyway, it can't be Marva. She and the girls are up in Sarasota visiting Marva's mother. She's in the hospital having her colostomy reversed! I got a text from Marva yesterday! They're fine! I don't even know why I told you all that." She reopened the heavy door, peeked out, then closed it again and said, "I'm sorry, Dr. Colburn, I'll go check on your order."

"It's fine, Jeannie! I understand!" Dr. Colburn pulled his phone from his pocket and began reviewing the news of the day.

The police lights were slicing through the narrow gaps around the wooden doors, periodically catching his attention and redirecting his thoughts to what might be going on just three hundred fifty feet east of his table. They were refracted into the restaurant from two directions. First, from the parking area behind the loading zone of the Municipal Services building, where the many mooring field residents use the city facilities for their laundry, showers, and bathroom needs. Another set of lights came from the Dock Master's conch and concrete dock area, where the turtlers, historically, pulled their carts beside the turtle boats to offload their catch. Dr Colburn was familiar with the layout! He wondered if the victim might be one of his clients and in need of his assistance. He determined that after breakfast, he would walk over to see if he could help.

Jeannie had just set Dr. Colburn's plate on the table when Calvin's voice bellowed from the sundeck above the icehouse. "Oh My God! I know who it is! It's Billy! Shit! That's Billy's dinghy!" Jeannie was in an instantaneous panic as she jumped to the harbor-facing door and pushed it open. "Are you sure?" She called out as she strained to see as deep as possible through the waning fog. Calvin was at the railing, directly above her. From his raised vantage point, visibility across the dock was less obscured, and he called down with confidence, as he described what he was witnessing, "There's a police evidence van with a flat-bed trailer hooked on the back! It's parked over on the turtle dock! I just saw four cops pull Billy's dinghy out of the water and carry it up the gangway to the van. They put it on the trailer." He hesitated, and softened his voice as he said, "Jeannie," he paused as he choked on his next words, "There's blood! All over it!"

2. OLD FRIENDS REUNITE

By the time Dr. Colburn had finished breakfast and paid his tab, the fog conditions had improved immensely. He stood just inside the harbor facing doorway, and looked across the expanse of docked sailboats, and out toward the Gulf of Mexico. After exiting through the decorative archway, he crossed the wooden dock, then leaned over the railing to look down into the crystal clear water. A school of silver kings was gliding in and out of view from under the boats, anticipating the feast of discarded fish trimmings that would be tossed into the water under the cleaning station at the end of the day. A party-boat, loaded with tourists, rounded the breakwater, then turned West toward the Sand Key lighthouse, where they would be enjoying a few hours of snorkeling on the reef. Dr. Colburn mulled through the developments he had just witnessed and recognized how deeply Billy's death would soon be impacting many of his clients. Though he had never met the man, he had regularly heard of his generous contributions to the needs of the less fortunate in the community. Helping them through their grief would be a daunting task, and as he turned toward the dinghy dock, he wondered if he had the necessary chops to accomplish the job at hand.

Death was no stranger to Dr. Walter Arlin Colburn. The sound of its knocking had been a familiar rhythm throughout his life. No one had yet confirmed that Billy was dead, but as he stood watching the officers removing their caution tape and hosing the blood off the dock, he could feel Death's sacred cadence as it proved its veracity. There was only one reasonable summation: death had once again come ashore in Old Key West.

"Excuse me," he called out as he approached the two police officers standing at the closed back door of the Key West Turtle Museum. "I'm Dr. Walter

Colburn with the Depoo Hospital Mental Health Outreach Center," he introduced himself as he handed one of them his business card.

"I happened to be watching from the restaurant as your team addressed this morning's incident, and I thought you might want to have my contact information available, in case anyone you run into appears to need psychiatric attention."

One of the officers was reading the doctor's card as the other reached to shake his hand and said, "Yes sir! I met you over a year ago at the Spanish Garden motel on Simonton Street. I was one of the officers with Stookerelly!" The frown on Dr. Colburn's brow betold his failure to remember the officer's face.

"You had breakfast with five of us over at Camille's! I remember that you ordered the Eggs Galore omelet with Caribbean Hollandaise sauce. That's my favorite!" The officer was grinning like a kid as he told the story.

"Oh, I remember now! Great to see you again," Dr. Colburn was focused on the seriousness of the events at hand and redirected the conversation by addressing his concern for the community. "If you don't mind, could you please pass my phone number to any of your officers who might chance to come in contact with any of Billy's friends. I think there are going to be a lot of people suffering over his passing."

The older of the officers raised his eyebrows and said, "I'm sorry, Dr. Colburn, but we haven't identified anyone as being deceased! What happened here today is under investigation by the detectives, and any release of information will have to come from them!"

"Oh! Of course! I understand fully," the psychiatrist responded. "Well, thank you for everything, and don't forget, if anyone needs anything, my staff and I are available 24/7!" The three men shook hands, and Dr. Colburn turned toward the main dock from where he had come.

"Hey, Dr. C.!" As he stepped into his turn, someone called out from a small boat that was pulling up to the dinghy dock, fifty feet away. "What are you doing out here?" The young man called out as he jumped from his boat to the floating dock and began tying its rope to a cleat.

"Oh! Hey, Cai," the Dr. answered. "Breakfast! At Schooner's! Fantastic!" He kept his pace and threw a thumbs-up, hoping the young man would honor his intention to avoid engagement with clients when outside of the office.

Cai's voice faded as the doctor kept walking. The name, Cai, was short for Cairo, the Egyptian city! That was his place of birth! He was a card-carrying, certified member of The Key West Circle of Psychos! And everyone knew it!

As Dr. Colburn approached the entrance to the Schooner's Wharf bar, he heard the voices of several people engaged in an emotional discussion of what had taken place on the dinghy dock. The fog had almost completely cleared, and the sun was steaming out the moisture trapped in the cracks of the dock planking as he stepped into visibility.

"Oh, there's Dr. C.," Jeannie called to him. "Please!" She stepped through the doorway, onto the dock, and pulled him by the arm. "What did they say? Is he OK?" she asked, as she led him across the sand-covered patio to the edge of the stage where Calvin, Marty, Devin, the lead singer of the Schooner's Wharf house-band, *Devin McCollum and Slack Tide*, and two of his band's members were gathered.

"I really wish I could tell you something, but they wouldn't confirm or deny who it was, nor if there was a death. They did say that it was being investigated by detectives, though!". He felt uncomfortable, cornered, outside of his realm of comfort. He nervously leaned toward the trellised entrance, waiting for a pause that might offer him a convenient time to exit, then Jeannie tossed out a question that caught his attention and sparked his curiosity. She turned to Devin and asked, "Didn't Billy play with you guys last night?"

"Yeah! He did!". Devin took a deep swig from his coffee cup, then added, "He's been filling in for Tommy every night for a week now. Tommy's got an inguinal hernia and can't stand up without passing out from the pain. Billy set him up with a doctor in Miami to do the surgery. He was planning to drive him up there next week to get it done. I guess everything's gone to shit, now!"

Dr. Colburn graciously excused himself on the pretense of professional demands, which did NOT exist, and resumed his walk back to the Gallion.

It was a six-step rise, from the walk along Lazy Way to the bypass deck that bridged the east to west ends of Jimmy Buffett's studio. He placed his right hand on the railing and his left foot on the first stair. Then, as he pulled himself toward the next step, that's when it began to hit him.

"Oh, God! No, not here!" It started in the back of his head, under his hair, and moved like a waterfall, washing over his body. The feeling cascaded down his skin, then penetrated deeply into his nervous system, and morphed from a vibration into a shaking sensation. He felt weak, then dizzy and nauseous! He abandoned his climb and turned to sit on step number two.

"Walter, dear, you really need to deal with this, NOW!". He imagined her whispering in his ear, consoling his feeling of ineptitude over his dealings with death. "These people are going to need the best of what you have to offer! Sooner or later, you have got to come to grips with it." Amelia always knew how to tie off his mooring lines. He sat, dumbfounded, glaring into the chinked and tortured planking that had led him to this sacred spot and considered how deeply this loss would impact the people that he had accepted the charge of leadership for.

"May I take the helm for a moment?" She whispered from inside his head.

"Sweetheart, I need you to do that like never before!" he thought, as he fought to keep the words from spilling over his lip. It seemed imperative to him that he resolve all his personal grievances with loss before he tried to rescue others from the kind of crushing bereavement that would soon be washing over their lives.

"It's all there, inside of you!" She coaxed his thoughts toward her persuasion.

"What?" He tripped into the memory of her voice.

"The answers you're looking for! Trust me! What you were just feeling! That weakness, that feeling like you were going to fall off the dock, that lightheadedness, that instability. Your body is trying to get your attention! It's in the beat of your heart! It's deep in your brain! In your blood! It's even the breath as you let it out! It's all screaming at you! Listen!"

"OK, Yeah!" He started to pay attention to his thoughts as they conjured up their response, "Yea, yeah! Every time I have to deal with issues of death, I feel these feelings. I feel threatened! Chased! Like I'm about to be eaten alive! Like I can't run fast enough, and there's no switch to turn it off! Like what I'm running from might destroy me."

Amelia offered some sympathetic advice with, "All you can do, Walter, is stop in your tracks and take as many breaths as you need till the fog clears. Don't move till the fog clears! Stay put till all the fog clears."

"That's right," he thought.

It seemed the perfect place to sort through his thoughts. The stair! The second stair to the studio of Key West's favorite son. One breath, two breaths. Deeper, in! Now, out! It was therapeutic, and he knew it.

He leaned onto his knees and closed his eyes. He tasted the salty mist of the fading fog and the sweetness of broken coconuts that lay on the ground as he continued slowly breathing in the air.

"What was that?" he thought.

"What was what?" she pushed into his imagination.

"That thing! The one that always knocks me off my feet?" He was searching through his history of seemingly unanswerable questions that had haunted him since childhood.

"Which thing?" she asked.

"The one that always knocked me down!"

"Oh, that's simple!" He imagined her hand gently stroking his cheek as her voice whispered through his thoughts, "It's death! It's the thought of death. The possibility that death might find you before you walk from this end of the dock to the other. It's fear! It's the fear that death is the final truth, and you can't argue it away. You can't negotiate with its constant, always present, never compromising threat. Billy and I faced it! Tasted its kiss! Bought it hook, line and sinker! You only fear it, every aspect of it! Now, you're afraid you won't have the courage to lead your clients through their own fear."

He took another deep breath and exhaled, slowly, as he considered the hidden realities that were coming to light. Amelia poked his embers with one last thought, "The survival of mankind has always been tied to his instinctual understanding that death would be his final truth, and, as futile as it may seem, fear has always been his only argument against it!"

She mused deeper, "Those feelings, that weakness, that feeling like you were going to fall off the dock, that lightheadedness, that instability. It's your version of a self-engineered punishment!"

Dr. Colburn's thoughts began to wander back, two years, to the death of his wife, when they were on vacation in Key West. She had suffered an aneurysm while snorkeling in the lagoon out at Fort Jefferson, just seventy miles west of where he was now sitting.

"You know, it wasn't your fault!!" She offered. "It wasn't your decision to go out there!" He was remembering the day they had taken that boat ride out to the old fort. He had said that the sun exposure was too dangerous that day. She had insisted that his fascination with history was worth a little burn. She was snorkeling in the shallow waters, just beyond the fort's south coaling dock ruins, when she collapsed. "It just happened," she insisted. "It could have as easily happened in the hotel pool!" He realized the truth in her suggestion, but these feelings of guilt are sometimes as hard to dislodge from a fractured heart as the feeling of despair.

"Remember Nanna Mae?" Amelia probed. "Remember where she was buried?" He was twenty when his father's mother died. They were deeply connected! Her death was immensely traumatic for him! So traumatic that he blocked out the memory of her entire memorial service. He has never been able to bring to memory the funeral procession, or her graveside ceremony. No thanks to the ridicule he suffered from his brother, he has felt guilty ever since.

"What happened to Thumper?" That thought had not been in his head since the time he had told her about his childhood pet rabbit and how he had accidentally caused its death.

"I was six!" he said to himself as he stretched his legs and rose to resume his climb up the stairs.

Standing now, on the upper deck bypass to Jimmy Buffett's studio, he began to revisit one of the most impactful and painful events he had ever experienced. "We had two rabbits! I don't remember the name of Lenord's, but mine was Thumper. Mom and Dad gave them to us for Easter! Dad built a hutch, and we used to turn them loose to run in the backyard. Our dog, Tippy, used to like to chase them, and when they were worn out, they'd stop running and play dead. Then Tippy would lick them from head to tail. It was great fun, but one day, I threw a stick to make Thumper turn toward the middle of the yard. It hit him in the head. It was horrible! I went crazy! My dad buried him behind the backyard fence. It was my stupid fault! It still hurts to think about it! I caused Thumper's death!"

"You're going to need to keep this story handy, dear," she was preparing him for what might soon become the pinnacle of his professional career.

It was a slow walk back to the Gallion! For the rest of the day, he sat on his fifth-floor balcony, staring out at Christmas Tree Island and across the beautiful expanse of the Gulf of Mexico. It was a perfect vantage point for watching the comings and goings of the people that live in the mooring field. He knew that many of them would be deeply impacted by their friend's death, and many of them would soon be knocking on his door for help. He felt the weight of the responsibility he would be shouldering and, throughout the evening, fought the doubt that sought to undermine his confidence. It was a long and sleepless night for this island psychiatrist, and the reasons were clear!

It's a tenuous hold we have on life, he thought. Tenuous at best!

3. DR. GRANT CALLING

"**D**r. Colburn, there's a call for you on line one, from a doctor Grant in Washington, D.C. He insists on waiting." Rosa handed the doctor a clipboard with his Wednesday schedule and the most current admissions list, as he passed her desk. "Oh, and Jillian called! She'll be in late again!"

His door snapped closed behind him as her words ricocheted back to her desk. His heart skipped a beat as his memory raced back, more than forty years, in anticipation of hearing the voice of his old boss. "Thank you, Rosa," he called out as he dropped the clipboard next to the load of files on his desk and picked up the phone receiver.

"I can't believe it! Marcus, is it really you?" He said as he slid into his desk chair and reset the height, which, as usual, had been changed by Jillian after he had left for the evening on the day before. He knew it was her way of letting him know she had been in the office, even though she had not been there during "working" hours.

"Is this the same genius doctor Colburn that used to show up late to my Wednesday morning staff meetings?" Dr. Colburn smiled broadly as he listened to the voice of his long-ago mentor and friend, Dr. Marcus S. Grant. What a thrill it was to be hearing that beautiful voice in his ear again. He had worked for almost seven years under Dr. Grant's directorship at the NIMH (National Institute of Mental Health) and owed much of his earliest professional experience to the training and leadership he had provided.

"My lord, it's so good to hear your voice, Marcus! How are you, old friend?" Dr. Colburn leaned back in his chair and ran his hand through his thinning white hair as he staged himself for what he hoped might be a catching-up conversation. "Rosa said you were calling from Washington!"

Dr. Grant chuckled as he explained," Well, that always puts a bit of a glare in their eye, but the truth is, I'm right here in Key West, about three-quarters of a mile from you, in Old Town, sitting by my pool and sipping on a cold iced tea, with my foot propped up on a pillow. I need to talk to you about something important," Dr, Grant's voice became notably more serious as he added, "How soon can you break away?"

Dr. Colburn knew that his friend would never make such a demand without good reason, so he grabbed a pen, copied the address, and headed for his car in the parking lot. "Rosa," he said as he passed the receptionist's desk, "I've got to run an errand. I'll call you in just a bit when I know how long it'll take." There was no hesitation as he spoke. He knew something important was calling for his attention, and it could not wait.

The island traffic was always light at ten-fifteen on Wednesday mornings. The water in the Garrison Bight marina was like a mirror, reflecting the clouds that slowly billowed across the blue expanse of sky. As he pulled up to the stoplight at the intersection of Roosevelt and Palm Avenue, he placed his finger on the button in the center console and held firmly, while the top dropped into the trunk of his prized burgundy Z-4 Roadster, then accelerated around the corner.

A haggard old man on a three-wheeled bicycle, pulling a reluctant black and white dog, with two feet of tongue dragging along the scorching hot sidewalk, shouted in his direction, "That's my god damn car, you thieving son-of-a-bitch!" Dr. C. gave a smile and a back-sided wave as he glanced toward the man, then to the right at the houseboats, smoldering under the tropical summer sun.

His mind was paging backwards through years of fond memories of the days he worked inside the D.C. beltway, rushing through town from meeting to meeting. Those memories were so far in his past! What a pleasant surprise to find them nibbling their way into his mind. A quick glance to his left as he approached the bridge, he noticed that all the boat slips were empty along the dock at Charter Boat Row. On such a picture-perfect day as this, every concierge in every hotel lobby in town would have their tip jars filled by the end of the day. Gratitude, garnered generously by touristing anglers, for their well-placed bookings and their coolers full of Mahi Mahi and blackfin tuna.

Dr. Colburn drove over the bridge and toward his reunion with his old friend. He had moved to Key West just five months earlier from Chicago, after handing the sale of his apartment to his son and turning over his psychiatric practice to a young, ambitious colleague looking to break away from one of those huge, not-for-profit, government-subsidized and overly managed mental health services outfits.

The Depoo Memorial Hospital, a subsidiary of the much larger Lower Keys Medical Center Key West, had solicited his interest in assuming the directorship of their newly created Homeless Services Mental Health department. He had become acquainted with the facility, one year earlier, through a most unexpected happenstance that involved the rescue and recovery of a young, psychotic nurse named Jillian Bethany Dougherty and her newborn baby, Krismas.

Left turn on Francis, right on Southard, and there it was, 908 Southard Street. His eyes explored the privacy wall for a break in the thorny bougainvillea that would lead him to the hidden security gate that Dr. Grant had described as halfway down the block. Dr. Colburn sat patiently until the roadster's roof snapped closed, then crossed the street with a smile burning his lips in anticipation.

"It's me, I'm at the gate," Dr. Colburn called into his phone, then punched the access code into the security pad, as Dr. Grant called out the numbers. He pushed through the heavy metal gate and headed down the lushly landscaped path toward a wooden half fence that surrounded the pool area. He could hear people talking and water splashing as he reached for the latch to enter. He pushed the gate open, and was delighted to find himself face to beaming face with Darla, Dr. Grant's youngest daughter.

"Hi, Dr. Colburn," the young lady cheerfully greeted, as she took both of his hands in hers and firmly shook them up and down. "Come on in, Daddy's right over there. She turned toward the shade of the pool house, holding firmly onto his hand as she pulled him into the courtyard and cheerfully added, "he's waiting to see you." She led him across the pavers, around the shallow end of the pool, and over to her father, who rose with some difficulty from his lounge chair, and greeted his friend with great compassion and exuberance.

"Walter," the senior psychiatrist called out with delight, "You look great! It's so good to see you!"

Dr. Colburn was speechless! He choked in adoration as he embraced his friend. With the death of his wife, Amelia, such uplifting emotions had become a lost luxury. This one had popped to the surface, and he embraced it with delight! With a tear in his eye, he said, "Jesus, Marcus, you have no idea how many times I've wondered how you were doing. I am so sorry that I hadn't tried to reconnect! It was all such a painful mess! There's really no excuse" Dr. Colburn was referring to the shakeup when the National Institute of Mental Health, over which Dr. Grant had presided as director, was temporarily restructured under the NIH, (National Institute of Health), and Dr. Colburn, who since June of 1970 had been one of Dr. Grants most valued staff research psychiatrists, was reassigned as the head of the NIAAA, (National Institute of Alcohol Abuse and Alcoholism).

His reassignment had been commanded from outside the agency, and Dr. Grant was never consulted. As a direct result, valuable, groundbreaking experience was forever lost, and progress halted in the development of nationwide, community-based treatment of mental health-related programs. To say the least, many noses were jerked out of place, and though Dr. Colburn had no choice in the matter, he left behind an agency full of ill feelings.

"Listen, Walter," the senior psychiatrist explained, "I'm the one who should be apologizing, not you! I should have taken the time to explain about all the bureaucratic crap that I was dealing with back then." He leaned forward and rested his hand on his friend's shoulder. "I'm still haunted by some of those ill-advised decisions I was forced to make."

Darla had walked up to the condo and returned with a tray and two glasses of iced tea. She smiled at Dr. Colburn as she arranged the glasses on the little table next to her dad, then returned to the towel at the edge of the pool deck under a banyan tree and resumed her tai-chi exercises.

Dr. Grant straightened himself in the lounge chair and began the explanation for his call. "We will have lots of time to dredge up all that stuff, but right now, I've got to talk to you about something very important. I believe you've become familiar with a close friend of mine, Carl Dixon, over at the sheriff's office." Dr. Grant took a swig of tea while Walter confirmed the friendship, then the older psychiatrist explained, "Last night, I got a call from

Carl that has me extremely upset. It seems that one of my dearest friends met with a horrible accident yesterday morning." Tears were in the old doctor's eyes as he reached for the corner of the towel that hung on the back of his chair. As he wiped his eyes, his lower lip quivered the painful words, "He's dead!"

Dr. Colburn's sympathetic heart absorbed as much of his friend's pain as it could, and as he reached to place his hand on his shoulder, he offered his condolences, "Oh, Marcus, I'm so sorry! I know how much it must hurt! I'm so sorry!"

The older doctor courageously fought back his tears and said, "There's no time for this right now!" He rolled to one side and reached into his back pocket for his handkerchief. He fumbled to unfold it, then, with both hands, held it to his nose. "A lot of people are going to be hurting over this. We've got to get up and going right away."

Walter sat back in his chair and asked, "Was your friend the guy that the police found on the dinghy dock behind the Turtle Museum yesterday?"

"Yes! Billy was a very dear friend of mine!" Marcus answered. "Carl said he appeared to have passed out on his dinghy sometime in the night, as the fog was building. Apparently, it had floated under the dock at low tide with his head resting on the bow. By early morning, the tide had risen and the fog was thick. Billy was still asleep when the first of the commercial lobster boats headed out of the harbor, and as their waves rolled under his dinghy, they pounded his face into the underside of the dock." He choked from his grief, then added, "I just pray that he was unconscious after that first wave."

"Oh my God, Marcus, that's horrible!" Dr. Colburn listened in astonishment to his friend's description of the events that he, himself, had partially witnessed, while having breakfast at Schooner's Wharf the day before.

"I'm afraid, it gets worse!" Dr. Grant took a deep breath and let it out slowly, then continued, "If you've ever walked the dock behind the Turtle Museum, you've probably seen those white boxes that stand about three feet high. They're set about twenty-five feet apart and usually placed adjacent to the antique-looking light poles that light up the harbor walk. Well, those boxes cover up the water and power supply hook-ups that supply utilities to the boats that pay for dockage in the slips. They're each bolted to the dock by four or five long bolts. The bolts are, apparently, supposed to be cut off and filed, underneath the dock for safety, but Carl said that the contractor that installed them never came back to do the cleanup, and all the bolts are still hanging down by about four inches. Billy's face was impaled on the bolts every time a wave rolled in. It must have been horrible for everybody involved in his recovery!"

Walter's jaw was dropped throughout the entire accounting. "Marcus, I don't know what to say! This is just horrible!"

Dr. Grant was wiping his eyes while Walter searched for words that might console his old friend. They both grabbed their glasses and finished the last of their tea. As they sat recovering from the effects of Billy's story, the older psychiatrist reached into his front pants pocket and retrieved a set of keys, attached to a rubber Southern Most Point floater keychain, and tossed it onto the table top. "What are these?" Dr. Colburn asked.

"Those are the keys to a 1978 Swan 43, the *Psyched Out*. Dr. Grant was smiling as he answered. "Do you remember Senator Theodore Langford? Older fella, walked with a cane, got shot down in Korea? You remember him, don't you?"

"Yes, of course," Dr. Colburn had attended many political events and social functions during his time in Washington, and Senator Langford was a very respected and well-liked figure in his day. "I've met him many times, and his wife too!"

"Well, Theo and I became good friends in the early sixties, when I was working at the Whitehouse for President Kennedy." We met at the Norfolk Naval Sailing Center, when Jan and I had that Bermuda 40 docked over at the base marina, behind the golf course." Dr. Grant relaxed as he reminisced! "You and Amelia met us out there once! If I recall, it was in '74, when you were still working for me at the department! We sailed up to Chincoteague for lunch, then up to Cape May. You said it was your first time seeing whales! Remember that right whale, with her calf?"

Dr. Grant reached for his tea glass, giving opportunity for Walter to inject, "Marcus, I really don't want you to think I'm not enjoying getting together this morning, but I'll need to get back to the office to prep for my afternoon group session. Was there some specific issue you wanted to talk to me about?"

Dr. Grant set his glass on the table and leaned forward to pat his hand on his friend's knee, then apologized for not getting to the point of his call. "Thank you, Walter. I'm so sorry!" He took another sip from his glass, then continued, "In the sixties, I had helped Theo with a few family matters, and he always saw to it that the right ears, in Washington, were always bent in my direction while I was at the helm of the NIMH. He was a wonderful friend and an avid sailor, but because of his Korean War injuries, he couldn't handle much more than sitting at the helm and turning the wheel with his one good arm. Jan and I took Mitzi and him out on our boat as often as we could, and they eventually bought their own, and kept it two slips over from ours. Mitzi managed everything about his life, back then. When he wanted to go sailing, she would arrange for a captain and crew to handle the boat while she attended to Theo. It meant the world to him, and when he died in 1983, he left it to me in the hope that I would keep it sailing."

Darla approached once again, with two more fresh glasses of tea, patted her dad on the shoulder, removed the two empties, and headed back to their second-floor condo. The elder doctor took a sip, then continued, "In the mid-seventies, Theo and Mitzy had become deeply concerned with certain litigation that was becoming popular within the Reagan administration, that sought to dismantle all the great work that you and I had been working on since the Kennedy days. Support and funding of the national mental health programs we had built under President Kennedy, then expanded under President Johnson, was about to be cut, and all the mental health facilities that were dedicated to housing and treating patients diagnosed as dangerous to themselves or the public were going to be closed."

"I remember all that, Marcus," Dr. Colburn glanced at his watch, hoping his friend would recognize his restlessness and segue out of the history lesson and into the point of their meeting.

Dr. Grant held his index finger in the air as he continued, "I was the fall guy for all of that!" His voice cracked with emotion! "They hung every bit of it on me, and Theo watched them do it." He took another sip of tea, then sat back in his chair. "When the administration began to finalize their deinstitutionalizations, Theo and three other Senators fought like hell against it, but, as you know, we failed! Over the next thirty years, all federal mental health facilities had been closed, and the patients were kicked out onto the streets to, hopefully, fall into the sympathies of state, religious, and municipal care programs."

Walter was getting restless! He wondered if perhaps the years had caught up with his old boss. Maybe the trouble with his leg had him on medication and was causing him to be delusional. Perhaps the Twilight Zone cast was about to pop out of the bushes.

Dr. Grant noticed his discomfort and offered his final pitch. "Theo and I had started a foundation for the homeless and mentally ill patients living in the Keys. We started it back in '81, and now its assets are over sixteen million dollars! We fund everything from apartments to pup tents, diapers to dentures, shoes to shuttle rides for medical appointments. Many of the boats in the mooring field were purchased by the foundation, then donated to some of the working homeless who were trying to survive the cost of living down here." He paused for a sip of tea, then continued, "When I retired in '79, I sold our home in Arlington and moved down here full-time. A year later, we sailed the Swan down and registered her under her new name, *Psyched Out*. A good friend of mine is a retired Key West Marine Patrol Officer, and for the next eleven years, he and I sailed her out to a spot on the backside of Christmas Tree Island, where we'd drop anchor and raise a signal flag, to let everyone living on their boats in the mooring field know that I was available for counseling. There were never any charges, and until my leg turned me into a cripple, it was easy for me to climb on and off the boat. But, for the past six years, I've been in the full grip of gout, and can't even climb the stairs to my front door without calling on somebody for help. That brings me to why I called you! I need your help! I need you to be the new psychiatrist on the *Psyched Out*. If I've counted my wager correctly, tomorrow afternoon you'll be one mile offshore and open for business!"

Dr. Grant had finished his presentation and sat back in his chair, waiting for his friend's jaw to close.

"Oh, Marcus," Walter stuttered out his defense, "I don't know how to sail a boat!"

His friend replied, "Don't need to! It's got its own captain, and a crew ta boot!"

"I've got my work at Depoo," was his second excuse!

"No worries! The older doctor exclaimed. "The Depoo family and three of the hospital's board members are already on board! Besides, many of the clients you have now live out there in the mooring field! We're just moving your office closer to where they live! You'll still be seeing patients at the clinic, and making rounds over at the main hospital when needed!"

Dr. Grant struggled as he pushed himself up from the chair and gently set his injured foot in place before rising. Dr. C. rose to assist him with a stabilizing hand on his upper arm. Once up, he offered the following: "Walter, I've known where you were and what you were doing for all of these forty years. My greatest enjoyment in life has always been watching the people who worked for me climb their way up their life's ladders. When we heard that Amelia had died, Janet and I were completely devastated. We cried that whole week. I knew that someday you and I would reunite, and I would have the opportunity to tell you this. I just had no idea things would develop as they have. Unfortunately, I've got a full day of phone calls to make so we can have the infrastructure in place to start helping these people." He was now fully standing with his hand tightly on his friend's shoulder, and added, "We've got a lot of onions to peel before we can serve up this stew! Meet me at Louie's tonight for dinner, at nine, so I can bring you up to speed. Then, maybe afterward, we can spend a little time catching up. What do you think? You on board?"

Dr. Colburn was drenched in sweat and completely dumbfounded! He felt as though he had no option but to say, "I guess, yes! The doctor is IN!" The two friends embraced hardily, then Darla stepped to her father's side and, arm in arm, helped him across the pool deck, through the gate, and disappeared down the pathway, through the lush, tropical foliage. Left behind was a bewildered Chicago psychiatrist standing in the burning tropical sun, drenched in sweat and lightheaded from an encounter with his past.

He had good reason to rush back to the clinic. Wednesdays were group therapy day, and his session was due to begin at one o'clock PM. Normally, he would work on his case reviews for two hours prior to beginning, but today he was, understandably, pinched for time. It was almost noon!

He pulled into the Circle K gas station for a cup of coffee and a cheerful smile from his favorite morning team, Chris and Dawn. He left the car running and the A/C on high, locked the car door, and waved to Stan, 'The

Paintin' Man', with whom he had made acquaintance on his first day of moving to the island. Stan had panhandled five dollars from him with a story of how he was living in his broken-down van behind the gas station and was trying to save up enough money to have the carburetor rebuilt and the windshield replaced so he could go back home to Albuquerque where his mother was dying of cancer, all alone, in her paid for, two story house, that needed a paint job. The truck was still parked out back, the windshield was still shattered, it now had two flat tires, and God only knows how the mother was doing. Stan looked great though, paint splattered jeans, white Sherwin-Williams Paint logoed T-shirt, fresh pack of Marlboros rolled into one sleeve, big cup of fresh Columbian Blend coffee sitting on the top of the trashcan where Stan stood proudly, ten hours every day, ready for any painting jobs that wanted to fall in his direction.

As Dr. C. approached the glass door, Stan jerked his head back and called out, "Say doc, you wouldn't happen to have a five you could spot me? Would you?" He left his mouth half open even though the question was finished.

Dr. C. knew this posture all too well as a common ploy of manipulative engagement, meant to hold the subject indebted to respond with a helping gesture or offering. Children use this tactic as if it was crafted in the womb! One hand out, mouth open, head leaning forward, and 'plop', candy gets tossed right in the mouth. Sad thing, after every swallow, the posture is immediately resumed. Like a monkey in a zoo, he thought.

"Sorry, Stan," he replied as he held the door for two school girls on their lunch break, "I give at the office!"

Stan's mouth closed in disappointment, as he fondled the eight quarters that sat at the bottom of his pocket, waiting for the five-dollar balance that would tender him his favorite six-pack of brew.

"Hey, two times in one day? What's the occasion, Doc?" Dawn had been the store manager until a month earlier, when she decided to cut back to a clerk position. She missed having time to socialize with her clientele and hated having to boss her employees into shifts they didn't want. Now, she had it made.

"Just can't get enough of that delicious house blend you guys brew!" he said while pouring a cup, then topping it off with some cappuccino from the coffee machine. He broke line to toss two dollars on the counter as Chris smiled from behind the register. The price was a dollar seven! "See ya tomorrow!" He called out to them both as he pushed through the door. Ten minutes later, he was back at work.

"I believe you said you would call!" Rosa wore a frown as she gave him the evil eye and a crooked grin.

"Oops! Things got pushed," he said as he walked through the open office door and sat down at his desk, then asked, "Any emergencies?"

Rosa followed behind him, then stopped just inside his door and asked, "I noticed that all this week you've been leaving your computer on when you leave. Are we supposed to start doing that now?"

"Oh, no," he answered, as he searched through his desk drawer for an ink pen. "I think Jillian must be playing games on it after hours or something. I don't think it matters. Whatever keeps her busy is fine." He shuffled through the stack of files that Rosa had set on his desk, waiting for his review, then directed that she close his door while he got ready for his upcoming session.

4. GROUP

"Good afternoon, everyone," Dr. Colburn addressed the circle of patients as he dropped his notebook and pen on the little table beside his chair. Then, as he took his seat, announced, "We will be going over a few issues that we left hanging last week, then we'll open the floor for any concerns that have come up since." This was a closed ward group! The attendees were either voluntarily admitted, or ordered into treatment by court order. Two of the patients had been admitted after their initial Baker Act evaluations had proven they were a threat to themselves. Dr. Colburn and his staff structured their days and nights to keep them occupied with activities that would force them to develop constructive and acceptable ways to cope with the stresses they faced. Psychotropic medications helped to stabilize the patients as they fought to gain control of their resident demons and forge their way back to a safer and more manageable life on the outside.

Rosa had pulled the door closed, then, as soon as the latch clicked shut, it reopened, and Jillian quietly slipped into the room. She made her way to the back, where she began pouring juice into cups and rearranging the oatmeal cookies that sat on plates on the refreshment table. It was just Jillian, trying to alleviate her feelings of nervousness. Oh, and of course, in her usual way, avoiding every possibility of making eye contact with anyone.

Jill was allowed to assume the posture of "staff assistant," but in reality, she was Dr. C.'s "pet" patient. He scheduled her psychotherapy on an "as needed" basis, and for him to keep an eye on her, she was given the complete run of the clinic. Rosa held the assignment of Jillian's immediate supervisor and kept a mock work schedule on the wall behind her desk, that designated twenty hours per week for Jillian to be engaged with insignificant duties. Having a place to "be" every day kept her from withdrawing back into isolation, and her participation in the group sessions helped Dr. C. to monitor her progress. Each day at four P.M., she would walk across Kennedy Avenue to the Poinciana day-care center and bring her daughter, Krismas, back to the clinic where she would, hopefully, clean the doctors' office, the two therapy rooms, and Rosa's reception area.

Jillian had come to Key West two years earlier after graduating from Boston College and accepting her first nursing job at the Lower Keys Medical Center. Unfortunately, she had not adjusted well to being on her own in such an unfamiliar tropical environment and, after just two months on the island, she sank into a dismal episode of culture shock and had completely disappeared. Unexplainable circumstances had subsequently arranged her admittance into the care of Dr. Colburn, and let us just say that her care, and the care of her beautiful baby daughter Krismas, had fallen into the hands of a most qualified and generous doctor of psychiatry.

"Dr. Colburn, I am sorry to interrupt, but Dr. Grant is on line one, and asking for you." Rosa nervously called through the door into the therapy room. "He says it's urgent!"

"It's ok Rosa!" Dr. Colburn assured her, "I'll get it in my office."

As he rose from his chair he apologized to the circle of patients, "I'm sorry, this will just take a minute. Please help yourself to some refreshments and hang around till I get back." He exited the side door that led directly into his office and answered the phone, "Hey Marcus, what's up?"

"Walter, I'm sorry to bother you," doctor Grant began, "but I just got off a conference call with two old colleagues of mine, Dr. William Keegan at Catholic Charities, Archdiocese of Miami and Jim Norwood, Deputy Director of Community Based Care, for Wesley House Family Services. They'll both be driving into Key West this afternoon, and joining us at Louie's for dinner! I just needed to let you know that I've had to move the time to five-thirty, and need you to pick me up at five-fifteen! OK?"

There was no time for questions! Dr. Colburn answered with, "That will be fine! I'll pick you up at your gate at five-fifteen", then, he returned to his session.

In the short few minutes that he was away from the circle of patients, things had spiraled into complete chaos. Of the original seven participants, only four remained, one of which was Jillian. For the next ninety minutes Dr.

C. waded through petty arguments over who had longer access to the second-floor smoking balcony, who had one more pillow issued than everyone else, who was allowed to retreat to their room to steal afternoon naps, who kept everyone else up all night with incessant chatter and who was spending too much time in the bathroom stall. At the end of the session, Dr. C. returned to his desk and sat wondering if his decision to trade his successful Chicago practice for this was nothing less than ludicrous. He took a breath, let it out slowly, tossed his pen on the desk, leaned his chair back and let his eyes roll around the office till they panned back to the desk top where they met hers. Oh! Those enchanting blue eyes! Amelia! She was never far away! Always ready to lead his hand back to the tiller! No hurricane could fowl his anchor when Amelia was there! Everything else passed into superfluous dribble when she was around! All he needed was to look at that picture, waiting dependably, at the edge of his desk.

"Have you figured it out yet?" She asked as she straightened her hair in the evening breeze.

Taken on the oceanfront deck of Latitudes restaurant, Sunset Key, on the night before they had boarded the *Yankee Freedom*, and sailed out to the Dry Tortugas for a tour of the Fort Jefferson National Monument, it was the last photo he had taken of his wife before she died.

She was so stunning, in that blue chiffon dress! He was never comfortable taking pictures of her in public, but that moment was worthy of capture. After dinner, she had posed under a half-moon, with a trillion diamonds shimmering in the waves behind her. Little did he know just how much he would cherish this last picture of his beautiful wife, the love of his life, Amelia.

"You mean why I'm here and not in Chicago?" he could hear the words forming in his mind, as he directed his attention deeper, into the picture.

"No, sweetheart! How you're going to help these poor people, in the mooring field, while they deal with the loss of their friend!"

"Jesus," he thought! Will the rest of his life be spent waiting for his deceased wife to inject reality into the vacant spaces of his unreality? Not that he would resist her intersession, but all the training, and all the experience he had had in the development of a keen understanding of the human psyche had led him to a place where the dead would be calling his shots? My

God! This was the kind of stuff he had spent his professional lifetime leading clients away from. Talking to dead people, listening to dead people, expecting that existential intervention could help pave a clearer path through life's turbid and treacherous waters? He might as well just choose an AKA and sign himself in under the Bakers Act. Lost it!! Lights out!! This one's belly up!! Then he began to consider the possibilities! What if? What if everything about the psychiatric teachings he had studied so reverently over the years were only half true? What if the one truth missing in life was that life doesn't stop with the closing of death's door.

Oh, these were dangerous considerations for a tutor of temperance and mentor of good mental health! Still, he could not negate the indulgence he so enjoyed, revisiting fond memories of how Amelia always seemed to know just how to lead him to where he needed to be. He decided to let it ride, as he sat there, leaning back in his fully adjustable, lumbar-supported, brown Italian leather desk chair. He answered his deceased wife out loud, "well, I think I'll let these people peel their own bananas"!

He put both hands behind his head as he leaned back and swung both feet up to the edge of his desk and finished with, "when all we got left are the seeds, we fertilize!"

The remainder of his day was spent updating case records and responding to e-mails. At four-forty-five, he bid goodnight to Rosa and Jillian, then walked across the parking lot to his beautiful roadster.

"Right on time!" Dr. Grant was grinning ear to ear as he watched his friend ease over to the curb and drop the top on the sporty little two-seater. Darla helped her father closer to the car as Dr. Colburn opened his door, then climbed out.

"You want the top up, or down"? He asked, jokingly, then paused for the giant old man to respond. Darla and her father laughed in unison at the seemingly preposterous assumption that Dr. Grant might be able to squeeze into such a little car.

"You wouldn't expect to fit a buffalo in a baby carriage, would you"? The older doctor asked as he surveyed the burgundy Beemer.

Dr. Colburn rounded the front of the car, then opened the passenger door and beckoned to his friend, "What say we give it the old college try!"

Darla and her father navigated their way to the open door, then, with Walter's help, slid him into the plush leather seat. "Oh, my God"! He exclaimed as he ran his hand across the leather upholstered dashboard, then flipped the tiny visor down, and back up again. "Is this a spaceship, or what?"

Darla closed the door while Dr. Colburn climbed back into the driver's seat, then asked his old friend, "Well, up or down?" The trio laughed in unison, as the engine roared back to life, then pulled away from the curb. Darla heard her father bellow out his preference as they drove away, "Down boy! Down!"

5. THE MEETING AT LOUIE'S

"Have you discovered Louie's yet?" Dr. Grant asked as they made a left turn onto Simonton Street.

"Oh, Yeah! I think I'm addicted to their Bohemian conch chowder! Just unbelievable!"

Dr Grant held his right arm high into the air above his head and felt the afternoon breeze as they drove south toward Louie's. "I'd imagine you've started compiling a list of questions about what I've pulled you into, but if you'll just hold on until after tonight's meeting, I'll make sure you get the answers you'll need."

They turned right, onto Vernon Street. Two blocks later, they pulled into a sandy parking spot beneath the dog beach street light, where frisbee-carrying retrievers, and their sunbaked owners, had tracked sand halfway up the street on their trek back to their cars, blurring the distinction between roadway and beach. The sun was just beginning to set and a purplish, orange sky painted a surreal backdrop to the palm tree lined approach as the two psychiatrists climbed from the roadster and turned toward Louie's Backyard Café.

Dr. Colburn pressed the lock button on his key fob, and stepped into the glow of the streetlight. "Hey Doc!" A familiar voice called out from across the street. "Are you the ring leader of this circus?"

The two doctors turned to find an approaching police officer walking toward them.

"Nice to see you, Stookerelly," Walter responded. "What circus are you referring to?" He asked as he retrieved his hand and shook it gingerly free of the pain left by the officer's crushing grip.

Sometimes brains get trumped by brawn with no better reason than an attempt to mask one's insecurities.

Officer Stookerelly pointed his finger toward the second floor of the restaurant and explained, "I got this assignment at four-thirty this afternoon and came straight over. Detective Dixon got here a few minutes before you, and is already upstairs. I was wondering if you might have a suggestion on what I need to be watching for."

Dr. Colburn looked toward the glimmering waves that gently lapped the dog beach sand, then flicked his finger against the officers' badge and said with a smile, "Well, I'd be watching out for dog crap if I were out there!"

"Good evening, Doctors!" Jamal greeted them, as Dr. Grant's better foot landed on the top step of the landing, while his friend assisted his climb from his left side.

"Let me help you!" Jamal offered as he reached for Dr. Grant's forearm and took a supportive posture. "The upstairs dining room is ready for your meeting, and I've made the usual arrangements with our servers to minimize interruptions."

Jamal was Bahrainian-born, but raised in the South Bronx by his aunt and uncle, who owned a popular Arabic restaurant on Second Avenue. He had learned every aspect of restauranturing from them, and thoroughly excelled in all facets of the business. At the age of twenty-seven, he had left New York after a rather brutal and embarrassing escapade was uncovered, involving Jamal and a well-endowed sixteen-year-old neighbor boy who, according to Jamal, had lied completely about the incident, which had left Jamal suffering such damage that he would be forced to limp through the rest of his life. He had found his way to the "end of the road" in the nineteen seventies when the island mecca for misfits was redefining itself as a sanctuary for society's love-struck outcasts. After twenty-some-odd years of working every job in every eatery on the island, this gaunt and graciously elegant dark skinned Muslim gentleman had earned the esteemed title of maître d' of one of Key West's finest eateries.

Doctor Grant was as comfortable with this establishment as one might hope to be in their own home. His "hellos" to staff, as the threesome passed them by, were as cordial as greetings to his own family members. He had grown to love his Caribbean island life, and was thrilled to now be sharing it with his long-lost friend from Chicago!

As the trio climbed the beautiful mahogany stairway to the second floor, Dr. Grant briefed his friend on the upcoming gathering. "Welcome to S.H.A.L. (Southernmost Homeless Assistance League)." Then, he added, "We've been holding these meetings for over ten years, always on the first Wednesday, every third month." When they reached the top of the flight of stairs, Dr. Grant hesitated, stretched his shoulders back, then leaned toward Dr. Colburn and whispered, "You, might already be familiar with some of the people we'll be meeting with, but sit tight. After we get through with a few formalities, I think you're going to find it particularly enlightening."

As they approached the open doors to the upstairs dining room, several voices grew increasingly more distinguishable. "Hello, everyone," Dr. Grant called into the room as they entered. Jamal turned loose of the doctor's arm and quietly backed away, as several of the attendees approached to offer their greetings. The younger doctor stood supportively at his side, as Dr. Grant became pressed upon by friends and colleagues, anxious to gain his attention. Dr. Colburn gestured toward the only people that he recognized, Detective Dixon and Natelie Reize, the director of the Families in Transition division of the Florida Department of Children and Families.

Two gentlemen entered the room, and Dr. Grant turned to welcome them, then motioned to Dr. Colburn for help getting over to his chair. Within a few minutes, everyone had made their way to their seats and as the chatter subsided, Dr. Grant tapped on his water glass and announced, "Good evening, everyone! Thank you for, once again, putting your lives on hold to help our little island community find solutions to some of its unique challenges!" He took a sip of ice water, then continued, "First, I'd like to apologize for any inconvenience you may have had, from my changing our meeting time to five o'clock. As many of you may already know, our friends over at Catholic Charities have secured approval from the city for their nine-million dollar expansion to the Saint Bede's homeless facility on Flagler Avenue. As hard as it is to believe, there's an entire congregation of church members, on the other side of the street, that just can't seem to tolerate the thought of homelessness carving a path through their neighborhood. I decided to move tonight's meeting forward, after receiving an anonymous tip that some of those parishioners intended to demonstrate at tonight's meeting. Detective Dixon was kind enough to arrange for a police presence out front, to help deter any of their overly ambitious early arrivers." He took a sip from his glass and listened to the murmurings of the group. The "Not in My Backyard" sentiment had long been established in Key West, and passionately defended by the islands taxpaying property owners, who fear their property values might plummet if thirty-seven more apartments were to get added to the island's affordable housing roster.

When the chatter died down, he moved on to the next issue, and announced, "If you don't mind, I'd like to introduce you to our new sea-bound psychiatrist, Dr. Walter Colburn. Walter and I have been friends and colleagues since the early seventies, when he worked for me at the National Institute of Mental Health in Washington. Walter holds a PhD from Duke University and was awarded the Hofheimer Award for his 1974 landmark study in the pathophysiology of psychiatric manifestations of wartime trauma. We had first met at Bethesda Naval Hospital. I believe it was in 1967, when Walt was head of psychiatry at the trauma center. His work paved the way for what would, ten years later, be formally recognized as PTSD (Post Traumatic Stress Disorder)!" Dr. Grant leaned toward his friend and tipped his head in respect, then continued, "I could not be more pleased that he has agreed to become a part of our little island cadre, and I'm sure his contributions will soon be appreciated by us all."

Dr. Grant turned to his left and led the group in applause as Dr. Colburn graciously rose and bowed respectfully to their acclamation, then said, "Thank you! I am honored to be a part of this wonderful initiative and hope I can live up to your expectations!"

As his friend sat back down, and the applause subsided, Dr. Grant unfolded his notes and addressed the next issue on his list. "By now, you have all heard that we lost our dear friend Bill Chapman yesterday morning. His body was found in his dinghy, under the dock, behind the Turtle Museum, where apparently he was waiting for the fog to clear before heading back out to his boat in the mooring field. Bill was a long-time member of S.H.A.L., and his contributions to our mission were invaluable, to say the least. He was generous beyond imagination, both in his time and his never ceasing commitment to helping the people he knew and loved." Dr. Grant leaned forward and placed his hands, palms down, on the table to help carry the weight of the grief that burdened his heart. He pulled a handkerchief from his pants pocket to clear his nose, then, with tears in his eyes, shook his head and struggled to gain composure. He then continued, "Billy was like a son to me!" He took a drink of water from his glass and cleared his throat, then, with his hands clasped across his chest, he began to explain the reason his grief was so deep. "I met Billy and Carla in the summer of 1995, at the Officer's Club, on Sigsby Island. It feels like it was just yesterday! He had just retired after twenty years in the Navy and they were exploring the idea of moving here from their home state of California. They were buying a sailboat in North Carolina and thinking about bringing it down here, where they could sail the Caribbean. Janet and I were celebrating our thirty-ninth anniversary! We met them on the dance floor! They were so cute together, so happy to be in Key West! It was their first time here."

He took another drink of water, then continued, "They were sitting at the table next to ours, and at some point, I invited them to join us for champagne. By the end of that night, Janet and I felt as though we had known them all their lives. We were captivated by their love for life." Dr. Grant wiped his eyes and looked in the dozen-or-so attentive faces of the S.H.A.L. members, then continued. "I know that many of you were familiar with Billy's Navy history, but you may not have known about the tragic loss of his wife Carla."

Dr. Grant's leg was now painfully demanding he sit down, so he eased himself back into his chair as he talked. "I was the reason they moved here! Jan and I invited them to sail with us out to Fort Jefferson, the day after we met them, and they came over to the condo for dinner when we got back. I've always felt that I was the one who sold them on the whole "Livin' Life in Paradise" idea, and before they left that night, their minds were made up. It took them about a year to sell their house in Mendocino, and then to get their Morgan outfitted in North Carolina for their new life in the tropics." He took a deep breath and exhaled slowly, then continued, "They were sailing south through Georgia, on the Intracoastal Waterway. It was late in the night when a storm drove them into an oyster bed near Cumberland Island and bent their rudder stock. Billy told me that Carla was in a panic and having an anxiety attack, so they put out a mayday call. Within an hour, a Coast Guard response boat from Saint Mary's base pulled up on the other side of the oyster bed and called to them on a bullhorn. Carla had just come up from below, and made her way to where Billy was standing at the bow with a hand-held spotlight, when the Coast Guard threw him a weighted heave-line. Poor Carla hopefully never knew what hit her! According to Billy, she had died within minutes."

Dr. Grant blew his nose, then dried his tears, and explained, "I'm sure that you can see how Billy's death holds twice the pain for me! Sometimes, it just seems like this island is cursed! So many beautiful lives come to their end here! I felt it was important that I talk about Carla's death so that all of us might have a better understanding of why Billy was so deeply committed to helping others as they navigate the cruelties and unfairness that living down here, on the edge of disaster, can bring. He was relentless in his generosity and compassion for others. I don't think any of us could argue that." He took another sip of water and concluded with, "Thank you all for your patience! I've asked Detective Dixon to give us an update on his investigation so that you will be able to answer your client's questions with as much accuracy as possible." He stood and gestured toward the detective and said, "Thank you for joining us, Carl," then sank deep into his chair.

Detective Dixon stood and addressed the group, "Thank you, Marcus! On behalf of Sheriff Acosta and all of us at the Monroe County Sheriff's Office, I offer our sincerest condolences for your loss and assure you that we are readily available to respond to any need that may arise, so please, feel free to keep my number on your speed dial. To begin, let me tell you that the chief and I met yesterday afternoon to go over some of the possible fallout that might be expected once the formal announcement of Mr. Chapman's death is made public. That should take place early tomorrow morning, once we get a chance to review the coroner's report. I've been advised that it's been completed and, as of three o'clock, is waiting on a signature before getting handed to a courier for delivery. Dr. Grant, Sheriff Acosta, and I had a conference call with Dr. Phillips, who did the autopsy, and we collectively decided that because of the extent of impact Mr. Chapman's death is expected to have on the community, I'm now authorized to release some of our findings here with you. Before I get into it, I'd like to say that I knew Billy! My wife Barb and I have sat at Schooner's Wharf and enjoyed his guitar playing since he first moved here. I can't count the number of times that we danced to his rendition of Tennessee Whisky! Anyway, I want to say that yesterday morning, when I discovered it was Billy, I was deeply affected. Very deeply! And Barb and I share in the grief that you and everybody else on this island are feeling. More than that, I worked with Billy on several projects that he championed! I remember once, after Hurricane Wilma, there was an older couple living on their boat out in the mooring field that had lost their dinghy, and Billy arranged for a brand new one to be towed out to them by our Key West Marine unit, so they wouldn't know he had bought it for them. He had it outfitted at West Marine with a new fifteen-horsepower Yamaha kicker. He wanted the police department to get credit for it. I don't know why he did that, but over the next several years, I came to learn that it was just his way of living his life."

The detective reached for his water glass and took a sip, then began his presentation. "Our office got a 911 call at 0440 hours on Tuesday from a Julian McCarthy, who reported that while walking his dog along the dock behind the Turtle Kraal Museum, his German Shepherd strongly alerted to a smell that seemed to originate between the cracks in the dock. Mr. McCarthy reported that he explored the area and observed the back end of an inflatable dinghy sticking out from under the dock. He also reported seeing what appeared to be blood in the water around the boat. Our office dispatched two deputies to the scene, and at 0459 hours, they called in a 10-97, confirming they were on scene. At 0507 hours, they 10-25 with Mr. McCarthy at the Turtle Museum back entrance and began inspecting the area. At 0509 hours, dispatch put out a signal-7, and I got a phone call at home to respond. I arrived at 0540 hours, and the area was already secured. After I inspected the scene, I joined our chief of Special Response, the senior officer of evidence, the two responding deputies and our chief of forensics for a debriefing and review of facts. I interviewed Mr. McCarthy, then cleared his dismissal from the scene. Upon the completion of evidence procurement by the gathering team, Billy's body was removed by city EMS, and his dinghy was secured for transport to the inspection center on Stock Island. I interviewed five boat residents from the proximity of the dinghy dock, including one resident who was employed as an assistant dockmaster, and all reported they heard no alarming noises within the time frame of the suspect incident. At 0823 hours, I took another walk through the scene, then headed over to Harpoon Harry's for some breakfast and to sort through my notes. The fog had significantly lifted by 0900 hours when I left Harry's and proceeded to the dockmaster's office, where dockmaster Donald Hargrove provided me with the harbor activity logs, fueling records, transient dockage manifests, and all city dockage registrations covering the five preceding days."

The detective took a long drink from his water glass, then continued his dissertation, "One interesting piece of data that Don was able to provide was a printout of the tidal rise and fall record for Tuesday morning. He told me that NOAA had installed a tidal monitoring device under the dock beside the dockmaster's office in 2005, after Hurricane Wilma. It records and transmits tidal and wave changes as small as 1.00337 centimeters. I'll be referring to this data later on, when I discuss the case summary, but the most relevant information that Mr. Hargrove was able to provide was a list of which of the commercial boats, docked in the harbor, that were equipped with the necessary navigational electronics that would allow them to navigate safely through the breakwater under the heavy fog conditions that we've had this week. That information was particularly important in our final determination of causality, which I will be discussing in detail later. I arrived back at my office at 1006 hours and prepared a list of people I would need to interview by phone, and by 1400 hours, yesterday, I had discovered that out of the seven commercial vessels that are docked in the Key West Bight, only one is equipped with the combination of thermal camera technology, radio-based AIS, and the type of radar that could navigate through fog. That vessel is the lobster boat *Routine,* captained by Corey Delaney. I talked with Captain Delany yesterday afternoon, and he confirmed that he and his crew had idled past the Turtle Kraal area at approximately 0430 hours on Tuesday, and had maintained an idle speed until clearing the rocks of the breakwater."

Dr. Grant rose from his chair and offered, "If you don't mind, let's give Detective Dixon a short break, while we take a few minutes and place our dinner orders." As he spoke, he motioned to Jamal, who was standing just outside the closed French doors at the entrance to the room. Jamal opened the doors and stepped toward the doctor, who then suggested they were ready to order. Jamal exited the room and shortly returned with two waitresses, who began dutifully attending to the patrons while Jamal topped off their water glasses.

There were fourteen attendees at the meeting! Ten official members of S.H.A.L., Dr. Colburn, Detective Dixon, Dr. Bill Keegan from Catholic Charities, Archdiocese of Miami, and Jim Norwood, the Director of Community Care at Wesley House Family Services. After the dinner orders were taken and the restaurant staff had left the room, Jamal closed the doors and Dr. Grant stood back up and explained, "With consideration to our guests, I feel inclined to explain that tonight's meeting has a particularly unusual agenda that came upon us rather unexpectedly. Captain Chapman was an integral part of our efforts at S.H.A.L. He changed a lot of lives, and a lot of people are going to suffer over losing him. We will be the hope that many of them will be reaching out to, as they move past what happened yesterday morning. Thank you, everyone!" As he lowered himself into his chair, he extended his right hand toward Detective Dixon and said, "Thank you, Carl!"

Dixon rose and resumed his dissertation. "Thank you. Before I left for the day on Tuesday, I made a call to the coroner's office to see if there had been any progress toward a suspected cause of death. The technician that I talked with verified that the subject had been through cleanup and the initial medical inspection, but at that time, there was no determination as to any evidence other than his death being due to accidental frontal trauma to the head. As I left the station, I stopped by the forensics office and met briefly with Tim Bucannon, our department chief, to get an update on the inspection of Mr. Chapman's boat. He told me that his field team had motored out to the mooring field at approximately 1100 hours and were unable to board it. He explained that Mr. Chapman's dog ferociously guarded the boat and that the officers felt that her aggression was enough of a threat that they should abandon their attempt to board. They reported that a neighboring boat was moored about two hundred yards away, and a man was watching them from its bow. The officers motored to his location, and the man said that he was a close friend of Mr. Chapman. He then offered to assist with their effort by taking the dog over to Christmas Tree Island while they conducted their inspection. The individual dispatched his dinghy and retrieved the dog. After she was removed, the two Marine Officers proceeded to board, then inspect Mr. Chapman's boat. They made a routine search for evidence that might support any potential causes related to Mr. Chapman's death, then they took forty-seven photos of the interior and exterior of the vessel. While the deputies were securing the customary crime scene tape, a Coast Guard Defender Class 25 arrived on scene, and Chief Warrant Officer Colline Di Cantalupo engaged with the deputies on the case specifics necessary for her to file a CG-2692. That, officially, opens a Coast Guard investigation."

"Why would the Coast Guard have any interest in a death that took place under a dock in Key West"? It was a reasonable question! It had come from Genine Mackley, the director of the Samuel's House Shelter for Homeless Women. It was the first of many questions that would soon be propelled into the evening's discussion!

The detective cordially answered with, "DOSHA, the Death on the High Seas Act, was passed in the early 1920s. It's a federally enacted law that protects the interests of surviving family members when the deceased was engaged in a maritime activity at the time of death. It has a three-mile out limitation, and since Mr. Chapman was on his dinghy, in what legally is considered international, navigable waters, the local police are under statutory obligation to notify the Coast Guard within the first five days of the death. In Florida, we also make it standard procedure to notify the Florida Fish and Wildlife Commission so they can investigate possible incidental consequences that might have impacted the environment during the incident. I had placed those calls yesterday afternoon, before leaving for the day. It's standard operation!"

He lifted his water glass to take a sip, and Dr. Grant took advantage of the pause and stood briefly to interject, "In the hope that we can get off the property before the protesters show up, I think we should hold our questions till Carl finishes his reporting. Thank you, everyone!"

Detective Dixon resumed his accounting of the case chronology with, "The marine unit field team had confiscated Mr. Chapman's laptop to look for any reason to believe there might have been foul play involved in his death. There's no need for a warrant when the subject is deceased! His 4th amendment rights are forfeited upon his death! This afternoon, I checked with Tripp Hughes, our forensics' IT specialist, to see if he had found anything that might be suspicious, and he reported that after reviewing the data on the hard drive, nothing seemed to indicate a need for further investigation. We cloned the hard drive after Tripp finished running his FTK (Forensic Toolkit), and I inspected the list of personal belongings seized from the incident site and checked again with Tripp for his assessment of Mr. Chapman's phone and Fitbit data. He conveyed that due to the facial trauma Billy had endured, his access to the phone might take another day, but the Fitbit data had transferred to the corresponding app on the laptop, and he will be sending me a printout with that information for review." He took another quick sip from his glass, then continued, "I think I've provided enough background on the case for you to get an idea of how we will, soon, be forming our conclusion. What we believe the evidence is providing, so far, is that Billy's death was an unfortunate accident. If you don't mind, I'll try to summarize the developments. He had reported to Schooner's Wharf Bar and joined his fellow bandmembers on stage at approximately 2100 hours, Monday night. Staff reported that the patronage was unusually light and by midnight there were three local fishermen left at the bar, so the band ended their performance and proceeded to pack their instruments. Witnesses confirmed Billy had stayed to visit with staff until approximately 0100 hours, when he bid them goodnight and exited the property through the dockside exit. Several staff members verified that the fog had begun to move into the area as early as 2100 hours, and had continued to slowly build in intensity. The conditions were also verified through a review of the NOAA Hazardous Weather Outlook Data reports."

The audience was deeply engaged as he talked!

"We believe Mr. Chapman proceeded directly from the Schooner's Wharf bar to the Key West Bight dinghy dock, where he probably considered the threat of navigating through the fog and out of the harbor, then out to his boat in the mooring field. We feel it would be reasonable to deduce that, while waiting for the morning sun to improve the conditions, Mr. Chapman made himself comfortable and fell asleep with his head resting on the forward area of his inflatable dinghy. The tidal charts revealed that the lowest tide was recorded at 0627 hours. Also, the moon was in its last quarter, making it a "neap" tide. With this data in hand, we can say with confidence that the water level would have been low enough for Billy's boat, with his head resting on the bow as it was found when he was discovered, to drift under the lowest dock beam at, or after, 0335 hours."

Once again, he reached for his water glass to quench his thirst, then continued. "As I had mentioned earlier, it was approximately 0430 hours. when the lobster-boat, *Routine,* motored through the marina and turned West toward the deep-water channel, then accelerated as they rounded the end of the breakwater jetty. When Captain Delany powered up, the propwash sent a large wake back into the marina. That wave moved past the dockmasters' building, and caused Billy's dinghy to be jolted into the underside of the dock, where his face became repeatedly impaled on the bolts that secure the base of the electrical box on the upper side of the dock. Hopefully, he died with the first wave."

A collective gasp filled the room! The image of their beloved friend finding his end in such a horrible way brought tears to several of the attendees' eyes. Dr. Grant stood to his feet and thanked the detective for his detailed briefing, then announced, "I think this might be a good time for us to take a break. We'll reconvene in about fifteen minutes and, with a little luck, dinner will be served."

Several of the group headed for the first-floor restrooms. J. B. Markum, from City H.U.D., and Tyrone Salamante, the longtime S.H.A.L. attorney, stepped through the French doors that open onto the second-floor deck, lit cigarettes, then began discussing the developments that had befallen their friend.

Detective Dixon crossed the room and stood between the two doctors who had remained seated. "I hope that was helpful," the officer directed his comment toward Dr. Grant, then put his hand on Dr. Colburn's shoulder and said, "Good to see ya, Walt! How's things over at Depoo these days?"

"Well," Walter responded with a warm grin as he turned and looked up at the giant of a man standing over him," I've just found out that tomorrow morning they're rearranging my office! They say it's to give me a better view of the water!"

Dixon laughed, "Yeah! We were hoping you'd accept that challenge. Back when Marcus and Witt were out there doing their psych-thing, we saw a remarkably significant drop in incidents that involved the boat people. Whatever they were doing sure made our job a hell of a lot easier!"

Dr. Grant smiled as he leaned to his right, then turned his head toward the officer, and said, "I'm pretty sure you'll be seeing those numbers start dropping again real soon!"

Louie's staff began staging trays along the back wall, then delivering wine glasses and plates of food to their respective places, as the guests made their way back into the room and took their seats. Conversations began to develop between several small groups and as they settled into their places, Dr. Grant stood up, raised his glass of wine, and proposed a toast, "My dear friends, we could search for days trying to find the perfect words to honor Captain William Blain Chapman's life, but I am sure we would all be embarrassingly humbled by our incapacite'! Nonetheless, I could say that Billy was a generous man, a loyal friend, a talented artist, a leader worthy of following, a champion for the rights of the most downtrodden of our community, or that he will be missed by all of us who knew and loved him as deeply as we did. As true as those words may be, none of them capture the full essence of who Bill Chapman was, or how deeply he will be missed." He wiped his tears from his eyes, then continued. "If you please, let's take a moment to honor our dear friend's memory!" He reached into his jacket pocket and retrieved his phone, then, after setting it face up on the tabletop, he pushed play. It was Billy, singing his song, "My Remedy"!

When my soul has left this earth, for what it's worth,

I believe that in tha hearts of tha ones I loved, forever held, in memory!

I climbed these mountains, sailed these seas, painted sunsets of all of these,

cast my shadow on every wall, reached my hand out to everyone that took a fall!

I've been broken, and I've been down, been stepped over, and kicked around,

I've been desperate, and hopelessly searchin' for my remedy!

Rusting ships upon tha shore, stain tha sands, and sail no more,

Set to stare, eternally, across tha oceans of history!

I've been desperate, and hopelessly searchin for my remedy!

Tell my children, tell my wife, as I lay here, beneath tha fading light,

All I thought of, all I could see, was livin' forever, in their memory!

I've been broken, and I've been down, been stepped over, and kicked around,

I've been desperate, and hopelessly searchin' for my remedy!

When my soul has left this earth, for what it's worth

I believe that in tha hearts of tha ones I loved, forever held, in memory!

Oh, I've been broken, and I've been down, been stepped over, and kicked around,

I've been desperate, and hopelessly searchin' for my remedy!

There were no dry eyes in the room! By the second verse, half of the listeners were mournfully crying into their napkins. Dr. Grant took a deep breath, dried his eyes again, and respectfully addressed the group, "Forgive me if this has caused anyone discomfort! I assure you, that was not my intention! I think that we are all sharing the same sadness, as we face the reality of Billy's passing. It's that grief and sadness that we'll need to be calling upon, as we seek to find ways to alleviate some of the pain that our clients are going to be feeling." He raised his wine glass high into the air, and beckoned a toast, "Here's to our friend, Captain William Blain Chapman, a man of deep empathy! May we find inspiration in his every memory!" He seated himself, slid his dinner plate closer, picked up his fork and offered, "Thank you, everyone, for your patience! Please, let's eat this fantastic food before it gets up and walks away!"

After a few bites of his dinner, Dr. Grant suggested that if anyone had questions for Detective Dixon, they might wish to offer them for the group to hear.

Mallory Stockton raised her hand as she finished a sip from her wine glass. She had been a close friend of Billy's since he first joined S.H.A.L. They had collaborated on hundreds of projects over the years, and together, were a commanding force for changing the lives of the island's neediest residents. Her family was deeply rooted in the establishment of some of the earliest not-for-profit social service organizations in the Keys. Her grandfather, Colin James Stockton, had co-founded The Stockton & Morland Maritime Shipping Co. and, after retiring, was a cofounder of The Wesley House Family Services of Key West, and a major benefactor to the early Depoo Foundation, where Dr. Colburn now practiced psychiatry.

"If you don't mind, "Mallory set her goblet down and asked, "I was just wondering if someone will be taking care of Flow?" Mallory and her husband were the owners of two doodle-dogs, and regularly met with Billy and his wolf-dog, Flow, at the dog park, where the three pups romped and ran like littermates. "If no one's available to keep her, Gene and I would love to have her! Permanently!"

Officer Dixon responded, "I believe she's still over on the boat with the young man that took her over to Christmas Tree Island yesterday. I'm not sure if that's going to be the best place for her, but I was told she had responded to him as if she knew him when he took her off of Billy's boat yesterday. I guess we can check on that for you!"

"Was it Cai?" She was obviously familiar with the layout of the Key West Harbor's mooring field, and its residents! She added, "I can get in touch with him this afternoon and see what he wants to do with her!"

"Ya know, Billy keeps two vehicles over in the public parking garage!" Tom Bozeman had been a friend of Billy's since taking over the directorship of the Keys Overnight Temporary Shelter, (K.O.T.S.) just three years earlier. He had been a valued resource for Billy whenever he was helping the homeless transition from sleeping on the beaches or in the mangroves, into a safer, healthier housing situation.

"We had them both towed over to impound this morning!" Carl responded! "I appreciate it, Tom! Our evidence team is already making headway on their findings. As of this afternoon, when I left the office, we hadn't found any evidence that might lead us to suspect anything beyond Billy's death being an unfortunate accident."

Dinner was fabulous! While they ate, several people presented questions to Detective Dixon, while others were directed to Dr. Grant! The tables were eventually all cleared, and the doors were, once again, closed for privacy. For the next hour, the group reviewed issues relevant to the usual administration of their program's interests, then Dr. Keegan presented the latest updates on the Saint Bede's shelter expansion project, and Dr. Grant announced the acceptance of S.H.A.L.'s recent Social Services Block Grant filing application by the Florida Administration for Children and Families, in Tallahassee.

He ended the meeting with his heartfelt condolences and encouragement, "It's been a very sad and trying week for all of us!" He stood to his feet and, once again, leaned forward to support himself on the table. "We have no way of predicting how deeply Billy's passing will impact the people who loved and depended on him! My greatest hope is that we can bring their ships into harbor safely without any further losses." He reached his hand to remove his glasses, then panned his watery eyes, slowly, through the audience of attentive faces and added, "As we go forward, may the memory of our beloved friend be the beacon of hope and inspiration that guides us all to a better shore." The elderly psychiatrist stood crying into his handkerchief as several members made their way toward him to lend comfort. It took another half hour to end the meeting! Under the streetlight, a group gathered, sharing their remembrances of past times with Billy.

No protesters showed up that night! The rumor never bled into serious intention, but the sentiment would live on in the fear-fed hearts of the few people who would never understand their island's highly celebrated mantra of "One Human Family".

6. NIGHT OWL

"Would you mind if we just drive for a while?" Dr Grant asked his friend as they pulled from the curb and turned right, onto Alberta Street. At the next corner, the Spottswood Waterfront Park availed them a picture-perfect view of the moon sparkling across the southern expanse of the Caribbean approach to Key West. Dr. Colburn slowed as they pulled toward the park and prepared for the left-hand turn, when Dr. Grant asked, "Do you remember when I introduced you to John?"

"John?" Dr. Colburn had no idea who his friend could be talking about.

"Senator Spottswood! John Spottswood!" He held his hand out the window and pointed his finger at the green sign that memorialized the Spottswoods, then continued, "You and I played golf with him a couple of times back in the early seventies! Remember?"

"Oh, yeah! Nice guy! Did he live down here?" Dr. Colburn asked.

"He was a conch!" the older psychiatrist answered. "He was born here! You probably didn't know that before he was in Congress, he was the island's sheriff." He motioned to a parking place in front of the entrance to the park and suggested, "What say we take a few minutes and check out the view?"

Dr. Colburn pulled into the vacant space, then circled the car to help his friend climb out of his seat. They made their way across the decorative pavement, beyond the landscape planters, and over to the sea wall that faced the southern expanse of ocean.

"There's no place on earth like this!" Dr. Grant exclaimed. "Not anywhere!" He leaned against the seawall, looked up at the moon, and added, "No other place has this much beauty, this much inspiration, or this much love!" The dock lights on the Cassa Marina pier shone down into the emerald waters. Two night herons were poised on ropes that hung from the pilings,

47

intent on spearing minnows that come to the surface to feed on bugs attracted by the lights. "I can't tell you how thrilled I am that you and I have reconnected!"

Dr. Colburn smiled, "It's been a long time, Marcus! I've had so many regrets over the way the agency was dismantled! It's still painful for me to think about all those years of research just thrown away."

Dr. Grant understood his friend's angst completely and proposed, "I'm sure we'll have plenty of time to unravel that ball of twine later on, but tonight we need to focus on the daunting task that has, unfortunately, befallen us." He stretched his shoulders, then arched his back and suggested, "What say we drive around for a little while! I don't think I've ridden in a convertible in over sixty years!"

Dr. Colburn was happy to oblige and after helping the old fellow back into the car, they drove toward the southern side of the island and Higgs Beach.

"I'd imagine that by now you've gotten familiar with a lot of the scenic places on the island, but have you had a chance to explore any of the history behind them?" The older doctor asked.

"Well, as much as I'd hoped that I could forget it, I did take a boat ride out to Fort Jefferson about two years ago." Dr Colburn was referring to the boat ride that he and his wife, Amelia, had once taken out to the Fort Jefferson National Park. Amelia had suffered an aneurysm while swimming in the shallow waters beside the fort, and had died one day later.

"I'm so sorry, Walter!" His friend offered a consoling sentiment, but before he could find the words that might further his concern, Dr. Colburn insisted, "No, it's fine, Marcus! It took me a while to get to a place where I could think about it without being emotionally crushed by grief. I finally came to realize that grief is often a consequence of death, and that by embracing it fully, and allowing it to freely evolve without expectations, it finds its own natural resolution."

The older psychiatrist smiled as he relaxed into his seat and said, "You and I have had this discussion before, you know! It was about forty years ago! We were at the Ebbitt Grill, eating lunch and discussing Joe Kennedy Sr's recent death. I was working closely with his daughter, Eunice, back then, and some of the Shriver kids were having trouble with the loss of their grandfather. You had suggested something that sounded remarkably like this, way back then!"

"My God, Marcus! I think your memory may be stronger than the Fort Knox vault!" Dr. Colburn chuckled. "I do remember that Ebbitt's was one of your favorites, but how you can remember details about one specific time, that long ago, completely baffles me." Dr Grant's phone rang as they passed by the entrance to the West Martello fortification.

"Hey, sweetheart!" His wife was calling! "Yes, dear, it went very well!" Then, "Yes, I'm riding with him now, enjoying our visit and going over some of the things he's going to need to know for tomorrow." He turned toward his friend and called into his phone, "Here, I'll put you on speaker, so you can ask him yourself!"

From the phone came a most delightfully charming voice, "Walter, is that really you?"

"Hi, Jan!" Dr. Colburn answered, "So nice to hear your beautiful voice again!"

Dr. Colburn leaned to his right and listened intently as she expressed her delight that the two doctors had reconnected. "Marcus and I are thrilled to have you back in our lives again! We're hoping you will join us for a little dinner party on Sunday night. It'll be here, at the condo! Just a few friends! I believe you already know some of them. Anyway, there's a lot to catch up on, but don't let me tie you up, now! You boys have a lot to talk about." Dr. Grant pointed toward a parking place near the White Street pier, and Dr. Colburn turned in, as they said their goodbyes and finished the call. "Do you know this place?" Dr. Grant asked.

"You mean the pier?" Dr. Colburn responded.

"No!" He lifted his arm out the window and pointed toward a wrought iron fence that bordered a large slab of concrete set in the sandy beach. Beyond was the seawall that held back the waves of the Atlantic Ocean. The beach was well lit by the glow of the moon! The ocean was calm and glassy! They could hear the waves gently lapping against the other side of the stone seawall. The pier lights illuminated the rocks of the breakwater below the concrete pier. Forty feet to their right was the eastern entrance of the West Martello tower. It was constructed of brick in 1862. "This is considered to be a sacred place, and the fort is said to be haunted by the spirits of the two hundred and ninety-five African slaves that were buried here." He paused while his friend tried to grasp the gravity of such a claim.

"Slaves?" He paused, then added, "In Key West?"

"That's right! Three ships, loaded with almost 1,500 slaves were captured by the U.S. Navy in 1860. Key West was the nearest American port, so they brought them here, and the locals built temporary housing, provided medical services and food, donated clothing and, effectively, took on the responsibility for their care while the Federal Government arranged a ship to take them back to Liberia. Three hundred died from the brutality of the slave ship journey and were buried in shallow graves on the beach. For over a hundred years, the only clue to where they were buried was on an 1861 map. A friend of mine is the archaeologist for the Mel Fisher Maritime Museum, and in 2002, he and his team ran ground-penetrating radar all over this area and finally found fifteen burial sites. This cemetery was dedicated to commemorate the plight of these poor victims of a horrible era in American History."

"That's amazing!" Walter sat with his hands on the steering wheel, staring out at the scene, and envisioning the despair and grief that must have been suffered by the poor, unfortunate, inhumed souls. "It's hard to imagine how you could be lying on the beach, soaking in the sun, sipping a cold drink, completely oblivious to the human suffering that lies just a few feet directly under your towel. It's truly amazing to me!"

Dr. Grant was pleased that his friend had realized the depth and the significance that he had hoped might be provoked by stopping at the site, and said, "Billy knew more about this island than anyone I've ever known. I used to sit with him over there." He pointed toward the circle of chairs in the dog park across the street, where they would rendezvous whenever Billy brought Flow to town, to romp with some of her lesser K-9 buddies. "He loved history! More than that, he had a way of infusing emotion into the history he was talking about. One evening, he was describing how the enslavers used to link the leg irons of the slaves onto a massive anchor chain that ran along the deck to the back of the ship, where a huge anchor was set for a quick dispatch in case the slave ship needed to dispose of their illegal cargo quickly. Imagine the terror when a slave ship captain shouted for the anchor line to be cut, and you, your family, and friends were dragged across the bloody wooden deck and into the depths of the ocean. It was a horrible era, and few people these days can face the realities of its brutality!"

Walter listened intently, then presented a very insightful question, "Why do I sense there might be some inference that this story is leading toward?

"You certainly know me well, old friend!" Dr. Grant sank deeply back into the plush leather seat, and motioned with his hand for the doctor to resume the drive, then responded cordially, "This 'One Human Family' thing goes way back! When word made it from the docks of Key West to the stock yards on Stock Island that there was a ship with fourteen hundred hungry and destitute slaves in immediate need of life-sustaining assistance, the three thousand citizens of Key West, under the leadership of U. S. Marshal Fernando Moreno, heeded the call and selflessly offered remedy to their pain and their suffering. It was an exercise in empathy, and it was that same empathetic compulsion that Billy brought to this community every day. You're going to need to know all about him, and the impact he made on people, if you're going to be successful out there on the boat, tomorrow!"

They turned right, onto Bertha Street, at the Southernmost Hockey Club and drove the one block stretch toward Smathers Beach.

"Did Billy have any health issues before he died? I mean, that you knew about?" Dr. Colburn asked.

Dr. Grant was thrilled to see his friend's eagerness and answered, "For the ten years that I knew him, he was in perfect health, but about a month ago, he had filled in at the Turtle Museum when his friend, Alex Coleman, flew up to North Carolina to help his mother move down to Sebring, Florida. Billy was inside the open-air museum for five days, and on the fourth day, one of the charter boat captains started sanding his boat while it was tied up in the dock slip, directly across from the front door of the museum where Billy was sitting. Apparently, the wind blew the dust into the museum, where Billy ended up breathing it for those last two days, and it made him horribly sick. I suggested he see a pulmonologist friend of mine, and I believe he was able to help Billy recover from the exposure. I can't say how successful that was, though! I only talked with Billy on the phone once since then, when I called to invite him to Sunday night's dinner party. Other than that, he was in great shape for a man of sixty-four years!" He turned to his friend and asked, "I'm curious, why did you ask about Billy's health?"

Dr. Colburn was cordial in his answer, "Well, truth be told, I was more interested in your professional assessment as a psychiatrist. I was particularly curious to know if you observed any unresolved issues of delusional grandeur or any clues that he might have suffered from a hero syndrome. I wondered if there was any clinical evidence of psychosis that might have driven his compulsions toward messianic rescue behavior. That would be my starting point for understanding what drove Billy to be so deeply involved with programs that support the homeless and downtrodden of the community."

Dr. Grant obligingly responded, "Well, I can certainly understand the reasoning behind your interest, but if you'll be patient and humor me for just a bit, I think you'll have your curiosity satisfied."

The eastbound drive along South Roosevelt Boulevard, on such a beautiful moonlit night, with the coconut trees and the white sands that stretched out to the sparkling water, was a perfect place for Dr. Grant to begin telling the legend of Three I'd Billy.

"As you already know, I met Billy and Carla back in the mid-nineties, at the Sigsbee Naval Air Station Officers Club, and over the next sixteen years, I was honored to be considered one of his best friends and a confidante. I knew Billy better than anybody, and he felt the same toward me! I came to love him like the son I never had!" Dr. Grant wiped his eyes, then continued, "If you don't mind, I think I'd like to take some time to give you some of Billy's history. Maybe it will help you when you start seeing clients out on the boat tomorrow. There's no doubt it will help me deal with his passing."

Dr. Colburn asked, "Shall I keep driving, or would you rather we pull off the road and sit for a while?"

"Oh, my! I'm enjoying this more than you could imagine!" He proclaimed. "Let's keep driving for a while, if that's OK!"

As they approached the Key West Airport, a plane was making its low-altitude approach over the glistening water.

"Billy grew up in Santa Cruz, California", Dr. Grant began. "His dad was the assistant director of the University of California Marine Science Center, and his mother was an Adjunct Professor at San Jose State, Department of Music. They were always huge supporters of Billy's passions! His love for the ocean, his fascination with marine animal life, his concerns for environmental issues, and his enthusiasm for music were all highly encouraged by them both. In the early nineteen-sixties, his maternal grandfather had purchased several acres of land in the famous Laurel Canyon area of the Hollywood Hills, where he built a beautiful, sprawling house with a recording studio in the basement and several guest cottages, where his musician friends could stay for extended sessions as they recorded their music. When Billy was a teenager, he often visited his grandparents' home, and became close friends with people like Graham Nash, Joni Mitchel, John Mayall, Jackson Browne, and Frank Zappa. It was there that Billy made friends with drummer Aynsley Dunbar, who encouraged him to further his love of the guitar and begin formal studies in music. That led him to apply to, and be accepted by, Berklee College of Music. Most of Billy's friends don't know that when he was a boy, he suffered from a severe stuttering problem. Billy credited Aynsley with helping him overcome it by teaching him how to sing scat over his guitar scales. There's no scientific proof that it works, but there are lots of accounts of famous singers using the technique to stop their stuttering. With Billy, it worked beautifully! The only time his stuttering returned was when he drank too much. After two glasses of wine, if someone had asked him a question, like "Billy, how are you doing?", he would answer "Well, I, I, I'm OK!". "That's how he got the nickname, Three I'd Billy! I'm pretty sure it was his reason for avoiding alcohol like it was poison!"

The two psychiatrists chuckled, then Dr. Grant suggested, "What say we drive over to Hogfish Bar for a nightcap in Billy's honor?"

Dr. Colburn responded, "It's tricky to find, but if you do the navigation, I'll pilot tha ship!"

They turned right at the light, then crossed the Cow-Key Bridge. It was a six-minute drive through the commercial fishing area, then out to Hogfish Bar and Grill. The smell of dead shrimp and rotting fish entrails permeated the air as they passed the packing houses and docks, where the catch of the day had earlier been unloaded and processed for shipping. Their repugnance was, thankfully, short-lived, and as they pulled up to the chickee-hut roofed restaurant, their suffering and torment completely faded away.

"I love this place!" Dr. Grant said, as he struggled to unlock his seat belt. Dr Colburn was already at his door to help him exit the car. They entered at the harbor-facing side of the building and took a table on the dock, next to the water. Houseboats, catamarans, sailboats, and fishing boats of all sizes lined the docks. As they situated themselves onto the benches, a waitress approached and set two menus on the table, then asked if they were ready to order drinks. Dr. Grant knew that Billy's first choice would have been Chardonnay and ordered a glass for him, then a Bahama Mama for himself. Dr. Colburn ordered a Raspberry Guava Mojito, and after the waitress walked away, Dr. Grant returned to his account of Billy's life.

"Did you ever get a chance to hear him play at Schooner's?"

"Several times!" Dr. Colburn answered. "He was one of the best guitarists I think I've ever heard!"

"Well, when he first moved to the area, he docked his boat over at the Boca Chica Naval Air Station. He said that after the first six months, he realized that if he was going to work his way into the Key West music scene, he would be better off moving over to the mooring field out by Christmas Tree Island, so that's what he did. Before long, he had established himself as a dependable stand-in guitarist for all the best local bands, and was constantly in demand. Jan and I were big fans and regularly went to Schooner's or Hog's Breath to hear him play."

The waitress showed up with their drinks, and once delivered, he resumed his story. "While Billy was establishing his reputation in the Key West music scene, he was also becoming deeply connected with the community of boat people who lived out in the mooring field. He and I talked regularly about the difficulties his neighbors faced, living on the water, fighting the elements, running from the hurricanes, and such. I began relying on his recommendations, as I administered financial support from the trust that might help their situations. We began working in-depth on many cases. Between his input and my sessions out on the boat, I think we really began to make a difference in their quality of life. Billy always insisted that his efforts remain anonymous! He felt that if his neighbors discovered he was their benefactor, or if anyone discovered how wealthy he was, his life in Key West would be over. There's this thing they call the "free wall", over near the dock, beside the public bathrooms and laundry facility. He would leave things on it that he knew people needed, like kitchen appliances, light fixtures and tools. He used to spend his own money on specific things that he knew they needed, and have them delivered to the dockmaster's office with the intended person's name printed on the package.

He ordered boat motors, engine parts, equipment, sails, safety lines, there was no limit to his benevolence. It was inspiring!" Dr. Grant took a sip from his drink, then continued. "He used to have breakfast over at Harpoon Harry's almost every day, and sit in the last booth on the left, where he could see everyone as they came in. Lots of people knew him, and many times they would join him at his table. He became a local celebrity, so to speak. What no one knew was that he was not just there for the great breakfasts, nor for the tremendous customer service. Nope, he was there to do reconnaissance. He was always listening and watching for cues that might indicate someone was in dire straits, and needed a helping hand." He took another break to nurse from his straw, and after a satisfying exhale, he went on. "Conrad Gilmore, the owner of Harpoon Harry's, was the only one, other than me, who knew what Billy was all about. On many occasions, Conrad would be walking through the restaurant and overhear a customer talking about some devastating situation that he knew Billy might be interested in helping with, and he would advise him, then Billy would pick up the ball and arrange for the necessary relief to be delivered on the person's next visit. There was one case of a young couple whose child needed to be seen by a neurosurgeon in Miami. They had no car and no money for the trip! They also had no insurance. Billy arranged for everything! He set them up in a hotel, two blocks from Jackson Memorial, prepaid their bus tickets, round-trip, then he arranged for their medical bills to be paid from his own account. Only Conrad and I knew about it." Dr. Grant took another sip from his drink.

Dr. Colburn was dumbfounded, and asked, "What happened to the child?"

Dr. Grant sighed deeply, then answered, "He didn't make it! When the doctors at Jackson Memorial evaluated his condition, they admitted him immediately. Sadly, he only lasted another two months. He hung on just long enough to see his tenth birthday. I knew the family! Beautiful people! His parents were devastated! They had an older daughter who would be about sixteen now. She's very gifted! You may be seeing the parents out on the boat after word gets out that we're back in business. I made a few calls today that should help spread the word through the mooring field, that you've taken over for me."

Questions were building in the younger doctor's brain, "Marcus, this is an awful lot for me to process!"

Dr. Grant placed his hand on his friend's arm, leaned into the table, and said softly, "Walter, I can't offer you any deeper apology for all those years we lost, and I will never be able to find the perfect words to describe my sorrow over Amelia's death, but I believe that if you can just trust me for the next few days, you're going to find that your journey was worth the pain."

The waitress approached the table and offered, "The kitchen will be closing in thirty minutes! If you gentlemen wanted to place an order, now would be the time."

Dr. Grant looked at his friend and asked, "How do you feel about conch fritters? They're better than the ones you get in Nassau!"

"Oh man, sounds great!" Dr. Colburn answered. After the waitress headed for the kitchen, the senior psychiatrist resumed his briefings about Billy.

"People who live on the fringe have limited access to the fruits of a successful society! When that society's fruitfulness begins to decline, it's the people on the fringe who feel the suffering first, and sometimes they feel it the worst! Billy understood that the people out on the fringe may, or may not, be there due to consequences of their own bad decisions, but are, more often, victims of completely unforeseeable circumstances. He never judged anyone! He just provided a steady hand and a secure foot as he tirelessly lifted them to a better place. This was the core value that drove him! It's why we all loved him! He was a constant remedy, and he will be deeply missed!"

Dr. Grant was in tears, again, as he finished talking and turned his head toward the harbor as he dried his eyes with his napkin. After a few moments of somber reflection, he continued, "I think, maybe I should start orienting you in what you might expect from some of the people you'll be seeing, out on the boat."

Dr. Colburn had been anticipating the arrival of just such a briefing, and eagerly asked, "Do you know what time I should show up at the dock tomorrow?"

Dr. Grant explained, "I had a lengthy conversation with Captain Witt this afternoon. He says that, with the water temperatures rising, the fog is starting to dissipate earlier each day, and he expects the visibility to be clear enough to sail by 0800 hours. We had the bilge pump replaced last week, and he did a full shake-down yesterday afternoon to make sure she was ready to go if you agreed to join us." Dr. Grant drew the last of his drink from his glass, as the platter of fritters was delivered. "Can I get you gentlemen re-fills?" the waitress asked. Dr. Grant needed no time to consider his answer, "Please!"

As they sampled the fritters, Dr. Grant continued his briefing. "As long as the weather stays good, you won't need to do anything but enjoy the ride. Witt takes care of it all! She's rigged for single sailing, and he knows her inside out! About three years ago, he overhauled her engine and, while she was on the hard, he sanded her hull and gave her a fresh paint. She's all set to get back to work!"

Dr. Grant motioned toward the waitress for the bill, and after slipping fifty dollars inside the check holder, they stood to their feet and gazed across the moonlit Marina.

"Billy had a friend who lived on a houseboat with his girlfriend, some-where out here. He was a local musician who had an addiction to Oxy-codone. I met the guy once!" Dr. Grant turned to walk the dock and contin-ued as his friend joined him. "His name was Jimmy Borg, and he had put to-gether a little band. I went with Billy one night to hear them play over at the Irish Pub on Grinnell Street. Way too loud for me, but Billy was concerned that his friend was a high risk for suicide. On the Friday before last, Billy got a call from this guy's girlfriend, who said she was scared that Jimmy was about to kill himself, and asked Billy to come out here and check on him. Billy called me that Saturday to talk about what he had found when he got to the boat. He had arrived there at about ten o'clock pm, and all the lights were off. He said there was no sign of anyone on board. He called for his friend, but there was no response. He stepped onto the back deck and called through the partially open hatch, but no one answered, so he opened the door and stepped inside the cabin. His friend jumped up from a hidden area and start-ed screaming wildly as if he thought Billy might be the girlfriend. When Billy got him to calm down, he saw that Jimmy was naked, and that the cabin was in shambles. He told me there were piles of ropes, coiled and sorted, lying on the mattress. Billy said that his friend convinced him that the girlfriend was trying to cause trouble for him by lying to all his friends, and that he had no intentions of harming himself. Billy left the boat with apprehension, and the next morning, unfortunately, his friend was found hanging in the cabin of the houseboat. Billy was inconsolable! I was eating my lunch that afternoon when he called. We talked for several hours! One of the things I had suggested was for him to write an epitaph that might capture how he felt about the loss of his friend."

Walter's interest was duly heightened, and he asked, "Did he?"

Dr. Grant nodded his head and answered, "He did! He texted me a copy of it on Monday afternoon, before he headed over to *Schooners* to join up with Devon and the band. When I read it, I cried! On Tuesday, after I heard Billy had died, I changed the name from Jimmy to Billy, then sent it over to Russell Napier at *The Citizen Newspaper*, with a note asking him to put it in circulation as soon as he can. I'm expecting that it might hit the stands in the morning. It's probably going to upset a lot of people who knew him, but I think they should know."

It was one o'clock AM when Dr. Colburn dropped his old friend off at his condo. Darla met them at the gate and helped her father out of the little roadster. Then, after goodnights were exchanged, Walter returned home to the Gallion.

It had been a long and exhausting day, and he was glad to see it end.

7. FIRST COME, FIRST SERVED

"Good morning, Marcus. What's up?" Dr. Colburn answered the call as he climbed through the hatch and stood beneath the mainsail boom of the *Psyched Out*, then pressed the speaker button.

"Are you on the boat?" His friend's voice was clear and full of expectation!

"I am!" Dr. C. responded with heightened anticipation. "The fog has almost completely cleared, and Witt says we're casting off in five minutes!"

"Have you had a chance to see the paper yet?" The senior doctor asked.

"Not yet! I grabbed an egg sandwich over at The Cuban Coffee Queen for when we get out to the mooring field, but I didn't think to pick up a paper. Why?" Dr. C asked.

"That's OK! Witt always has a copy with him when he's on the boat. See if he'll..." as Dr. Grant's voice was delivering its message, a copy of the *Citizen Newspaper* flew through the hatch and bounced off of the back of the binnacle, and dropped at the doctor's feet.

"I've got it right here!" Dr. Colburn called into his phone as he picked up the paper and set his phone on the hatch cover. "What am I looking for?" He asked.

Dr. Grant directed, "Page three, *Local News*! See that headline, "Beyond the Bounds of an Earthly Domain"?

"Yeah! I see it! Do you want me to read it now?" Dr. C. asked.

"Please, and tell Witt to listen up!"

Dr. C. turned toward the captain, who had been listening through the open hatch, "I'm here Marcus! What's up?" Captain Witt called out!

"I want you both to hear this before you head out. Some of the folks you will be seeing today will be showing up as a direct response to this piece. It's a eulogy! Billy's eulogy, and.." his voice broke up as he struggled to finish his words, "...he wrote it!" Captain Witt climbed up from the cabin and sat on the cushion behind the wheel, and listened intently as Dr. Colburn read:

Epitaph for William Blain Chapman III
Beyond the Bounds of an Earthly Domain!
Billy has taken his passion for music, his love of freedom, his dedication to the seeking of universal answers to the haunting questions of who and why and how, his hunger for a greater and truer self-awareness, his skills, his creativity, his love of all things worth loving, his voice and all the songs it could ever sing, with him on a journey that leaves no footprint. May he find his final rest in peace while he sings to the wind!

There was somberness in the silence as the three men reflected upon their shared tragedy. "Well, Gentlemen," Captain Witt reached to push the start engine button. Then, as the motor began to rumble, announced, "Time to cast off!"

Dr. Colburn stepped to the gangway and climbed down to the dock. "Bowline first?" He called back to Captain Witt.

"That's great!" The captain answered. He threw the line over the railing, then proceeded to the back of the boat and unhooked the stern line, then swung himself back onto the boat and locked the safety rail into its closed position. "Marcus didn't tell me you had boat savvy!" Captain Witt exclaimed.

"My wife and I sailed with Jan and him several times around the Hampton Roads area, and the Chesapeake, in the seventies. Other than that, sailing has been just another hole at the bottom of my bucket list!"

The captain chuckled, then said, "I don't suppose Marcus has had time to tell you much about me, but you and I might want to get together for drinks sometime, and talk about how I could help you plug that bucket." Captain Witt leaned to the port side to eyeball the clearance as he steered the boat away from the dock, then proudly proclaimed, "My wife, Kitty, and I, started the Southernmost Sailing School here in 1986 and have graduated over nine hundred students since we began!"

"Really!" Dr. C. exclaimed. "Maybe we're going to need to talk about that sometime soon!"

The captain steered the boat carefully around the granite breakwater, then turned to the North, toward the city's mooring field, where they would soon be tying up to mooring ball number thirty-six. "We'll be about fifteen minutes in route till we tie off. If you have any questions about how this thing's going to go, feel free to ask me now."

Dr. Colburn appreciated the captain's offer and asked, "Oh, great! Is there some protocol for how the clients get situated so that I can begin their counseling sessions?"

"There is, but I take care of all of that! When I took on this gig, I signed on as a charter for hire, and legally, as a licensed captain, I have full responsibility for the safety and security of everyone who boards this vessel. When Marcus and I hammered out the contract, almost ten years ago, I had to attend HIPAA training, over at the Human Resource office at Depoo Hospital. It was specifically stipulated in the contract that I be familiar with, and follow, all HIPAA guidelines. Once we're on site, I'll get everything set up! All you need to do is keep your coffee from spilling!"

"Well! It's sure nice to know what my responsibilities will be!" The doctor said with a laugh.

"I'd expect we'll be seeing a lot of the same people that Marcus was treating before his gout got bad. Some of them, I understand, are already clients of yours over at the clinic, but for a few of the others, this might be their first time seeking psychiatric help. I'll be screening out the ones that are just looking for opioids or other prescriptions they can abuse. Markus has trained me well over the years! I think you'll catch on real quick!" The captain turned into the main channel and pointed toward the cluster of boats beyond Christmas Tree Island, then announced, "There's the mooring field!"

Dr. Colburn looked to the west and counted twenty-three boats moored in the field. "Is that a usual number of boats for this time of year?" He asked.

"There is no usual number of boats in Key West!" The captain responded as he pointed his finger toward a larger number of boats anchored off Fleming Key, then added, "Over there's where most of the people you'll be seeing live. We call it all the 'Mooring Field', but the only area that's officially a mooring field is the city-owned moorings that were established a long time ago. They're anchored to the seabed by huge concrete blocks. That's it, over on the North East side of Christmas Tree Island. Heavy chains are embedded in the block and secured to ropes that are tethered to floating white balls, that have a steel eyehook on top where the boat can be safely secured. Each mooring ball is numbered, and the dockmaster keeps track of every boat that ties up. He collects a daily fee and issues a sticker for tying their dinghy up at the dinghy dock. He also issues a combination, so people can access the laundry room and the showers when they come ashore. Though the city wants to get rid of the mooring field, they can't! It's protected by Florida maritime law, and statutory mandates! People traveling on their boats have the right to stay off-shore, if that's their choice. I think it's one of those American freedoms that makes traveling by boat so romantic!"

A pod of bottlenose dolphins was racing with the boat, as it motored through the deep-water channel. Dr. Colburn leaned over the railing and snapped several photos with his phone, then asked, "Do you know where Billy's boat is?"

Captain Witt pointed toward the back-side of Christmas Tree Island and said, "It's that Morgan Out Island Ketch 51 with the Conch Republic flag hanging from the stern staff. It looks like it still has the police tape in place." He steered left and idled down, as the boat entered the no wake zone and said, "If you look closely, you can see a group of dinghies and kayaks clustered next to a mooring ball on the back side of the field. That's number thirty-six! Those are your first clients of the day! Their waiting for you!"

Dr. Colburn stood to his feet, for a better look, and anxiously remarked, "We can't have all those people on the boat at the same time!"

Captain Witt chuckled as he directed, "Steady your mug, sailor! They know it's first come first served! Marcus and I went over some things he wants me to address with them before we get started. Sit tight! You'll see!" He killed the engine and climbed onto the upper deck, then made his way to the bow where he retrieved the mooring line and tossed one end to a young man standing in a dinghy. "Thanks Cai! Been a while since I've seen you, you doing OK?"

The lanky young man called back as he hooked the line to ball number thirty-six, "Things aren't so good Witt! Everything's kinda fucked up!".

The captain tugged on the line to test its hold, then offered an assuring suggestion, "Be sure to talk it all out with Dr. C. when you get with him! I'm sure he can help!" He made his way back to the starboard gunnel and called out to the crowd of people, "Good morning, everyone! Give us a few minutes to get things set up, then we'll go over the rules and get started." He turned to Dr. C. and nodded for him to follow as he opened the hatch and climbed into the cabin. "I think I ought to bring you up to speed on a few things you need to be watching out for. Are you familiar with that kid that hooked us up to the mooring ball?"

Dr. C. responded, "Cai? Not really! He's been over to the clinic a couple of times to pick up a hygiene kit or to ask about our prescription assistance program, but I've never personally interacted with him. Why?"

The captain explained, "Out of all the people that Billy was involved with, Cai was the most fragile! It was about six years ago when he first showed up. He was emaciated and sleeping under some bushes in Clinton Square. Billy took him under his wing and got him fixed up with one of Marcus's boats to live on. I'll tell you more later, but just be aware that nobody out here was more dependent on Billy's generosity than Cai!"

The doctor was keenly attentive and appreciative of the captain's warning and responded, "Gee, thanks, Witt! I'll keep that in mind!"

As the captain reached for the ladder to pull himself back up to the hatch, he suggested, "You can see your clients up in the cockpit or down here in the air conditioning, but if you bring them down here, you'll have a hell of a time getting them to leave!" He raised his eyebrows and tilted his head to assure the doctor had fully grasped his inference, then added, "having them in here would be safer, though! I'm always right there, in the forward berth, working on my laptop and keeping an ear peeled, in case somebody starts trouble!"

"Well, that's great to know!" Dr. Colburn was thrilled to find that his new partner was not only competent but conscientious too.

As they climbed up the ladder, toward the closed hatch, they were startled by the voice of an angry man yelling profanely. "Oh, Oh! That sounds like trouble!" There was a loud splash, then more yelling. The captain rushed through the hatchway, and leapt to the starboard rail in time to see J.C. pushing Cai under water with the end of an oar.

"J.C., what in the hell are you doing?" The captain shouted authoritatively at the man with the oar.

"He's a lying thief, god damn it! He was over on Billy's boat, looking for stuff to steal!" Cai was struggling to pull himself back into his boat, while J.C. continued with his accusations, "I saw the little son of a bitch in the fog, about an hour ago! He was paddling his piece of shit dinghy over here from that direction." J.C. pointed toward Billy's boat, then continued, "Tell them, you little bastard! Tell the truth for once, you little creep! You're going to jail this time, bitch!"

"All right, J.C., that's enough!" The captain was concerned for the other clients that were now, widely dispersed in the waters around the boat. "Any more outbursts and you'll be banned from these sessions." He leaned toward J.C. and said, "Am I being clear enough for you J.C.?"

J.C. begrudgingly nodded his head and sat back down in his boat. Cai dug through his satchel for a towel, then wiped his face and blew his nose.

"All right, listen up!" The captain announced as the crowd pulled their boats back into a half circle. "Dr. Grant has asked me to let you all know that he shares your sorrow over losing Billy, and he wants me to assure you that our services will be available to you anytime, anywhere, while we try to find our way through this pain! Some of you may already be familiar with Dr. Grant's longtime friend, Dr. Walter Colburn." The doctor stepped to the railing and smiled as he bid good morning to the flotilla of new clients. "He will be our shipbound psychiatrist here on the *Psyched Out*, and will be able to provide you with all the same services that we've offered in the past. Now, with the temperature climbing toward ninety degrees, I think we should get started putting together a schedule!"

He leaned low, over the railing, and handed a clipboard and pen to a lady in a green kayak, then continued with his instructions, "If you don't want to use your real names, you don't have to! We just need a way to figure out who goes before who, and a cell number so we can contact you when it's time for your appointment. We will need your real name for prescriptions or if you need to be referred for other services. If you need refills, we'll need you to bring your prescription numbers or their empty bottles with you, when you come for your session. For those of you who haven't been with us before, we already have arrangements with the Walgreens Pharmacy, over on Duval Street, and if we write you a prescription, they bill it to us, not you!"

The captain reached to recover his clipboard, and as he scanned through the list of names, he announced, "If you have any questions, feel free to ask them now!"

An older gentleman with a small white dog sitting in his lap asked, "What about my dog? Is it ok for him to come on board?"

Captain Witt placed his finger on the side of his forehead, then turned to Dr. Colburn and said, "Well, I don't know if the doctor has much experience with counseling dogs, but I think he'd be willing to try!"

Everyone but J. C. laughed as the captain finished with his orientation. "Once we work out who was ahead of who, you are free to go back to your boats and wait for my call. Also, if you want to wait over on Christmas Tree Island, that's up to you, but keep your phones charged and listen for my call! I will try to give you at least thirty minutes to get back here for your appointment."

The captain spent the next few minutes assigning appointment times and verifying corresponding phone numbers, then he finalized his orientation. "I've hung a cooler with ice and water from the transom, so take what you need and leave the rest. Each of you will have an hour for your session, so please stay within thirty minutes of getting back to the boat and wait for my call."

J.C. angrily pulled twice on his engine's start cord, then sat back down in defeat and began cussing out loud, about Cai being first on the list.

"J.C.!" The captain scolded, "Knock it off, now! If you want us to help you with anything, you'll need to dump your anger off at somebody else's boat!"

Moments later, the crowd had disbursed and Cai was left standing in his dinghy, waiting for permission to board.

8. CAIRO

"Well Cai, I guess you're up first!" Captain Witt called down to the curly-haired string bean of a man. "Toss me your line and I'll get it tied off, then we'll help you climb up."

Dr. Colburn reached through the boarding gate and grabbed Cai's backpack, then the two men pulled him onto the boat.

"When was the last time you ate something, Cai?" Asked the captain as the young man took a seat on the port side of the cockpit.

"I had a can of soup last night with some potato chips!" he answered, hoping that the captain might offer something to help tame his growling stomach.

The captain opened the ice-cooler that was sitting on the deck and retrieved a bagged sandwich, and a bottle of water, then asked, "Turkey and cheese sound ok?"

Cai eagerly accepted and sat eating as Dr. Colburn situated himself with his coffee and Cuban sandwich, then, before taking a bite, initiated Cai's session by saying, "Cai, I know we've met a couple of times over at the clinic, but I don't think you ever joined us for group! Were you able to get what you needed?" Captain Witt climbed back down, into the main cabin, and pulled the hatch closed from inside.

"Oh, yes sir!" Cai answered. "I usually get my bus pass, and toiletry bag, over at DePoo! That's really the only reason I've ever been over there."

The doctor asked, "How are you feeling this morning? Are you having any difficulties that you and I might need to talk about? Any thoughts that people might want to hurt you, or that you want to hurt yourself?"

The young man seemed agitated, nervous, and evasive as he answered, "I wish somebody would kill J.C.! Is that what you mean"?

66

The doctor's curiosity needed to be satisfied! He asked, "Is there any chance that you might act upon that impulse?"

"No! I just wish he was gone. You know, blow away! Him and his fuckin boat just get sucked into a hurricane and disappear. That's all!". Cai seemed to relax a little after unloading. He thumped his foot against the hatch to the gear locker he was sitting above, and slapped his hand against his upper left thigh, waiting for the doctor's response.

The doctor was focused on finding the best way to lead his new client into, what he hoped, might be a productive psychotherapeutic first hour of counseling. "I really don't know much about you, Cai." The doctor began! "If I understood correctly, you were close friends with Billy. Is that an accurate way of putting it?"

"He was more like a father to me!" He continued chewing as he talked! "Nobody ever gave a shit about me till Billy!" He tilted his head back and emptied the water bottle, then added, "I'd probably still be sleepin in tha bushes behind the parking garage if I hadn't met Billy!"

Dr. Colburn wadded up his sandwich wrapper and tossed it into the can by the helm, then asked, "Did you know Billy before you came to Key West? Were you in the Navy with him?"

"Uh-uh!" Cai answered. "I met Billy about three months after I got here. I met him over on Mallory Square! He stopped his bike and asked if I was OK! I don't know why, but he just stopped and asked me a bunch of questions. I thought he was after something, but after a minute or two he handed me six dollars and told me to go get something to eat, then he rode off through the crowd. That was about five years ago!"

"Did you?" The doctor asked.

"Did I what?" Cai responded.

"Get something to eat, with the six dollars?" Dr. C. asked.

"Oh! Yeah! I walked over to Denny's on Duval Street, and got a burger." The young man answered.

"Did you have any money left over?" Asked Dr. Colburn.

Cai frowned! He wondered why the doctor might want to know such a thing. "Yea! I left it for the girl! I felt bad that I only had a little bit of change left over for her! She was nice to me! She's always nice! She thinks we're gonna get married, but I'm not sure about that!"

Cai had no way of knowing that Dr. Colburn was using this dialogue to assess his ability to stay focused on facts and follow the flow of normal social discourse, nor that Dr. C. was continuously evaluating Cai's body language and facial responses as he watched for clues that might be symptomatic of mental health issues that needed attention. No, poor disheveled Cai had paddled over to the *Psyched Out,* looking only for something he could grab hold of! Something, anything, that might offer him a sure grip, then pull him safely away from the intolerable fear that his future now offered. In a flash, all of his hopes had washed away! He was drowning in an ocean that had no interest in the tears of his eyes, or the screams of his soul.

Dr. Colburn was always cognizant of how quickly these one-hour sessions could dissolve into unproductive chit chat, and how this one hour could be the only chance he would ever have to significantly impact this friend of a friend of his friend. He pressed further and asked, "Why don't you tell me a little bit about yourself, and how you came to be living here, in Key West."

"Well, you know Dr. Grant already knows all that stuff! We spent lots of time talkin bout it years ago! Right here, on this boat."

Cai was nervous about having to talk about his past with a new doctor, but this doctor knew how to handle it and offered, "Ya know, I'm pretty sure that there might be a lot of stuff that I can help you with! Maybe some things that might make living out here a lot easier for you." He reached into the cooler and grabbed Cai a second bottle of water, then asked, "Were you born here in Key West?"

Cai downed half the bottle, wiped his lips, then opened the flood gates to his life story. "No, sir! I was born in Egypt!" It was like watching a fiery spark pop skyward out of a burning pit! "My mother was Egyptian, but my father was Greek!" He swallowed the remaining water, then went on with his questionable tale, as the doctor heightened his attention. "He was an assistant to the Greek Ambassador sent to Cairo by the Hellenic Republic Consulate office of Foreign Affairs in 1995. Billy did the research! He said he was a barrister-at-law and graduated from the Kapodistrain School of Law in Athens and when he was working in Cairo, he met my mother!"

Dr. Colburn's tongue pulled slowly off the inside wall of his right cheek as he considered the confident nature with which this sweaty, dirty, highly disheveled, and potentially misconstrued man described his past. Could he be delusional, he wondered! Cairo had presented the information succinctly and without the least hesitation. These attributes are not often found when patients are observed exhibiting delusional constructs! The possibility that Cairo might be describing his true family history had to be considered, and if so, what else about this young man might bewilder the doctor as he proceeded? He was interested in exploring further the origins of the information and asked, "You said something about Billy having provided you with some of your father's information?"

"Yeah!" Cai was eyeballing the cooler, hoping that the doctor might offer him something else to eat. As he began to describe how he had come under Billy's tutelage, Dr. Colburn pulled a second sandwich from the cooler and handed it to him. "I didn't see Billy again for a long time! I was walking by an open door at Harpoon Harry's one morning, and saw him sitting in a corner booth. He must have seen me, cause by the time I was halfway across the street, he had come outside and called for me to join him. I didn't really want to, but he insisted, so I followed him back to his table, where he ordered me a big breakfast." Cai shoved the last bite of sandwich in his mouth and kept talking, "I was sleeping behind the parking garage on Grinnell and Caroline Street back then! Billy wanted to know all about me. It was weird! Nobody ever asked so much about my life. I didn't know why he was interested, but later, after he and Dr. Grant got me fixed up with a boat to live on, and we'd become friends, he wrote me into one of his songs. It's great! It's about me sleepin' behind tha parking garage on Grinnell and Caroline. Anyway, nobody ever did so much for me! When I first got to Key West, my teeth were so bad that I could hardly chew anything. If I had a burger, I had to take little bites and smash it all up with my tongue before I could swallow it. They were horrible! Billy took me to a dental school in Bradenton! They pulled out all my teeth and gave me new ones! See!" He used his fingers to pull back his lips, and showed Dr. Colburn his teeth, then stretched proudly and proclaimed, "I'm gonna be a dentist"

Dr. Colburn was beginning to see indications of psychosis that gave him concern! He reached into his bag and retrieved a small note pad and pen. As he adjusted his seating, he leaned forward and said, "Amazing! They sure did a great job!" He continued talking as he wrote his notes. "It sounds like Billy was a powerful help to you! I'd imagine losing him might leave you feeling uneasy about the future. Can you tell me a little more about how much his friendship meant to you?"

The young man leaned his upper body forward and rested his elbows on his knees. "Billy was more than a friend, he was my only family! If it weren't for him, I'd probably be dead by now! He took care of me! He did it for everybody out here! He was the guardian angel of the mooring field. I can't believe he's really gone!" The boy was whimpering as he talked. "I got nobody now! Nobody at all!"

Dr. Colburn redirected the man's thoughts toward a more productive narrative. "Tell me about your childhood and any memories of people and events that you felt strongly about."

Cai sat up and looked across the water, toward Key West, then began, "Some of this I remember, but lots of it comes from the research Billy did! My younger brother and I were sent to foster care when I was five years old. There was a newspaper report, in New Jersey, where my father and mother were arrested by the FBI, and later sent back to Egypt where they went to prison for stealing a lot of money from the government. I think they're still probably in prison! Billy contacted the child welfare agency in New Jersey and finally learned that they couldn't get my mother's brother to accept either of us, so we both grew up changing families till Aman was six and got adopted by some Arab American couple in New York. I never heard from him after that."

Dr. Colburn's phone was sitting on the cushion next to him and Cai pointed at it, "You can see the house I grew up in on YouTube!"

Dr. Colburn's curiosity was duly aroused! He picked up his phone and opened the app, then asked, "What should I search for?"

Cai stood to his feet and excitedly directed, "Crime Family $7,000,000 Abandoned Beach Mansion! You'll even see my Dad's BMW and my Mom's Mercedes! They're still in the garage! My toys are still on the floor next to my bed! Some guy took a camera inside and made a video. Billy was going to drive me up there to clean it up and let me live there."

It only took a couple of seconds for the video to load. "That's it!" Cai was jumping like a little kid. "That's my house! I'm a Goddamn millionaire!" Cai was euphoric! He began pacing from one side of the salon to the other, leaning far out over the water as he shouted into the salty air, the words, "I'm a millionaire!"

The doctor let the video play for several minutes, then suggested, "We can get back to this sometime soon, but since we've only got another thirty minutes till my next patient shows up, how about you tell me more about the people closest to you. Is there anyone other than Billy that you feel might be supportive, as you move forward?"

Cai settled back into the cushion and shrugged his shoulders, then said, "There's Ken, in Fort Pierce! He said I could come stay with him anytime I want. He's my best friend! He's got a huge mansion on the river, looking out at the cape. He said we can watch the rockets launch from his boat dock and go fishing whenever we want!" Cai reached into his back pocket and pulled out his tattered leather wallet. "Here's his card!"

The doctor took the card and read aloud, "Kenneth T. Hartmann Sr., Luxury Yacht Brokerage, Fort Pierce, Florida." On the back side of the card was a handwritten address! "Is this his home address, on the back?" The doctor asked.

Cai leaned across the deck to look, then answered, "Yeah! He wrote that on it so I could find him when I get up there. Billy showed me where it is on his computer. He went right down onto the street, and we walked it like we were there."

"That might have been Google Earth!" The doctor suggested.

"Yeah! That's what it was!" Cai seemed pleased that Dr. Colburn was engaging with his story. "He and his wife have plenty of room, and I'm going to help them fix up their garage so they can rent it out."

"Is there anyone else you can think of that might be able to help you if something comes up that you might need help with?" The doctor was hoping to provoke him into exploring resources that he may not have, as of yet, considered to be viable.

"I don't get along with too many people! Usually, I try to stay to myself. When I was a kid, I had to change schools every time I had to move to a new family. I kept to myself to keep from getting picked on! I got beat up a lot! Usually 'cause of my skin being so dark! Sometimes by kids, sometimes by my foster parents. It was tough!"

Dr. Colburn had been waiting for an opportunity to question Cai on his relationship to J.C. and asked, "That fellow that pushed you off your dinghy this morning, have you had trouble with him before?"

Cai was more than happy to talk about that relationship and explained, "J.C.'s a low life, son-of-a-bitch! He came here from tha mooring field in Sarasota about two years ago. I heard that they told him to leave or they'd put him in jail and impound his boat, and I believe it! He's mean to everybody! Somethin's really wrong with that guy!"

"Why do you think he attacked you this morning?" Dr. Colburn asked.

"That's the third time he's tried to kill me!" Cai said angrily. "He shoved me off the dock one night, and I got scraped up by the barnacles when I hit the pilings. Tha guy's just dangerous! He swerved his scooter into me one day in the parking lot behind Turtle Kraals. I didn't see him coming! He hit me from behind! It knocked me down, but I wasn't hurt so bad."

Captain Witt opened the hatch and stuck his head through the opening, "Excuse me, doc, but your next client is twenty minutes out!"

"Thank You!" The doctor said, then proceeded to wrap up his session. "Cai," he started, "have you been having any difficulty with sleeping?"

Cai raised his eyebrows and exclaimed emphatically, "Hell! You can't imagine! I usually drag my comforter up on the top of tha cabin at night, ya know, to try to catch a breeze. That is, if it's not lookin' like rain. The boat I'm on doesn't have electricity, so tha fans don't work. Billy buys me candles for light and Sterno for cookin' food. Sometimes he brings me Tylenol PM, but I've been out of that for over a week."

The doctor pulled his prescription pad out of his bag and held his pen in the air as he asked, "Would you like me to write you a prescription for something to help you get to sleep?"

"Well, that would be great, but I don't have any money!" Cai replied.

"That's no problem," the doctor said. "We cover it entirely! I will have to use your full name, though. It's got to match what's on your legal I.D."

Cai seemed concerned and offered, "I always thought my last name was Amberdon, but Billy found out it was, really, Katsaros. The Amberdons were the foster family that Aman and I lived with for several years when we were first sent into foster care! We always used their last name for school stuff! Billy once researched to see if there were any court records that legally changed my name, and there weren't. He found out that, in New Jersey, it was illegal for them to change my name unless they adopted me! He got a copy of the naturalization form my mother used to get citizenship, and we used that to get a Florida I.D. for me. It's got my real name as Cairo Tanopolis Katsaros. I guess you can use that name!"

"Ok!" The doctor said as he began to write the prescriptions, "Spell that for me!"

Cai pulled his I.D. out of his wallet and began to spell out his full name as it was printed on the card.

Dr. Colburn handed two prescriptions to the young man and explained, "This first script will help you get to sleep. It's for fifty milligrams of hydroxyzine! I want you to take one tablet, at night, before you go to bed. This second script is Seroquel one hundred milligrams. Take two capsules at night after you eat something. This will help you keep your thoughts focused, so that you can get more things accomplished every day! It might take a month or so before you start to feel the full effects, but start tonight, and if you need a refill, just get in touch with my office. They'll be sure you get you what you need."

The doctor stood to his feet and handed Cai an envelope with two-hundred dollars inside, and instructed, "Hand these prescriptions to the pharmacist at the Walgreens store on Duval Street. He'll get them filled for you, and there won't be any charges. Then use the money in the envelope to buy a bottle of good-quality multi-vitamins and any personal items that you need to keep yourself clean and healthy." The doctor led Cai over to the boarding gate as Captain Witt climbed back up from below deck. "I want you to plan on seeing me again in two weeks, over at the clinic. I think there's a lot of progress to be made here!"

Cai climbed back into his boat with no indication that he heard anything the doctor had said. The two men watched him as he struggled to paddle his half-deflated dinghy toward the deep-water channel.

Captain Witt couldn't resist offering a parting comment and said, "I'm pretty sure that guy's anchor line got tied with a slip knot!"

9. JAZELLE'S GOT A BUG

Captain Witt turned and looked to the west! He lifted his finger and pointed, "Here comes your next client!"

Doctor Colburn turned and ducked his head under the edge of the dodger for a better view.

"I called her when Cai was thirty minutes in! That's how we keep on schedule! I'll call your next client at her thirty, whether she shows up on time or not."

Dr. Colburn was amazed at how deeply involved the captain was in managing the clients and asked, "Is that how you did it for Markus?"

"Well, Markus and I were out here for almost ten years. The clientele seems to have changed a little, but I think I'll be doing the same for you as I did back then." He tapped the LCD screen on the weather monitor and exclaimed, "Wow! It's already over ninety degrees! You might want to move this next session inside!"

Dr. Colburn raised his eyebrows and agreed, "Yeah, I think that's a good idea!"

The girl in the dinghy was about three-hundred yards out when Captain Witt asked, "Did Markus get a chance to brief you on any of these client's histories?"

Dr. Colburn answered, "No, he didn't! After the S.H.A L. meeting, we drove out to Safe Harbor but never got around to talking about clients. He told me about a guy that Billy was helping with an addiction problem. I don't remember the guy's name but Markus said he had committed suicide on his houseboat."

"Yeah! That was Jimmy Borg!" The captain explained. "Poor guy! I met him a few times. He used to hang out a lot with Timmy Wegman over at the music shop on Caroline Street. Tim was the owner of tha shop! Before Jimmy died, all the best local musicians would hang out in the breezeway beside the shop and jam. Tim had a baby grand piano out there and this little girl that's about to climb onboard was the only one, besides himself, that played it. Anyway, used to be Jimmy's girlfriend! She's tha one that found him hanging on his houseboat. It tore her up, and Markus helped her through it."

"Hey Emmie!" The captain called out as she cut her motor and drifted toward the boat.

"Mornin Witt! Tie me off?" The girl called out as she tossed her bow line across his outstretched arm.

Dr. Colburn steadied his foot on the gunnel and reached out his hand to help pull her up. "Good morning! I'm Dr. Colburn!"

The girl climbed on board, then turned to shake the doctor's hand and said, "I'm Emmalea! Emma Lapierre, I think you might remember my sister, Jazelle. She did a tarot card reading for your wife at Mallory Square once."

Dr. Colburn's heart skipped a beat! A familiar flood of emotion rushed through his body, then buckled his knees. Captain Witt jumped to his side and grabbed his arm. "Woah! You ok, Doc?" he asked as he lowered him into his seat.

The doctor took a deep breath, then let it out slowly, "I've got a bit of a balance problem that sometimes hits me from out of the blue." He reached for his bottle of water, and added, "I'll be fine, as long as I keep my hydration up."

Captain Witt opened the hatch and suggested, "What say we take this project inside where it's twenty degrees cooler." Once the trio had made their way into the cabin, Captain Witt excused himself and disappeared into the forward berth, while Dr. Colburn and Emma situated themselves in the main salon.

"Tread softly, darling!" He felt the breeze wash across his ear as Amelia imposed her silent concern. "You don't want to shake that crystal ball right now!"

"Well, Emma," He seemed a little disoriented as he reached to adjust the fins on the air-conditioner vent, then pulled two cold water bottles from the cooler on the floor. "Yes, I do remember Jazelle! She read for me once, later, after my wife passed. Wonderful girl! Is she still doing her readings over on Mallory Square?"

"No, she's not well!" Emma explained. "She was living up on Ramrod Key, for the past three years, in kind of a hippie/rainbow commune set up, way out on the North end of the island. She had sliced her leg open on a rusty piece of an old car that was dumped into the canal back in the seventies, and she didn't get it seen by anybody till it was infected. When she finally went to the Lower Keys E.R., they did a wound culture, and two days later, it came back positive for flesh-eating bacteria. They flew her up to Jackson Memorial in Miami, where she was isolated for three and a half months and had to have a bunch of surgeries. Now, she's sleeping in her car and begging for gas money to go back and forth to Miami for treatments. Billy had gotten involved a week ago, and was working on getting her into a room over at Samuel's House, but now, with him gone, I was hoping that maybe you and Dr. Grant might be able to help her."

The doctor puffed out his cheeks as he exhaled a deep breath and gave the girl his assurance, "Oh. Emma, I'm so sorry! I'm sure we can get something going right away on this. Give me a moment!" He stood to his feet, then stepped to the closed door to the forward compartment and called to Captain Witt. "Witt, could you join us for a minute, please!"

The door opened, and the captain stepped into the main salon and asked, "What's up doc?" "Emma was just telling me about her sister, Jazzell's, medical condition, and wondering if we might be able to help get her into a room at Samuel's House. I was wondering if you knew anything about how we might be able to help with getting that expedited?" Before the doctor finished his question Capt. Witt had his phone to his ear, "Hi Courtney, it's Witt! Oh yeah, we're out there now! Yeah, he's taking to it like the pro Markus said he'd be. Listen, we're with Emma Lapierre right now, and she's asking if there's any movement on her sister's placement. Any chance we could get a status report? Yeah, that's right! No, she's still in her car! Oh great! Thanks! Yeah, that would be fine, I'll wait for your call! Thanks!"

He turned toward the doctor and his client, then explained, "Courtney says that Billy had dropped off Jazzell's paperwork on Monday, and she'll check with the director to see if the background check has come back, then she'll call and let us know what to expect."

Emma was overcome with gratitude and began to cry, "Thank You! Thank You! Thank You!" While she was whimpering, the captain's phone rang and he answered, "This is Witt! Oh great! Thank you Courtney! Sure, she's right here! Ok, hang on," he pushed the speaker button and dropped his phone from his ear, "Go ahead Courtney!"

"Dr. Colburn, Emma, this is Courtney Ashcroft over at Samuel's House! I'm the intake coordinator that handles Jazelle's case." She listened as they each offered their return greetings, then continued, "I've just finished reviewing her file and am happy to tell you that she's all set. If she can get here by six pm, she can sign her resident's agreement, and we'll do her orientation, then she can settle into her new room. From what Billy told me, she's been through an awfully tough time this year! We're thrilled to be able to offer her a shot at making her life better, and we look forward to helping her in any we can."

"That's just astounding!" Dr. Colburn's voice resounded throughout the cabin. "We can't thank you enough!"

Emma was ecstatic and called out, "Thank you so much! I'll get the news to her right away and should be able to be over there by three or four o'clock, if that's ok."

Courtney obligingly offered, "That's great! I'll personally make sure she gets everything she needs!" Then added, "I'll see you when you get here!"

The doctor and captain added their thanks, and once the call was completed, Emma gave them each a grateful hug. Captain Witt returned to the forward berth, and the doctor turned his attention toward any other issues of his client's concern. "So, I understand you are living out here in the mooring field with your two children. How is that working out for you?"

"Well, I don't think I'd have it any other way!" She explained. "I've been out here for sixteen years! I think that having the kids grow up so close to nature will prove to be the best choice I could have ever made! We don't have a TV, so there's nothing to distract them from developing their talents and looking for creative ways to keep themselves entertained. I think living out here builds character and is making us stronger and closer as a family."

Dr. Colburn's curiosity led him to ask, "How did you come to be living in Key West?"

Emma took a drink from her water bottle, then began, "My boyfriend and I came here from Toronto so he could be close to his father, who was living dockside on his boat behind Schooner's Wharf. We lived out here in the mooring field on a trimaran that he and his dad had built for us. While they were building it, Ethan and I rented an old Hunter thirty-three sloop. It's still out here! Ethan's friend Rollye and his wife Melinda bought it in 2010 and fixed it up. It's a dream boat now! They moved up from Saint John when he lost his maintenance contract with the National Park Service. You'll probably meet Melinda at some point! She's the community care coordinator for Wesley House Family Services! Dr. Grant knows her well! Anyway, Ethan's dad worked in the banana industry in the Caribbean and with many of the countries in South America. When he retired from that, he moved his boat up here and lives on it for four months out of the year, then flies back to York University in Toronto to teach. He has dual citizenship with Canada and the U.S., but Ethan never applied for his. He said he owed restitution to the Toronto courts for some kind of trouble he got into when he was about eighteen and feared he would be extradited back there. He never talked about it, and I never asked. We never did get married, either! He didn't want anybody, "official" to have a reason to do a background search, and risk being arrested, then get sent back to Canada." She finished her water and continued, "It's the only regret I think I've ever had, not pushing him into getting his citizenship. If I had, maybe the kids would have been entitled to his survivor benefits."

Dr. Colburn's brain did a backflip. He raised both hands in the air to beckon her to pause her story and said, "Wait! Are you talking about the same Ethan Hall that was spotted floating dead, twelve miles offshore in 2009?"

"Yeah, that's him!" Emma answered.

"Well, I'll be a son of a gun! Your two kids would be half-siblings to Jillian Daugherty's daughter, Krismas, right?" He exclaimed.

"Yeah! That's right! We know Krismas! I watch her for Jillian sometimes when she needs me to. I assumed you already knew all that."

"No!" Dr. Colburn exclaimed. "Well, I mean, I never knew about your kids. I never met Ethan. I just knew who he was from the newspaper articles when he was found by that cruise ship. Jillian told me about him, but I never knew he had two other children. Did Dr. Grant ever meet Ethan?"

"No!" Emma answered. "He didn't know Ethan, but I brought the kids out here to talk with him when we found out he had died. Dr. Grant was very helpful! He suggested some things for me to start paying attention to, so that Mallory and Kinsey could get a better grip on what death is all about. I still use some of those techniques when we come across something dead in the water. I try to always keep it real. Billy was also helpful back then. He had a unique way of explaining things like death and God and life. I really liked his take on things that are hard to explain."

Dr Colburn took her pause as his opportunity to redirect the discussion back toward its therapeutic intent and asked, "Were you and Billy close?"

"We were friends for almost ten years! I covered for him when his dog, Flow, needed to get over to Christmas Tree Island to poo, or if she needed feeding, and he couldn't get back out to the boat in time. Usually, though, she was with him wherever he went." She sipped from her bottle, then continued, "Sometimes, he'd ferry the kids back and forth from the docks when I had to stay at work late or got caught up somewhere and couldn't get to them on time. I think he helped us a lot more than we helped him, though!" She drank the last of her water and sat the bottle on the table, then added, "I love to cook and would take him dinner regularly! He was like an uncle to me and a grandpa to the kids. I'd say our relationship was like an extended family! I could call him anytime and he'd be there for me! It was the same with him! We're all going to miss him deeply!"

"Do you have concerns for how the children will react to the news of his passing?" The doctor asked.

She took a moment and was noticeably troubled as she answered, "Actually, they're already having trouble! I got a call from Jeannie about ten o'clock yesterday when she and Calvin saw the cops pulling Billy's dinghy out from under the Turtle Museum. I think that everybody knew he was gone by noon! We're a tight little community out here! We look out for each other, generally! There're a couple of people we stay clear of, but for the rest of us, we hang together, and when something big happens, it goes out on the Coconut Telegraph. It's not long before everybody's got the news."

Dr. Colburn asked, "Are the kids out on the boat this morning?"

"No! We were up most of the night talking about Billy and life stuff. Remember when I told you about Ethan's dad and how he spends some time up in Toronto teaching, and some time on his boat down here?"

"Oh, yes! That was very interesting!" The doctor answered.

Emma explained, "Well, luckily, he's here till January, so we spent the night over on his boat and were up all night, talking and crying. They were sound asleep when I left this morning. I asked Don to call me when they wake up."

Captain Witt opened the forward door and called into the salon, "Excuse me doc, next up-ten minutes!"

The doctor pulled a business card from his pocket and handed it to her. "I want you to promise you'll call me if you think of anything I can do that might be helpful! My office can schedule appointments for the three of you and usually get you in within a day if needed. In the meantime, if you just need to talk to me by phone, I'm putting my personal number on the back. You can call me anytime and if I'm not available, leave me a message and I'll call you right back as soon as I can."

As they rose from their seats, the doctor reached into his bag and took out two envelopes. He handed them to her and said, "If you don't mind, when you see Jazelle, give her one of these and tell her to call me. I want to talk to her about her pharmaceutical needs, and see if Dr. Grant and I can't help her with the costs of her treatments. The other envelope is for you and the kids to use as you see fit." Emma's eyes welled up with tears as she gave the doctor a hug. Captain Witt entered the salon and the trio moved toward the cabin ladder to exit. Emma climbed back into her dinghy and turned to look up at the two men standing on the deck of the *Psyched Out*. With tears streaming from her eyes, she crossed her hands over her heart and mouthed the words, "Thank You," then started her engine and motored away, leaving one psychiatrist and his captain soaked in empathy.

10. SI JE PUIS (IF I CAN)

The doctor and his captain stood beneath the shade of the hardtop and waved goodbye to Emma as she motored toward shore. "Hey! Isn't that Cairo?" the doctor asked as he pointed toward a motorless inflatable one half mile out, bobbing haplessly in the channel.

"Ya know, I think you're right!" Captain Witt exclaimed as he reached into the helm locker to retrieve the binoculars. He adjusted the lens and studied the floundering boat, then handed the glasses to his newly found friend. "He's just sitting out there!"

Dr. Colburn raised the binoculars into place and asked, "I wonder why he stopped paddling? It doesn't seem safe to be out there just sitting, especially with no power! Wouldn't he be hard to see from those big boats that are cruising through the channel?"

"That's for damn sure!" Witt muttered through clenched teeth. Years of sailing these waters had hardened his will when it came to sympathies or condolences for people too stupid to run from a hurricane. "Here comes the real trouble!" ,he proclaimed as he tapped the doctor's shoulder and pointed to a small boat cutting across the waves. The boat took a hard turn to its left and drew a bead on the poor, crippled Cairo.

"You think he's gonna ram him?" The doctor asked.

"Naw! He knows we're watching!"

J. C.'s boat was at full bore when he threw his tiller to the left, missing Cairo by a mere three yards. The maneuver splashed a torrent of water over the boy and almost capsized his already floundering boat. J.C. recovered from the turn and redirected his course toward the *Psyched Out*. Minutes later, he idled up to the starboard side and cut his engine, then stood to his feet and held up his tether toward the two disapproving gentlemen with their arms crossed. "What?" J.C. felt a need to defend his action. "You don't know this guy! He's a fucking thief! He steals from everybody out here. He stole my hundred-dollar fishing rod and took it to the pawn shop. He's lucky I didn't ram him, tha little bitch!"

Captain Witt reached for the line and muttered to the doctor, "You got your hands full with this one, doc!" He turned to slide the hatch cover back, opened the hatch and climbed down the companionway ladder, then disappeared into the forward compartment.

"What's his problem?" J.C. halfheartedly asked.

The doctor tied the boat's line to the cleat and answered, "I think everybody's a little on edge this week! Let's get inside and cool off, then see if we can find you something to eat. Sound good?"

"Yeah! Sounds like that's just what I need!"

J.C. was noticeably on the take! That was no surprise to the doctor. He had already begun assessing the young man's temperament, and soon, he hoped to be developing a full psychiatric profile.

As they climbed into the cabin, the doctor asked, "Have you lived on your boat for a long time?" They situated themselves into the seats, then J. C. sarcastically answered, "Longer than any of these halfwits!" His eyes were scanning the interior of the boat as he talked. "You said you had something I could eat!"

The doctor reached into the cooler and offered, "Turkey and Swiss ok?"

"Great!" J.C. answered as he took the sandwich and began to unwrap it. "Can I have one of those waters?" "Oh, yeah!" The doctor grabbed a bottle and by the time it was in J.C.'s hand, the entire sandwich had disappeared.

"Can I get another one of those sandwiches?" He asked, then polished off the bottle of water with no hesitation.

"Sure!" The doctor pulled a second sandwich out of the cooler with a second bottle of water and set them on the table next to J.C. There was no display of appreciation, no recognizable regard for the effort made by the doctor on his behalf! He seemed detached, and solipsistic, and without any sign of compulsion toward gratitude. It was as if he willed the sustenance into existence, and some cosmic entity presented it for his satisfaction.

"What do we have here?" Amelia was tickling his hippocampus as he paged through years of psychotherapeutic sessions and lectures, searching for the necessary references that might lead him to his most accurate diagnosis.

J. C. devoured the second sandwich, and with one flush, bottle two was emptied and set on the table. In an effort to stave off a request for thirds, Dr. Colburn began his inquiry. "I assume, from what we witnessed earlier this morning between you and Cai, that you already know that Billy has died. Is that correct?"

J. C. straightened his back and raised one eyebrow. He glared at the doctor as he briskly raised his clenched fists to his beltline, then defensively asked, "Why are you asking me about Billy? You're not working with the cops, are you?"

In the millisecond it took for Dr. Colburn's mind to grasp the significance of his client's apprehension, he formulated his best defense with, "Good God, no! Not at all! I'm just here to help you, and anybody else who might have been impacted by Billy's death. You may not have been friends with him, but he meant a lot to many of the people who lived out here. I'm just hoping to offer support if you need it. If not, you are welcome to stay or go."

J. C. began to relax as he considered the presented option, then asked, "I still don't have to give you my name, do I?"

The doctor reiterated Witt's earlier announcement and answered, "Only if you need me to write you a prescription! Other than that, you're nothing but J. C. to me!"

The effect of his answer was immediately realized when the lad gendered a smile and asked, "You wouldn't have any mustard on this ol' tub, would you? I could use one more of those turkey sandwiches."

"I don't know! Let's take a look!" The doctor leaned forward and pulled out another sandwich, then stood to his feet and stepped into the galley, where he began pulling open drawers until he found a plastic baggie full of condiment packets. "Here, see if there's anything in here worth trying. I don't know how old they are, but maybe there's some flavor left in one or two."

J.C. sorted through the selection of packets and began squeezing the contents onto the opened sandwich he had balanced on his right knee. Within seconds, the sandwich had disappeared into his mouth, and as he washed it down with a swig of water, he proclaimed, "God damn! I needed that!"

The doctor was astounded when J. C. followed up with, "Thanks, Doc!"

"No problem, J.C. I'm glad you enjoyed it!"

J.C. wiped his mouth with the back side of his hand and asked, "So, you come out here just so people can talk out their problems?"

The doctor was beginning to see the opening of a door! It was a rewarding surprise!

"Well, it's what I've done pretty much for my whole professional life. When I graduated from Northwestern, I thought I was going to just stay in the Chicago area and set up a practice, maybe go in with another doctor and do general medicine and family stuff, but one of my instructors invited me to come back and work on my post-doctoral research in psychiatry, and I guess you'd say I got hooked. At some point, something I did got some attention by some people in Washington, and I ended up spending about twenty-two years helping to develop some of our nation's programs that helped make life a lot better for people in need."

Something the doctor had said seemed to strike an interest with the agitated and capricious young man. His leg had been nervously bouncing since he first sat down, and now it stopped. He straightened his back, then asked, "You been to Chicago?"

"I grew up in Lake View, about seven blocks from Wrigley Field! Chicago's my hometown!" The doctor proudly announced.

"Did you ever see tha Bulls play?" J.C. was referring to the Chicago Bulls basketball team.

"I had season tickets in 2001 and 2002! My son, Haydon, was one of the sports medicine doctors for the franchise, and I went with him to a lot of their games."

"Oh, that was cute!" There she was again. Popping in from those hollow spaces in his subconscious mind. "I like the way you did that!" He was hoping she would approve of the way he had substituted the name, Haydon for their eldest son Daniel's. True, it was! Daniel remained in his position with the Bulls until 2009, a mere eight months after his mother had passed, when he and another doctor opened their private practice. Amelia would have been proud of her firstborn baby boy. His dream had come true.

J.C. seemed excited when he asked, "So, did you ever see Michal Jordan play?"

The doctor knew immediately that their feet had landed on common sands and that his effectiveness with the young man relied on how deeply they sank. He dug in and answered the question with, "Not only have I seen him play, I've had the pleasure of dining with him and his wife Juanita several times, before they finally divorced. My younger son, Colter grew up shooting hoops with Michael's son Jeffrey."

You would have thought a lightning bolt had crashed through the cabin hatch! J.C. was like a little kid who had just trapped Santa unloading gifts from his sleigh.

"When the kids were little, my wife and Juanita used to take them all to the Shedd Aquarium for their birthdays. Colter and Jeffrey roomed together at U.C.F. the first year they were there, then Colter moved off campus to live with his girlfriend, over in Waterford Lakes. Colter told me, about three months ago, that Jeffrey had moved back to Chicago to work with his little brother in their family business. That's about all I can tell you about the Jordans! I don't know if it answers your question or not, but yes, I have seen him play."

J.C.'s mouth hung wide open! He slumped back into his seat, panting from amazement, then proudly bragged, "I bought a pair of Air Jordans for thirty-five dollars one time, at the Salvation Army over on Flagler Avenue. I had them drying out in the sun one day, and they got knocked off my boat by a wave! They were red with black laces!" He hesitated while Dr. C. pulled another water bottle out of the cooler and handed it to him, then added, "My dad was a big Bulls fan! He always hoped I'd grow up to be a basketball player, 'cause of my height, but I wasn't really any good at sports. I think I was tall enough, but I never finished the tenth grade and left home when I was seventeen."

J.C. was beginning to turn loose of his tongue, and Dr. C. expected that with this change in demeanor, he might get a better look into his client's deepest personality and emotional traits, personal values, and his fears and aspirations. They had arrived at this juncture with a full thirty minutes left in their session. "Were you close to your father?" Doctor Colburn began to delicately delve into J. C.'s cloistered psyche.

"Well, sometimes! Maybe in my earliest years, but I was the youngest of three, and he always seemed to like my brothers more than me. He was really mean, usually! He was a supervisor at The Naked Hog processing plant. Sometimes he came home feelin' good and acting nice, but there were other times that he came home mad and mean. Sometimes he came home drunker than a mule on sour mash, and when he was drunk, holy shit, you better be ready to run!"

J.C. lifted his water bottle to his lips and emptied its contents into his mouth, then continued, "He was really mean to mama! There were loads of nights that they'd be fightin' over stuff, and he'd start whipping her with his belt and callin' her a pig. He'd chase her into the back of the house, and the only way he'd let up would be after she'd start squeelin' like a pig. After a while of her squeelin' and screamin', they'd both start laughin', then they'd fall asleep. It used ta scare me to where I couldn't get to sleep, and then I'd be worthless the next day. That shit went on all the time since I was a little kid. When my oldest brother, Cayson, hit sixteen, Daddy brought home a lady named Maylene, who worked for him in the processing plant. He took me and my other brother, Julian, out to the garage behind tha house and made us watch while he taught Cayson how to, ya know, be a man! I thought it was nasty, but Julian got really excited, and from then on, he couldn't stop talkin' about it. He got in big trouble at school with Darleen McCrusky, when he got her to follow him out to Marlborough country, behind the football field. He was tryin' ta get her ta take off her shirt, but she ran away and told coach Naughten about what he did, and got him expelled. Daddy got mad as hell and beat tha shit out of him. Anyway, that's when I figured I'd better leave home before I hit sixteen, so I started makin' my plan. My birthday was commin' up in June, so in May, I hiked seven miles into Slidell and started hitchhiking toward New Orleans, where I told everybody I met that I was eighteen and had been robbed of all my stuff. I met this guy named Don, from Florida, who was tryin' to get back down there, to his mother's house. He said he had left his V.W. van there and we could use it to work the state fairs with a guy he knew who sells socks and T-shirts.

We were sleeping one night under an overpass on I-10 when a car pulled into the Shell Station and a guy got out and started pumping gas. It was still dark and there wasn't any traffic, so Don and I hiked down to the station and asked him if he was headed East, and if he might give us a ride. The guy talked it over with his wife and decided to help us out. He was a travelin' preacher, on his way home to Nashville, and they said we could ride with them as far as Mobile, Alabama. On the way, he and his wife asked all about our lives. When we got into town, he pulled into the Greyhound bus station, then asked if they could pray over us. We were grateful for the ride and both said yes. After they prayed, he walked into the station and bought us both tickets to Jacksonville. I can't think of anybody ever doing anything that nice for me in my life."

Dr. Colburn asked, "How did that make you feel?"

J. C. took another sip from his water bottle and said, "I thought it was stupid at first then, not knowing who we were, or if we'd do something bad, but then, when I look back, I just think there must be people out there who have no clue of how tough life can be and they just float along, expecting everybody else to feel like they do. It don't make much sense to me, but if they want to feel good inside by givin' me a ticket, well, God bless 'em!"

Captain Witt knocked, then opened the door to the forward compartment and stuck his head through, "Excuse me gentlemen," he said, "you've got fifteen!"

Dr. Colburn thanked him, then asked J. C., "Did you pick up the van?" "Oh, yeah! It was a piece of shit, but we got it running and worked the fairs and flea markets for over two years. We hooked up with an old guy in a Ford Econoline that he had converted for living in, and we worked with him all over Texas and Oklahoma, selling hats and leather belts, then Don and I came back to Florida, where we split up. He stayed in Jacksonville, and I hitchhiked to Orlando. I got arrested for hitchhiking on Interstate 4 and spent a month on a Florida chain-gang."

"Geezzz, J.C.! You have really had quite tha life so far!" The doctor exclaimed.

"Shit Doc, that ain't tha half of it!" The young man proclaimed. "I can go deeper into any of this stuff if you got time!"

Dr. C. needed to wrap up the session, but hoped to hold onto J. C.'s trust by directing his questioning toward the young man's more immediate needs. "We can revisit everything in greater depth the next time we get together, but today let me see if there might be some things I can offer you that might help make your life a little more comfortable and easier to manage." The doctor then asked, "How are you sleeping these days? Do you feel you are getting enough quality sleep?"

"Hell no!" J. C. answered emphatically. "You can't sleep out here! Not with this heat and not with all these jet skis speeding through the channel. Most everybody out here sleeps outside, under the stars, where they can catch a breeze, unless they have a generator and an A/C or a good solar system with plenty of batteries!"

"Would any of those help you to start getting better sleep at night?" The doctor asked. "Oh yeah, but all that stuff costs big bucks, and the only money I get comes from cleaning fish on the docks or poppin' heads off shrimp over on Stock Island. That's barely enough to pay my dinghy dock fee and flush-out costs every week. The rest I spend on food, water and my phone! I don't think there's ever gonna be a time when I'll have enough money to fix my boat up!" He seemed to be a defeated man. Life had beaten him into a hole and convinced him there was no way out.

The doctor told him to wait in his seat, then he rose and stepped to the forward hatch and knocked gently. Captain Witt opened the door and Dr. Colburn whispered, "Am I limited, in any way, with how much I can spend to help these people?" Witt grinned and said without hesitation, "From what I've been told, you have full control of the purse! You call the shot and I take aim and shoot! What kind of target are we lookin at here?"

The doctor turned toward J.C. and asked, "What shape is your boat in?"

Witt stepped into the salon and took control of the discussion. "Isn't that Jay Mann's old Hunter 33 you're on, over by Fleming Key?"

J.C. nervously answered, "Yes sir!"

Witt stepped into the galley, and began rummaging through a drawer as he talked. "If I recall, that's an 85 or maybe 86, right?"

"Yes sir, it's an 86!" J.C. answered.

Witt pulled a logbook from the drawer and began thumbing through the pages. "Here it is!", he said! "I was up in Homestead for some flight training in August 2006 while Dr. Grant was dealing with some leg issues. When I got back to Key West, I remember, that's when I helped Jay mount his new mast. His old one was blown off during hurricane Wilma." Witt had a mind like a steel lobster trap! "That's a God damn good little boat! He sold that to you, dirt cheap, too! Are you still paying him for it?"

J.C. shrunk in embarrassment as he made his admission, "No, sir! I'm behind on my payments by about a year now."

Dr. Grant asked, "What's the amount you still owe to Jay?"

"I think it's around three thousand dollars", answered J.C.

Witt was making his way up the ladder and stopped halfway, then turned his head toward the other two men, and announced, "I think you can go ahead and write that debt off now! I saw a post from Jay's cousin saying that he died of pneumonia yesterday at his coconut farm in the Philippines."

Jay had been a much-loved figure for the eight years that he had lived out in the mooring field. A retired trauma nurse from Hillsborough County, Florida, he often went back to Tampa, for short periods, to fill in at the hospitals when they were understaffed and overburdened. He said the money was good but would be worth ten times more when he moved to the Philippines. He moved! It was! He died! Dreams! You don't really know them till you live them, so *live your dream, while you can*!

"Dr. Colburn turned toward J.C., raised his eyebrows, and asked, "What kind of arrangement did you have with Jay regarding the legal ownership of the boat?"

J.C. stood to his feet and answered, "He signed it over to me before he left! He said he probably wouldn't be back and trusted me to pay it off when I could. He didn't seem to care if I paid or not, cause he was movin' out of the country and never gonna come back."

The doctor turned to climb out of the cabin as he shared his plan. "Ok, here's what I'd like to do." J.C. followed the doctor up the ladder and through the hatch. Once the three men had gathered on the deck, Dr. Colburn handed J.C. an envelope with two hundred dollars in it and finished with his proposal. "If you are willing, I'd like to have Captain Witt arrange for your boat to be towed over to the Three-D Boatyard, on Stock Island, and get it out of the water, where they can clean the hull and see if it needs to be painted. I'd like to have it completely overhauled and if there's anything that needs to be replaced, I want it replaced. I want it equipped with an adequate solar power system with top notch batteries and a generator that can power everything. I'd like to arrange for you to have access to medical and dental treatment for any conditions that may come up and, if you are willing, I'd like to see you get into an adult training program, over at the college, where you could work on learning a trade. You could get your GED if you like." The doctor was studying the young man's body language as he began imagining a life full of hope and positive opportunity. His face was morphing as he listened intently to the doctor's words. He was becoming more and more amenable! Tears began to well up in his eyes and his body began to shake. He fell into the doctor's arms, overwhelmed by the graciousness being offered to him by this stranger.

The doctor sought to console his client, and said, "Listen, J.C., I want you to understand that there are no expectations attached to what we are proposing here. You can take it or leave it! Witt will make all the arrangements, and I'll see to it that all the costs are paid by the foundation that we represent. We just want to see you in a place where you can get healthy and have better control of your life. Does that sound like something you'd like to do?"

J.C. regained his composure as Witt handed him a paper towel from the cabinet behind the helm. "If I can, yeah! I just don't know if I really can!"

The doctor knew just what to say! "Trust me son, you can change! We can all change!"

11. A TOUCH of DUTCH

Witt helped J.C. climb back into his dinghy, and pushed its bow toward the deep-water channel with his foot, then called out as J.C. started his engine, "I'll call you after I get with Lewis and see when he can get you scheduled over at the yard. Shouldn't take more than a day or two!" J.C.'s voice was drowned out by the whine of his motor, as he mouthed a thank you and pulled away.

"I haven't called the next client yet," Witt told the doctor, as he shoved the roll of paper towels back into the cabinet. "I wanted to check and see if you needed to break for lunch before I call Dutch and tell him he can come on over." Captain Witt pointed toward three sailboats moored just beyond Billy's, and said, "That's his ketch, over there. The one with that red tulip flag hanging from its starboard spreader. He and his wife moved here about twenty years ago. His wife drowned when she fell out of their dinghy one night. I'll tell you all about it later if you want. I've known him for years! Really nice guy! He's been through a lot, and I'm not sure he should be trying to live out here much longer. I think he might be in his early nineties!"

Dr. C. appreciated Witt's consideration, and after a quick glance at his wristwatch, responded, "Thanks Witt! It's just after eleven o'clock now! I think I'm good for one more if that's ok with you."

Witt grabbed his phone and dialed the next number on his list, "Dutch, this is Witt! If you're ready to get started, the doc says bring it on!"

After Dutch confirmed that he would be on his way, Witt propped a cushion against the starboard gunnel and sat down on the bench, then said, "We'll be calling Markus when we break for lunch! He wants us to give him an update on how things are going. I think he'll be particularly interested in how Dutch is getting along. After Annie died, he took a serious dive into depression, and Markus spent a lot of time with him. We were coming out here three times a week, back then, and he arranged for Dutch to come over every afternoon, after he finished with all the other clients. Dutch probably wouldn't have made it through that period if Markus hadn't been so attentive. He had him on a cocktail of Zoloft, Wellbutrin and Extra Strength Tylenol, if my memory serves me right. He can verify all that once he's onboard. I always felt that Markus and Dutch would have been close friends if they had ever gotten together outside of their therapeutic relationship, them being so close in age, and both being doctors."

"Dutch was a doctor?" Dr. C. asked in complete surprise.

"Yes sir! I heard him tell Markus, once, that he had studied at the University of Amsterdam and was a scientist in the Netherlands before he and Annie moved to England, where he taught marine biology and environmental studies at Cambridge."

Dr. C. was astounded that he would soon be interviewing such an esteemed and accomplished gentleman of the world.

Wit added, "When Mote Marine expanded their lab on Big Pine Key, Dutch came over as a consultant, specializing in atmospheric trace elements found in the Saharan Dust Layer and their effect on the Caribbean coral. He went back to England for a short while, then he and Annie bought that Frans Maas ketch and sailed it here to live in Key West. They used it to sail the islands and do research for Mote till Annie's accident. I knew them well and have helped Dutch with a few projects here and there. Great guy! I'm looking forward to seeing him again and finding out how he's getting along."

As Witt was talking, the two men watched Dutch climb into his dinghy and start making his way toward the *Psyched Out*. He was a huge and broad-shouldered man, but looked somewhat frail as he climbed down from his boat into his dinghy. He seemed to have considerable trouble when he pulled the cord to start his motor. In a few minutes, Witt's curiosity would be satisfied!

"Dutch, you ol' seadog, I thought you would have sailed that thing back to the Netherlands by now! It's good to see you again, my friend!" Witt knew well the value of making strong friendships. Living in a world where isolation could lead even a healthy person quickly into despair called upon people like him to grasp a higher level of responsibility toward his fellow islanders.

"How have you been?" He asked as he and Dr. Colburn lifted Dutch on-board. The old fellow had lost a lot of ground since their last time togeth-er. He was becoming frail and weak. He no longer stood fully upright and grabbed at the railing to steady himself.

"I'm not so bad for an old man, I guess!" He exclaimed as he looked be-hind him to see if he had remembered to tie off his dinghy. Witt introduced Dr. Colburn, and after they shared a cordial greeting, he and Dr. C. pro-ceeded to help Dutch into the cabin where they could enjoy a much-needed respite from the hot, salty air.

"It's an honor to meet you, Dutch!" Dr. Colburn began. "From what Witt tells me, you've had quite an interesting history living down here in the Keys!"

As he carefully lowered himself into the seat, the old man replied, "Well, I'd have to admit, if I were looking at my life through somebody else's eyes, interesting could be one way I'd describe it, but from where I sit now, I think I'd be more inclined to describe it as having been short, instead of interest-ing." Dr. Colburn chuckled as he took his seat. Captain Witt excused himself and retreated into the forward compartment.

As the doctor situated himself, Dutch continued talking. "Gill stopped by this morning and told me that you were starting your sessions again, so I decided this might be the right time for me to get some help with some prob-lems that I'm afraid might be too big for me to handle." Dr. C. was happy to see that his client was anxious to address his issues of concern so directly and asked, "By all means, how can I help you?" He reached into the cooler and retrieved a bottle of cold water for Dutch and unscrewed the cap, then set it next to him, on the cabin table.

The old man began to whimper as he explained, "I'm having serious trou-ble right now!"

Dr. C. leaned forward and listened intently. "It's ok, Dutch! We can get through this! Just relax and take your time!" Dutch was struggling! There was immense pain and distress with every breath he gulped into his lungs. Dr. Colburn reached for the hand cloth that lay folded on the galley counter top, and handed it to him.

The words fell slowly, one by one, "Eg...Vil...Deyja!"

There was so much pain behind his eyes as he lifted his head and looked in the doctor's face. "Tuesday was our fiftieth anniversary!" His whimpers broke into an uncontrollable freefall of tears. He moaned deeply, with every breath! "Fifty years!" He rocked from side to side as he cried into the towel and sobbed, over and over and over, "Eg Vil Deyja!"

Captain Witt clamored through the forward hatch and placed his hands gently on his friend's broad shoulders. "It's OK Dutch!" He offered his support. "It's gonna be fine, ol' buddy!" Witt looked at Dr. Colburn and gestured with raised eyebrows, and a distended chin to indicate his confusion.

They comforted him as he struggled to regain composure.

Finally, the old man leaned back and filled his lungs with air and said, "It's too much!" He fell forward and after a few seconds of quiet reflection, he said, "I've been too long in these waters!" He took a sip from his water bottle and relaxed his body, then explained, "Just before my Annie died, we discussed moving back home to the Netherlands where we hoped to live out the last of our days on our farm in Dordrecht. Annie was born there! We still own a little stone house on three hectares overlooking the Noord River! Her sisters use it as a guest cottage when friends come to visit. It's quite beautiful, and we had always hoped to restore the gardens to the way they were when she was a child. We had promised Billy that he would always be welcome to stay with us whenever he wished. There's an upstairs loft that was our daughter's room. It would have been a perfect place for him, if he had ever been able to visit." His tears welled up again as he reminisced about his deceased friend and how close they had become as neighbors in the mooring field.

"When Annie died, Billy was the first to come to me. He knew how deeply I was hurting. We stayed up for three nights, talking about love and the loss of it. If it weren't for Billy, I'd have tied a chain around my neck and jumped overboard. I'm sure of it!" He took another sip of water, then continued. "We played chess every night! While we played, we talked about life and the value of living it. He was in his early sixties then and I was in my mideighties, but he knew more about life than anybody I had ever met. Annie used to say that Billy had the soul of a Ghillie Dhu. I think she might have been right! That might be why he named his boat *The Ghillie Dhu*!"

Dr. Colburn and Captain Witt were both unfamiliar with the term and sensing their shared perplexity, Dutch volunteered a description, "It's an old

Scottish legend that got its beginnings around the Northwest coastal Highland forests of Gairloch and Kerrysdale. Billy had traced his family history to that region and studied it extensively. The Ghillie Dhu was a forest dwelling creature of great strength that rarely ventured out of the forest. He is depicted as a man-like creature, clothed in leaves and moss from head to toe, and is the protector of the forest and the animals that live in it. There are lots of stories of the Ghillie Dhu saving the lives of wild animals injured by hunters and sometimes the Ghillie would leave them on the doorsteps of people's homes that could help with their recovery. Billy just seemed to embody everything we know about the Ghillie Dhu! I think you'd have to have known him to fully grasp how much like a Ghillie he was."

"I think I'd have to agree with you!", the captain said. "Billy had a bigger heart than anybody I ever knew!" Dutch had calmed down significantly, so Dr. C. signaled the captain with an inconspicuous raised thumb that he was ready to begin the session. Witt patted Dutch's shoulder and said, "I'll be in my cabin if you need me for anything!"

"You and Billy were apparently very close." The doctor began to postulate, in the hope that he might provoke Dutch into some pertinent introspection. "I can't imagine how difficult the news of his loss might be on you." There was good reason to approach with caution as he led his client to the edge of such a trepidatious and emotionally unstable edge. "Do you think you might like to talk about some of those feelings with me today?"

The old man focused his eyes into the eyes of the psychiatrist and retorted confidently, "I'm ninety-two years old and seen more death than any three men my age!" He lifted his water bottle to the tabletop and left his monstrous hand around its belly. He squeezed it tightly, till the water had raised to the edge of its spout! The sound of the plastic crumpling under his grip was unnerving to the doctor, then as he released his hand, the bottle recovered to its original shape and he said, "Billy's came as a surprise, but he and I shared certain realizations about life and what to expect from living it."

"Oh! Oh!" He heard her whispering once again, from deep inside his brain! "I think you are about to get schooled!"

The doctor took a deep breath through his nostrils, then let the air out slowly through his slightly opened mouth. With carefully forged intent, he began to command parts of his body to stretch and relax. Fingers, toes, shoul-

ders, legs! It only took a few seconds for him to become pliable and recep-
tive. There was no tension, no apprehension! He was ready for his lesson and
said, "Expectations! They certainly have a lot to do with how people live their
life!" The old man leaned forward and reached into his back pocket to retrieve his billfold, then said as he slowly opened it, "When Annie died, Billy
and I sailed about twenty-five miles out, into the Gulf, where there's an an-
cient reef. It was the first reef that she and I studied when we moved here.
It's an isolated structure at a depth of about thirty feet and it's survived only by luck! Most of the reefs in that area have been destroyed by the shrimp
nets but somehow, this little patch has gone unscathed. It was always our favorite place to watch for the green flash." His eyes began to water again as he
talked about his wife. He wiped them, then continued, "It was almost sunset when we started to sprinkle her into the sea. The Gulf was like glass that
evening, and there was no breeze. I was pouring the last of Annie's dust from
the brass pitcher that we had brought with us when we came here, and as the
very last little pieces of her dropped into the water, Billy tapped my shoulder and pointed toward the horizon. I fell to my knees and dropped the brass
pitcher in the water. It was a kiss! My Annie sent to me a kiss! It was in a
green flash as the sun dropped over the edge of the earth. She sent me one
last kiss!"

He bellowed in pain as he bent his body over and buried his face in his
hands. The doctor fought back his own tears but lost full composure and began to wale. Captain Witt rushed into the salon and reached out to offer support. After several minutes, the men were still recovering when Dutch pulled
a piece of paper from his wallet and handed it to Dr. Colburn, then said, "It
took me a little while before I was able to move. Billy helped me back up
and we sat out there, under the stars, talking about how we had both lost our
wives to the sea and how so much of what we feel is important, really isn't."

Dr. Colburn began to unfold the piece of paper as Dutch continued to
talked, "It was about midnight. I was laying on the foredeck, staring up at
the stars and thinking about Annie when Billy climbed out of the cabin and
handed this to me. He said I might want to wait a few days before I read it,
but while we were motoring back to Key West, I opened it up and, well, if
you really want to know how much losing Billy hurts, this might show you."

The doctor wiped his eyes again, as he read aloud:

"With dust-packed golden urn, beckoning for pardon,
my love will walk on tidal sands, in search a fine release!
She'll drop a knee in tidal pool to gaze into the bliss,
then reconcile her depth of loss while longing one more kiss.
Upon the sea to roam the earth, to lands we never saw,
on crashing waves with rising sun to dust return us all.
Oh, hand me off to yonder sea and wait for clear of mist,
at setting sun a flash of green will be my final kiss."

William Blain Chapman III, August 4, 2010.

"Oh, My!" The doctor exclaimed! "I think I see what you mean. You were very close, weren't you?"

Dutch finished his water, then answered, "Billy was a good friend! Annie and I used to come ashore to watch him perform at Schooner's with Devin and Marty regularly. It was about the only time we ever stayed in town after dark. The night that Annie died, we were on our way back to the boat after having dinner with him during his break. He was as heartbroken as I was! Yes, you might say we were close! Very close!"

Witt moved over to the settee and, after sliding to the middle of the table, asked, "Do you feel up to telling Dr. C. about the accident?"

"If the doctor is interested, I have no problem with telling him what happened."

"Please!" The doctor confirmed his interest, and Dutch began to tell his story.

"Well, Billy and the band were playing on stage when we decided to head home. When we got up from our table, I waved goodnight to Billy, and Annie threw him a kiss. We left Schooner's about ten o'clock and walked over to Mattheessen's for ice cream, like we always did. It was about 10:45 when we cast off for home. The water was smooth and the moon was in its first quarter! It was a beautiful, perfectly clear night! Before we pulled away from the dock, I turned on my navigation lights, but my masthead light kept flickering on and off. I tightened the connections and pushed the bulb in deeper and it seemed to make a better connection, so we motored out of the harbor and into the channel. We were almost back to the mooring field when the light started to short out again, so I turned it off and pulled my flashlight out of the dry bag and tossed it to Annie for her to hold it up as a navigation light. She had just gotten her hands on the light when a Coast Guard RB-S Defender at full throttle side-washed us and knocked us both into the water. I had made the stupid decision to wear my leather shoes that night, and as I kicked my feet, they filled with water and were like anchors on my feet. I almost drowned trying to get them off, and once I did, Annie was nowhere to be found. I stayed out there all night trying to find her! In the morning, one of Fury's jetboat tour guides spotted her body in the mangroves along the Garrison Bight Channel. That was the worst day of my life."

He dropped his head in sadness as Witt picked up the story. "I had just left Sunset Key Marina in our Hunter 33' with four students on board. We sailed right past the Sheriff's Marine Patrol boat as they were doing the recovery. I didn't know it was Annie till later that afternoon, when I got back to the marina. It was such an avoidable accident! We were all saddened by the news."

Dr. Colburn sat dazed by the tragic tale. After silently contemplating the pain and grief Dutch must have suffered, he took a deep breath and offered his condolences. "I am so sorry for your loss, Dutch! I can only offer that I can understand how difficult it can be to get through something like that. It's been just a few years now, since the day my wife suffered her aneurysm while swimming in the moat out at Fort Jefferson. She died in my arms three days later. We were here on vacation. I know how tough it is to lose a loved one."

Witt added, "Billy's wife and Annie both died at the hand of the Coast Guard. I remember Billy telling me once that he had spent years in court fighting to get accountability. You had a case too, didn't you, Dutch?"

Dutch shrugged his shoulders, then offered the two men a disposition of his affairs, "American justice holds a different promise for foreigners! If you seek accountability from an American institution, you risk losing your green-card status. I had my attorney withdraw my petition before it ever got filed. At my age, it wasn't worth the risk, and now I've made my decision! Tonight, I'll be flying back to my beautiful little cottage on a hill, where I've got two great-grandchildren that I've never met. Key West and all the life it sucked from me will soon be just a memory to forget."

The captain and the doctor sat, listening attentively, as the old man went on. "I brought with me the title to my boat, *De Droom Van Mijn Engel* (*My Angel's Dream*), and her little dinghy." He pulled the papers from his shirt pocket, then clicked his pen open and signed the title and registration and slid them across the table for the two men to inspect, then said, "I know about the foundation that Dr. Grant and Billy managed! You can sell my boat, or keep it as a place for someone in need to live. I've cleaned it thoroughly, and it is in perfect sailing condition. When I leave here, I'm taking a taxi to the Miami International Airport and will never be back. Please accept *My Angel* as a donation in the name of my dear wife, Annie, and our dear friend William Chapman. Thank you, gentlemen for the generosity you bring to this community."

Dutch stood to his feet and extended his hands, one to the doctor, the other to the captain and said, "Mogen uw zeilen altijd een gunstige wind vinden en uw koersveilig en waarachtig zijn!" He leaned into each of them, with a one-armed embrace, then turned to climb the companionway ladder.

The two men were stunned! They followed Dutch up the ladder, then, while helping him climb back into his dinghy, they shared their appreciation and wished him farewell as he started his engine and turned toward shore.

"Lunch?" Wit asked.

"Oh yeah! I need a break!" Was the doctor's reply.

12. LOBSTER FOR TWO

The two men climbed back into the cabin. "Turkey and swiss?" Dr. Colburn reached into the cooler and retrieved a foil-wrapped sandwich as he asked.

"If that's your choice," Witt quipped as he stepped into the galley and opened the lid to the *Psyched Out's* refrigerator. "But before you take a bite from that crappy turkey and cheese, you just might want to look at what I've got over here."

The doctor stepped to the galley and gazed into the baking dish that Witt had set on the counter. "You have got to be kidding me!", he exclaimed as Witt turned to the gimbaled oven and lit the burners.

"We never kid when it comes to lunch on this boat!" Witt set the thermostat at 400 degrees, then waited while the oven began to preheat. "My wife, Kitty, was one of the original chefs at Blue Heaven. She never lets me leave without some special dish for us to have for lunch. Marcus used to say she did it to give me a reason to go back home for dinner. He used to say things like, 'What's for insurance today?' or 'Let's break for insurance', instead of saying 'lunch'". He slid the dish into the oven and asked, "You do like stuffed lobster, don't you?"

Dr. Colburn was ecstatic! "This is just too good to be true!" Witt lit one of the burners on the stove and grabbed a saucepan, then opened a plastic container and poured in the hollandaise sauce.

"She likes to put a little cayenne pepper in her sauce. I hope you're OK with that!"

The doctor leaned against the galley stanchion and crossed his arms, then answered, "Man, this breaks all the rules!"

Captain Witt smiled broadly as he pulled another container from the top-loading fridge and popped the lid off, then held it for the doctor to inspect. "She always precooks anything that might take too much time away from your sessions." The doctor gazed into the dish and smiled an approving smile, then popped his thumb out of a clenched fist, as the Captain placed the asparagus and potato dish into the microwave and asked, "Wine or beer?"

The doctor couldn't resist asking, "What do we have in wine?"

Witt moved to a teak cabinet in the rear of the galley and opened the door to inspect its contents. "Ahhhhh! This was usually Markus' pick when we had lobster." He held the bottle high for the doctor to read the label. "Oyster Bay, New Zealand, Sauvignon Blanc," then asked, "Think this'll do?"

The doctor grinned and replied, "Allez-y, oh Capitaine, Allez-y!"

"I don't know if that's a yes or a no, but it's sure gonna be my pick today!" He then pulled two cups from the upper cabinet and poured the wine.

"Oh, yeah! This is pretty good stuff!" The doctor exclaimed after taking a sip.

Witt pulled a thermometer from the drawer, opened the oven door, and stabbed it into one of the lobster tails, then closed the oven and announced, "Five more minutes should do it!"

"When do you think we should call Markus?" The doctor asked as he sat back down in his chair.

Witt reached over the galley counter and grabbed his phone from the edge of the table and commanded, "Siri, call Markus!" He set the call on speaker mode, then set it back on the table.

One ring and Markus answered. "What's for lunch?"

"Lobster tails and caviar from Odessa! You'd better get over here quick, though. The line is out tha door!" Witt quipped as he slid two plates piled with food across the counter. As he took his seat, he said, "It's been a very interesting morning, so far!"

From the phone came a short burst of laughter, then, "I can't wait to hear all about it. How's Walter taking to his new waterfront office?"

"Hey, Markus!" Dr. Colburn remarked. "I think I'm holding my own, at four hours in!"

"Well, I want you to feel completely comfortable with this project. I think that you'll fully adjust in short order! In fact, I'm sure of it! What do you think so far?"

The doctor wiped his lips, then remarked, "Something amazing seems to be going on!" He began. "I think that being removed from an office setting and having the freedom to relax some of the clinical expectations that come with seeing patients under a structured, regulated, and sometimes involuntary setting, is having a profoundly liberating effect on how I approach my clients. I'm feeling more compassionate and empathetic than I've ever dared to allow myself to feel before. Thank you, Markus!"

The senior psychiatrist was obviously pleased and responded, "I am thrilled to hear you say that, Walter! It was just what I had hoped might happen!"

Witt and the doctor continued to dine as they discussed with Markus the morning's developments. Dr. Grant was well familiar with all four of the clients they had seen so far, and took great interest in details about each, but it was obvious that his strongest concern was for Cairo.

"He's a very vulnerable young man!" he said. "Billy and I had discussed his condition many times over the past few years, and of all the clients I've seen out there, he was always the one that I hoped I'd get the opportunity to work with more. He's very fragile!"

"How do you want to handle this thing with Dutch's boat? Do you want me to go over to the DMV and take care of the transfer?" Witt asked. He had expedited several transfers of ownership for the foundation over the years, and was intimately familiar with every aspect of the Florida Vessel registration process.

"We can do all that together next week after you get back from Homestead," Marcus suggested. "First, I think I'll have you go out and do a formal survey of the boat, so we can establish its value. I need you to inventory everything Dutch left behind, too! At some point, we'll have everything moved to our warehouse facility and get Donna, and her team of volunteers, to sort through it to see what can be distributed back into the community. I sure wish Billy was still with us! He was so good at all that stuff! Here it is, just fifty-three hours, and I'm still thinking like he's just a phone call away. This business of livin's gonna kill me some day!"

It was one of Billy's favorite quotes! Using it now felt like giving tribute to the man who had always said it, grinningly, while he carried the weight of others' lives, so they might enjoy a little relief from the pressures that come with livin' in paradise. "What's scheduled for the rest of the afternoon?" Dr. Grant asked.

Witt grabbed his clipboard and read the next name on the list, "Kenyatta Morrison's next up! I'm sure you remember this guy, don't you? A tourist girl from Brazil fell in love with him two years ago, and sent him a ticket to visit her. He flew over and she married him. I think she sobered up and sent him back, two months later, though! He was busking on the streets in his boots and black wig, pretending to be Jimi Hendrix like he always did. I'm giving him a call as soon as we finish talking with you."

Markus laughed when Witt said the name! "Did I tell you that I ran across his real name?"

"No, how'd you get it?" Witt asked. "

"I was scanning through the arrest records like I regularly do." He paused for a second to say, "Walter, I'll show you how to do that sometime when you're over here. It's an invaluable resource for knowing what to watch out for with some of these clients." He then continued, "Anyway, I saw his mugshot! His name is Kenneth Raymond Morrison! I guess Kenyatta was his street name."

"Anything we need to be aware of?" Walter asked.

"Nothing physical! Just a few trespassing violations and one pot-related issue in 2009. You won't have any trouble with him, I'm sure!"

"Witt, what's the plan with hauling out J.C.'s boat? Do you need me to make the arrangements with Lewis, or do you want to take it on?" Dr. Grant was a stickler for making sure everything promised got done as quickly and as efficiently as possible.

"I'll be out there Saturday morning to pick up some hardware for one of my boats. I'll talk with him about it then. I like to go face-to-face on big jobs like this. I think it's the best way to negotiate a fair estimate. Lewis and I have done this so many times, I'll take care of it. When it's time to haul it out, I'll tow it over and get it set up in the yard, where J.C. can stay onboard while the work gets done. That'll be the cheapest way."

"You're a saint, my friend!" Markus and Witt had been together for a full decade. Their mutual trust and respect was a tribute to the caliber of men they were. There was no better team, anywhere, to champion the battles that they volunteered to fight. They saw the gaps in people's lives and sought tirelessly to make their fill. "Billy was so very proud to be working with you!" Dr. Grant added.

"Here's to tha 'Mooringfield Musketeers'! One for all, and all for one!" Witt was always prepared to lighten the intensity of embarrassment by injecting a little humor. He lifted his cup to Dr. C.'s and as they clacked together, he offered this heartfelt toast. "Here's to Three I'd Billy, may his legacy continue to inspire us forever!" The three gentlemen joined in a cheer of "Here! Here!" then bid a solemn fare thee well to their departed friend and downed their cups hard, on the table top. After they said their goodbyes to Markus, Dr. Colburn asked his new friend how he knew about the nickname, Three I'd Billy.

"Everybody knew him as Three I'd Billy!" Witt explained. "For lots of people, it was the only name they called him. He wrote a song about a California kid that grew up stuttering. In the song, the kid overcomes his stuttering by singing along to the notes he played on his guitar. As the song goes on, the guitar playing gets faster and faster and more and more complex. The singer is singing as fast as the notes on the guitar, and the whole thing morphs into a fantastic orchestra of tones. It's amazing how he does it and quite beautiful too. The man was a genius! He should have been famous for just that one song. We're all gonna miss him!" Witt picked up his phone and placed the call to Kenyatta. "If yer ready, we're ready!" He dropped his phone to his side, then packed it into his pocket. "One crazy Kenyatta, on its way!"

13. A ROCKSTAR FRAUD

"**I** don't mean to taint your objectivity with this next client, but there's a circus in town and the clowns are on the loose!" Witt wasn't sure how the new doctor might respond to his attempt at a humorous association being made about a client who he had not yet met, but his hopes were high that Dr. C. would reach an agreeable conclusion on his own, once the show began. He stood to his feet, then stepped to the starboard window and said, "Watch!"

Dr. C. joined him and leaned into the window. "What the hell is he doing?" the doctor asked in astonishment.

"He thinks he's a rockstar!" Witt calmly explained. "He's like this 24/7! He thinks he's in a music video that's running all the time. He never comes out of character!"

"Who's the woman driving the boat?" The doctor asked.

"Sometimes he says she's his 'manager'. Sometimes he calls her his 'old lady'! When she first started showing up, he was saying she was his personal trainer, but apparently, she thinks she's found her golden ticket and never lets him get too far out of her sight." Witt grabbed his binoculars and took a look at the couple in the dinghy, then passed them to the doctor and said, "I don't think you'll ever find a more motley crew than this!"

The waves had picked up considerably. As the little wooden boat pushed through them, it pitched forward, then rocked from side to side. The occupants were being jostled and thrown about, as it slowly pushed its way across the channel. Mr. Morrison was standing in the bow of the little boat, holding onto its anchor line with his left hand and fighting to keep his hat on with his right. He looked like he was trying to mimic George Washington in his crossing of the Potomac. Every time he fell over, he'd straighten his hat and stand majestically back up. "Yes! I think I'd agree!" The doctor dropped the binoculars from his eyes and proclaimed, "The circus is in town!"

"I take it you're Kenyatta?" The doctor called down to the fellow in the black hat, cowboy boots, wig, and leather vest, then reached to grab hold of his rope.

Witt joined him to help pull the duo up from the water-filled dinghy they had motored over in. As soon as Kenyatta got on deck, he turned and called to his friend, "Hey baby, pass me my guitar before it gets soaked."

Witt offered, "I've got a portable bilge pump you can use if you want. We can set it up now, and by the time you leave, it should have all that water back in the gulf where it belongs."

Kenyatta hung over the railing and almost fell off the boat trying to grab the dripping wet cloth gig bag with his beloved guitar inside. His friend tripped and fell in the dinghy, while trying to hold the bag high enough for him to grab. She was emaciated! Her skin was dry and stretched tightly across her bones. If she had once had muscle, it had long since withered away. The doctor recognized immediately how close she was to a tragic end, and he was concerned.

Kenyatta pulled himself back up and proudly held his guitar above his head as if it signified his championship in some great arena. It was a display of patheticism that could not be ignored. Witt hung from the gunnel and took the woman by her arm, then gently pulled as she climbed out of the little boat. Once they were on the deck of the *Psyched Out*, Wit explained, "There are privacy laws that we have to abide by while you're on board! If you want your friend to be able to sit inside with you while you and the doctor talk, you'll have to sign a waiver that gives her permission to be there."

Kenyatta turned to the woman and commanded, "Wait in the boat!"

The woman immediately turned and began to climb back into their dinghy.

"Wait! Wait!" Dr. Colburn interrupted. "It's too hot for her to be sitting in the sun with no protection. If Kenyatta doesn't mind, she can join us inside."

Kenyatta shrugged his shoulders and turned toward the cabin hatch, then mumbled, "She don't give a shit! She's too brain-dead to know if it's hot or cold!"

Witt helped her back into the shade of the bimini, and Dr. C. turned to better assess her condition. He was struck by what he saw. The old woman weighed about seventy pounds and stood dripping from the ocean spray. Her eyes were deeply clouded by cataracts, and the few teeth left in her mouth were broken and brown. Witt pulled a towel from the cabinet below the bench and handed it to Kenyatta, who reluctantly obliged by lightly toweling her off, then asked, "You got something we could eat? She hasn't had anything in her since yesterday morning."

Witt slid the hatch cover open and stepped onto the companionway ladder. As he descended into the cabin, he called over his shoulder, "Turkey and Swiss as soon as yer ready!" Witt was fighting back the cynicism that permeated through his blood. He knew well how dangerous it could become if he gave in to its influence. Once the trio had joined him, he reached to close the hatch, then stepped to the cooler and opened the top. "Help yourself!" he said, as he turned and stepped toward the forward cabin. "We're all out of mustard!" He stepped through the door and kicked it shut.

Dr. Colburn gestured for the couple to sit down, then pulled two sandwiches from the cooler and handed one to each. As Kenyatta and his friend began to eat, the doctor took a seat and asked, "What might I help you with today?" Kenyatta's mouth was full as he mumbled out his question, "You got any strings?"

The doctor was confused, and asked, "Did you say strings?"

Kenyatta grabbed a bottle of water out of the cooler and answered, "Yeah! I've got a gig this afternoon and need some strings! Guitar strings! Billy used to save all his old strings for me. Anytime I needed 'em, I'd pull over to his boat and he'd have them hanging over the side in a plastic bag. I went by last night and there weren't any. I checked again this morning, when you were tying up, and again, no strings! I was wonderin' if maybe he left them with you to give to me. You got some?"

It was now clear to the doctor that Kenyatta did not know of Billy's unfortunate accident under the dinghy dock, just two days earlier, so he asked, "When was the last time you saw Billy?"

"I saw him on Sunday!" Kenyatta exclaimed. "He was eatin' lunch over at Harpoon Harry's when I walked by. He was in that booth, the one in the back where he always sits. His wolf was there, on the floor next to him. I waved to him through the door. Why are you asking me that?"

The doctor leaned forward and placed his hands on his knees, then said calmly, "I'm very sorry to have to tell you, but Billy had an accident on Tuesday morning and didn't survive." Kenyatta's response was remarkably quick and surprisingly revealing!

"That no good, God Damn bastard owes me a hundred dollars, and where's my guitar?" He stood to his feet and clenched his fists to show his anger.

Witt burst into the cabin and shouted. "Sit your ass down before I bust you a new butt hole, you little con-artist! Billy didn't owe you a dime, and you're not gonna get your grubby hands on any of his stuff! Ever!"

Dr. Colburn watched in amazement as Kenneth begrudgingly returned to his seat and shrank under the captain's scolding.

Witt was furious! He saw through Kenyatta's scheme and wasn't about to let him tarnish Billy's reputation with low-life attempts to steal from his boat. He stepped to the middle of the cabin and crossed his arms, then, while standing over Mr. Morrison, asked him, "What brand of guitar are you saying Billy has that was yours?"

Kenyatta tightened his body and looked defiantly straight ahead. He knew he had been caught in a lie.

"Come on! You say Billy had a guitar of yours. What kind of guitar? Electric? Acoustic? Was it a twelve-string? How about a nylon string classical, or was it a parlor guitar? Oh, I know, was it maybe a travel guitar? A graphite? Come on, Mr. Kenneth Raymond Morrison! How am I going to get you your guitar back if I don't know which one to look for?"

Kenyatta stood up and grabbed his gig bag, then pushed past the captain as he reached for the ladder. His girlfriend stood to follow, and as they slid open the hatch cover, Captain Witt finished with, "Have a great gig, Rock Star!"

Dr. Colburn and Witt remained in the cabin as Kenyatta and his friend climbed back into their dinghy and motored away. Witt pulled a packet of hand wipes from the shelf above the settee and began wiping down the chairs where their guests had been sitting and said, "I'm sorry, but I couldn't let that lowlife con-artist think he might get away with running a scam on Billy that way."

When he finished cleaning, he tossed the wipes in the garbage can and added, "I've watched this guy pretending to be a guitar player for years, all over town! He's a total fraud! He was sitting on a stool one afternoon, on the sidewalk in front of Fausto's, when I pulled into their parking lot. He didn't see me, but I watched him for a full thirty minutes to get a better idea of what he was really all about. The guy doesn't even know how to tune a guitar! He strums it just lightly enough to not interfere with his voice as he rambles through a bunch of words that make no sense at all. When he catches some tourists' attention, he stops strumming and tells them that he was a close friend of Jimi Hendrix, and how he was in the studio with him when he recorded the Electric Ladyland album. He's just another bull shit artist who found his way to Key West, where all he needs to do is dress weird, act stupid, and get paid by drunken tourists to keep it up. Trust me, he wouldn't change in a million years!"

Dr. Colburn had no grounds to stage an argument. It made perfect sense to him. "Your astute observations are invaluable to me! Even though I deal with characters like this every day, I never really get to see them outside of a clinical setting. I'm at a disadvantage, I guess, having to assess them quickly, then evaluate their psychological profile while looking for ways to improve their conditions, all within a one-hour window. I appreciate you paying such close attention and looking out for my safety. Thanks!"

Witt straightened the chairs and asked, "Are you ready for me to call your next client?"

The doctor held his finger in the air and suggested, "Let's hold off on that for a minute! What's the chance that you and I could take a little time to get to know each other a little better first?"

"Yeah, sure!" Witt agreed, as he took a seat and grabbed two water bottles out of the cooler. "Anything particular on your mind?" The captain asked.

"I was curious! "The doctor began, "You seemed genuinely protective of Billy and his guitars, and I wondered if you and he were close friends."

The captain popped open the cap of his water bottle and took a long swig, then said, "Oh, yeah! When Billy moved here from Virginia, Kitty and

I owned three sailboats and kept them on Stock Island at the Sunset Marina. We lived on the Hunter-33 and kept the other two as boatels for rent. That's how we got started teaching people how to sail. Anyway, there was an available slip next to our Hunter, and Billy signed a six-month contract to dock his boat there. I had a Yamaha FG-150 acoustic guitar back then, and on the first night he was there, he heard me playing it outside, on the deck of my boat. Kitty was down below, and I was playing an old John Prine song that she loved. She was singing along, like she always did! I didn't know it, but Billy was listening from inside of his boat. He plugged in his electric guitar and started playing the lead parts of the song. He was fantastic! From then on, he was my best friend! Forever!"

"Well!" Dr. C. said. "Now I understand why you came to his defense so passionately. You never knew his wife, I suppose."

"No! She had died before Billy moved the boat here, but I know all about the accident they had with the Coast Guard. Billy told me the whole story one time. He was still involved with his tort claim for the entire first year he was living here!"

"Do you know why he and Markus put together the foundation?" The doctor's curiosity was in freefall. He was thrilled to be having it so well satisfied by his new friend.

Witt was happy to explain, and began, "Billy and Markus were friends from before Billy moved to Key West, but I met Markus through Billy one night, when Kitty and I were over at Schooner's Wharf. When Billy and the band took their break, Billy joined Markus and Janet over at their table. Kitty went over to say hi to Billy, and Markus invited us to join them. I knew who Markus was, but had never been introduced to him. When he asked about my sailing experiences, we instantly bonded. He's a very experienced sailor, but I think you already knew that. I did not know he was a three-star admiral then! I found that out once, when I rode with him out to the Sunset Grill on the Sigsbee Naval Base. He was driving his Toyota Land Cruiser and, when we went through the main gate, he didn't even slow down. The guard snapped into attention and saluted as we approached. I was surprised and asked him why. He pointed to the three gold stars down in the corner of his window and said, 'It's good to be the admiral'! Later, we were having lunch and he told me how he joined the Navy after he graduated from Cornell and, well, I think you probably know the rest of his history."

Dr. Colburn nodded his head as confirmation, as Witt continued. "Within the first few months of living at Sunset Marina, Billy discovered Harpoon Harry's, over on Caroline Street, and started going there for breakfast every day. It's the first pick for great food with all the locals. Billy was there so much that they dedicated his favorite booth as the Billy Booth. He and his musician friends used to sit and have dinner there before they had to perform. Anyway, give me just a second and I'll tell you how the foundation got started."

The captain set his water bottle on the table and stepped into the head to relieve himself. When he stepped back into the main cabin, he picked up where he left off. "Cristy is one of the waitresses over at Harry's! For years, she was the girlfriend of Tommy Too Low, the bass player and back-up singer for Devin's band, *Slack Tide*. Billy and Tommy were good friends, and Cristy was a strong part of that mix." He took another sip of water, then continued. "Billy told me that once, when he was having breakfast at Harry's and Cristy was his waitress, he was reading a copy of *The Citizen* and overheard Cristy talking with another customer who was sitting at the corner of the counter. I know who that girl was, but I'm not going to identify her now! She might be one of the people you'll be seeing out here sometime. So, this girl was in her mid-forties back then, rough around the edges, like lots of the people that live out in the mooring field. She used to work at the bookstore on Fleming Street. Anyway, the reason she was crying was because her only son had died in a wreck, on his motorcycle, and his funeral was coming up. She didn't have the money to get back to her hometown in Michigan. Billy walked to the bank, over on Whitehead Street, and came back with a thousand dollars and gave it to Cristy to pass to her friend. He made her promise to keep it anonymous and told me that it was the first time he had slept through an entire night without waking up from a nightmare, since his wife died."

The doctor sat speechless as he mulled over the story. Witt had more to add and continued. "I think that was the very beginning of the foundation, but there were several other generous episodes that we might credit to Billy's clandestine, philanthropic endeavors, before he and Markus began to see the potential of a partnership. I've gotten to know these guys quite well over the years! They operate on a higher level than most people. They have vision, and they both get their thrill by seeing those visions put into action. It's very rare! Without Billy, Markus probably feels like he's been blinded in his good eye. I'm worried for him right now! It's good that you came back into his circle when you did."

"Thank you for sharing this with me!" The doctor extended his appreciation for the captain's generous explanation. "This is going to help, as I become more deeply involved with the mission that the foundation was built upon. I don't think anyone else could have explained it more clearly. Thank You!"

Witt tendered a gracious smile, then asked, "You ready for your next challenge?" The doctor stretched, then said, "Bring it on!"

14. UNBOUND LOVE

"**H**i CC, this is Captain Witt, over on the *Psyched Out*"! Manny had stopped by this morning and put your name on our list to be seen today. Are you able to come over now, or do you want me to make arrangements for us to pull over there, later in the day, like we used to do sometimes, back when you were seeing Dr. Grant?"

The woman confirmed that she was ready for transport and that her friend would be assisting her with her appointment.

Witt responded cordially, "Ok, sounds great! We'll be watching for your arrival!" He hung up his phone and turned to the doctor and said, "Cassie Lynn Cunningham! One of the most amazing women I have ever met, hands down."

Dr. Colburn was smiling in anticipation over learning more about the next name on the captain's list, and asked, "What makes her stand out?"

"Well," the captain replied, "First off, she hasn't been able to stand up for nearly fifteen years, and second, that's never kept her from doing anything she decided she wanted to do! CC was one of the founding owners of The Key West Women's Center over on Truman Avenue. They've been providing health and wellness services to the community since about 2001. You'll probably be making referrals to them sometimes, if you haven't already."

"I have!" The doctor exclaimed. "I've referred several clients to them, and every one of them has reported back that they were thrilled with the help they received. What a great resource! Tell me more about this girl."

"Cassie lived with her girlfriend, Melissa, on their Catalina for the first five years she was here. She had bought the boat in Biloxi brand new and sailed it here when she took a state job with DCF, as the director of their Monroe County Adult Protective Services Division. Tough job, to say the least!" The captain moved into the galley and opened a cupboard door, retrieved a box of Vanilla Wafers, tore open the inside bag, and offered Dr. C. first grab. Then, while munching on cookies, he explained, "That was about 1987! My wife, Kitty, was the chef over at the Waterfront Market deli back then, and knew almost everybody who lived in the mooring field. Cassie and Melissa would come into the market for groceries, and Kitty became friends with them both. Cassie always had trouble with walking! It was a big struggle for her to get around! She looked like she was having to pull each leg forward to catch up with her other one. She never needed assistance until about 2004, when she tripped over a broken chunk of concrete on a Simonton Street sidewalk and fell into the path of one of the Old Town Trolley tour trains. After that, she had serious trouble with her motor skills and became completely dependent on Melissa. I helped build them a lift system so they could get her on and off the boat. I also modified the companionway and some of the interior compartments so she could get around inside. She has a tough life, but always meets it head-on." He stood to look out the starboard window and saw CC and Manny crossing the channel, then finished with, "Melissa moved to the mainland and never came back. CC doesn't talk about it, but used to counsel with Markus, back when we were coming out here regularly. She hooked up with Manny about five years ago. He's really been a great help to her. Big guy! Strong! He's completely dedicated to her, and she couldn't get around without him. He's from Guatemala, and when I first met him, he couldn't speak a lick of English. CC has taught him well, and now he communicates beautifully. Great guy! Very trustworthy!"

The doctor was eating from his pile of cookies and paused to ask, "Was she close friends with Billy?"

"Oh yeah!" The captain exclaimed. "They were very close! Ever since he first moved his boat over from Sunset Marina! They seemed to be of the same nature! Ya know, the way they care about helping people better their lives. You've really got to live in the center of something if you want to know how it spins! I think that's probably the reason they both lived out here in the moorings. Kitty says it provided them a fertile garden where they could grow their compassion flowers." He looked again, to check on CC's progress, then turned and asked the doctor, "We've got just enough time for me to tell you one more Billy story, if you want!"

The doctor insisted and Witt began, "It was in January, 2008, I believe, when he and his wolfdog, Flow, had left the dog park across from West Martello, and headed for his van that was parked next to the handball courts, when he spotted an older fellow and his wife curled up together against a concrete wall, trying to keep warm by staying out of the wind. Billy walked over and asked them if they were ok. They both sat up and told him they were fine, but Billy, being the conscientious crusader that he was, asked them when was the last time they had eaten, and the woman began to cry bitterly, while her husband insisted that they were fine. Billy knew better and asked if they had a safe place to get out of the cold, and the man said they had been living in their car, but that it had finally fallen apart and they left it up on Big Pine Key at a friend's house. He said they had ridden the bus to Key West and were staying at the Seashell Motel until their money ran out, two nights earlier."

The captain stood and looked out the window as he finished the story. "Billy pulled his van over to the couple and insisted they get in. They had bags full of their personal items with them, and Billy put everything in his van. He drove over to The Spanish Garden Motel on South and Simonton Street, and prepaid for them to have a room for two weeks. Over those two weeks, he and CC worked on getting them an apartment over at the Housing Authority. They're both doing well now! I know them and see them all around town. If it weren't for Billy's intervention and CC's connections, they'd probably both be dead by now!"

The sound of CC's motor grew louder, then stopped. "How's that for perfect timing?" He asked rhetorically, as he slid back the hatch and climbed out of the cabin. "There they are!" He called out as he grabbed the end of a looped line out of Manny's huge hand and secured it around the cleat. "How's my favorite maniac?" She was beautiful! Her smile could leave a sunset jealous!

"Witt, you ol salt lick, how've you been?" CC called up to her friend as Manny situated himself to saddle her securely on his back, then pulled her arms over his shoulders and began to climb. "Come on, Manny!" she ordered. "I can't wait to get my hands on that ol' dog!"

It was obvious to Dr. Colburn that there was much love between these two.

Once securely onboard, Manny unhooked the harness from his waist and leaned back to lower her onto the cushioned seat, then smiled as he shook the captain's hand, and moved out of the way for the two old friends to embrace.

"Oh, you don't know how good it is to see you, Witt!" There were tears in her eyes!

The captain knew perfectly well the reason! She loved Billy! He was like a big brother to her. The captain backed up and held both hands toward the doctor, then introduced him to the couple, "This is Dr. Walter Colburn, the newest member of our fleet! He and Markus worked, for many years, together at the National Institute of Mental Health in Washington. Markus wanted me to assure you that Dr. Colburn has his fullest endorsement!"

CC dried her eyes and looked up at Dr. C., then said, "I've been looking forward to meeting you ever since I first heard that your wife had died. I was working at the Women's Center back then, and knew the nurse who was assigned to her when she passed. I understand that she's now working with you at the Depoo clinic. Maybe you could update me on how she and baby Kristmas are getting along." She bent forward to stretch her back muscles, then added, "Markus told me about how close you and he were! I'm so happy to finally meet you in person."

Dr. Colburn smiled and motioned toward the cabin hatch as he responded to CC's greeting, "I'm looking forward to seeing how you and I can begin working together, but first, let's get situated in the air conditioning."

Manny moved into position and once CC was secured to his back, Witt opened the hatch and headed down the ladder to guide the duo safely in. Once they were all inside, Manny set CC on to the starboard couch, then stepped to the other end, and sat down. Dr. Colburn pulled four cold water bottles from the cooler and passed them around as Captain Witt closed the hatch, then sat down at the settee.

Dr. C faced his client and began, "Before we get started, I'm sure you are aware that HIPPA laws protect your privacy rights. Now, we can accommodate for that , if you prefer..."

CC raised both hands in the air and interrupted, "No problem here! I waive my HIPPA rights every time I climb off my boat, and if you need proof that I'm competent to do so, well, let me put John F. Kennedy's Whitehouse

Psychiatrist, Three-Star Admiral, Dr. Markus Grant on the phone and let him defend that for me."

Dr. Colburn and Witt laughed, knowing full well that the relationship she had with Dr. Grant, afforded her immediate access to his confirmation regarding her sanity. "Very well, then!" Dr. C began, "How can I be of assistance to you today?"

CC began, "If you don't mind, is it alright if I just relax for a few minutes? It's so hot outside, and I'm drained! I just need to cool off and relax first."

Witt grabbed two hand-towels from the head and handed one to each of their guests. Dr. Colburn adjusted the a/c vents toward the ceiling to bounce the cold air over to the couch, then offered, "You can take all the time you need! We're here for both of you!"

"So, tell me, how's Jillian doing?" CC asked, then popped the spout on her water bottle open, and took a long sip. "Krismas was such a gorgeous baby! I'll bet she's big by now!"

Dr C. grinned as he answered! "She's getting more and more gorgeous every day, and Jillian is an integral part of our operation now. I don't think we could get through a day without her expertise!" He was good at protecting his clients. Though Jillian was allowed to think of herself as a member of his staff, she would always officially be his client. "They are both doing very well!"

CC then volunteered, "Mellisa and I were good friends with Ethan! You know, Ethan's the guy that sailed Jillian down to Saint John and got her pregnant. We were out on Christmas Tree Island that night that he and Jillian first met. Ethan and I were singing the Wagon Wheel song, over at the fire pit, when Jillian caught his eye. I knew he was going to take her to his boat that night, and always regretted not warning her about how he operated. I used to think I could have saved her from all the troubles she's had if I had only warned her, but, if I had, she never would have had Krismas. Life's kinda funny that way!"

Witt chimed in, "Ain't that tha truth!"

Dr. Colburn took the opportunity to ask, "Are either of you hungry? We've got several sandwiches on ice, if you haven't had lunch yet! They're here for the taking!"

Manny looked over at CC and raised his eyebrows as high as they could go. CC smiled and said, "That would be great!"

Dr. C handed them both a sandwich while Witt stepped into the galley and pulled a tube of Pringles from the cabinet, then passed it to Manny and said, "Here, all we have right now are the bar-b-que flavor!" Then added, "I've got a jar of unopened sweet pickles in here too! They aren't cold, but you're welcome to 'em!"

As the two guests enjoyed their sandwiches, CC began to discuss the issues of concern that had brought her to the *Psyched Out*. "Ya know, Billy's passing is kind of prophetic. We were just talkin' about life and some of the trouble people bring on themselves. Somehow, we started to talk about the origins of how humans deal with loss and death. That whole conversation seems like a sandbar that I got stuck on, and now I've got to find a way to push myself back off, without breaking my rudder shaft." She reached across the couch and grabbed Manny's arm, and started to gently cry as she said, "It's the people that help to push us back into safer waters that we miss the most when they're gone."

She grabbed her knees and struggled to pull each leg closer, then rolled her upper body in wide circles to alleviate some of the pain that constantly pulsed through her spine. She was still weeping, when she said, "This is pretty tough for me," then buried her face into the towel that sat upon her lap.

Manny slid across the couch, draped his monstrous arm across CC's back and pressed his forehead against her shoulder as her cries grew more and more intense.

Witt looked over at the doctor, raised his eyebrows and contorted his face to signify his bewilderment. Dr. Colburn acknowledged that he recognized the captain's concern with a slight nod of his head.

Shortly, CC recovered and dried her eyes, then said, "When I was still working at the Elder Abuse Unit, I uncovered a case of fraud and had to wait on the Office of the Inspector General to finish their investigation before my team could intervene and remove an older gentleman from his son's home. The man was at high risk, but the OIG was dragging its feet. I told Billy how frustrating it was and the next morning I got a call from Tallahassee that the investigation was completed, and I could expedite the client's removal. I found out later that there was a Congressional Inquiry filed to the OIG's office that forced them to wrap it up. I can't tell you how many times that Billy helped me fast-track cases through the system. He just seemed to know what to do, every time! It took a while for me to figure out that Markus was Billy's power broker. Eventually, they let me in on how they operated their foundation and together, we helped a lot of people." She dried her eyes and took a sip from her water bottle.

Dr. Colburn asked, "When was the last time that you and Billy were together?"

She took a deep breath, looked over at Manny, then answered, "Last Saturday! Manny and I were dog-sitting Flow for three days when he went up to Miami, for a doctor's appointment. He came by to pick her up and we ended up talking for several hours. He had to meet with the guys in the band at six, over at Schooner's. He left about five-thirty. Manny and I had an early dinner, then went in to hear them play. We stayed till they took their break, then came back out to the boat. That was the last time we saw him! I just can't believe he's gone!" Manny had held her hand as she talked. He cared deeply for his friend. It was obvious that he didn't like seeing her sad!

Dr. Colburn offered, "Ya know, it's a wonderful thing that you both were able to spend some quality time with Billy before his death. That is something that can now be cherished and help to alleviate some of the pain of your loss. Too many times, when someone we care about dies unexpectedly, there's no recent, positive event to reflect on. That's a precious memory that you will always have. I can tell you firsthand how meaningful this will be later on."

CC smiled, "Yes," she said, "Billy leaves me with some wonderful memories!" She leaned to her left, and slowly twisted her right arm till it reached the leather pouch that hung from her belt. After fumbling to open the latch, she pulled out a billfold and began to awkwardly rummage through its contents, till she found what she was seeking, then said, "A little over a year ago," she talked as she unfolded a piece of paper, "My mother died! She was a social worker in Pascagoula when Hurricane Katrina flooded everything. She and my father had evacuated to my aunt's home in Memphis, but when they were finally able to get back, their little house was gone. That was the house I grew up in." She sighed as she brought back the memory of her childhood home, 3648 Cumberland Rd. "Anyway, Melissa and I evacuated and rode with Billy up to Pinellas Park. We stayed in the Best Western for about a week, and when we got back to the mooring field, we found that our boat's mast was completely folded over and the backstay and shrouds had pulled out from their chainplates and beaten the upper cabin to crap."

Captain Witt nodded his head as she described the damage, "I remember!" He remarked. "We pulled her up to D&D for repairs. Billy helped Lewis put her new mast on!"

"That's right!" CC confirmed his recollection, then added, "And neither of them charged me a dime!"

Dr. C. listened intently as the story of Billy unfolded.

"I think that was the last straw for Melissa, and she packed her stuff and moved back up to Michigan, leaving me to try to get by on my own. I was pretty eaten up with anger over it, and Billy, well, let's just say he saved me from going over a few edges!" She reached again, and patted Manny on his forearm, then continued. "When Mother died, I was trying to figure out how Manny and I could sail back home for her funeral, but with my condition being so much more debilitating, and Manny not having any sailing experience, it seemed I might have to give up any hope of being there. Billy came to my rescue. He and I drove all the way to Mississippi and back in his Town and Country van. It was a dream trip! Manny stayed here and had the time of his life." She looked over at Manny, who was grinning ear to ear, then went on with her story. "Billy and I stayed long enough for the funeral home to deliver my mom's ashes, then we drove over to La Pointe Krebs Museum and poured her ashes into the water off the dock. Billy walked back to the museum while I stayed down by the water, saying my goodbyes to Mama and when I walked back up, Billy was sitting on a bench next to the entrance. I sat down beside him, and after a minute, he handed me this piece of paper." She passed it to the captain and began to cry. "He wrote it while I was down by the water, saying goodbye to my mom."

Captain Witt seated his reading glasses in place and read aloud,
"She's a wonderous woman,
of unbound love,
who carries the world on her shoulder,
turn's to each morning,
with newfound way,

removing both pebble and boulder,

a path she will blaze,

through the whole of her days,

in hope of a brighter tomorrow,

alas her dismay,

while forging her way,

on sands to be kneeling in sorrow,

a pause in her life,

considered in rife,

the hand of a friend she would borrow,

to straighten her way,

as she tightens her stay,

and chastens her winds for the morrow,

onward we till,

with hope of goodwill,

we'll blunder our way to forever,

then bask on a shore,

we name evermore,

and live out our days there together.

William Blain Chapman III (March 3, 2010)

CC began to cry again, and bellowed loudly, "OH, Billy! Billy!" Then buried her face deeply into the towel on her lap.

The three gentlemen reached in unison to comfort her through her agony. It was a difficult yet compassionate offer that fell woefully short of their hope. They waited! Their touch on her shoulders, her head, her hands, led her through the painful darkness of the dreadful reality. He was gone! She was left only with the memory of him! She would hold onto those memories for the rest of her life!

Before CC and Manny left the boat, Dr. Colburn asked if she had any prescriptions she needed reordered and if they had their financial needs covered. She assured him that there were no other needs than the pleasure of his counsel and the love for her old friend, Captain Witt. They departed the *Psyched Out*, leaving the captain and the doctor standing on the deck, more bewildered than before.

"Well!" The doctor said to the captain, "I'm not sure I'm ready for another client, right now!"

The captain retorted gleefully, "I've got ten-year-old Scotch in the locker up front!"

"Oh, now! That'll be something to look forward to!" Walt said with a grin.

15. CHET ATKINS

It was 1:40 pm at the Monroe County Sheriff's office when Carl answered his phone. "Dixon!" he called into the mouthpiece as he looked up from the notebook on his desk. "Hang on, I'll check!" He removed the clip that fastened the photographs to the top of his file, then reported, "No! All I've seen so far are the ones from the dinghy dock. Have we got any from the marine team yet?" He got his answer, then brought his laptop to life. "Ok! Here they are! I've got 'em in front of me now! What am I looking for?" On the other end of the call was Tripp Hughes, the chief of forensics and evidence. "I'm not sure I'm clear on what I'm supposed to be seeing! Any chance you can come up and go over it with me?" He asked. "Great!" Then, he hung up his phone and returned his attention to the notes in his notebook.

Five minutes later, Tripp was standing over him, with a stack of 8" x 10" glossy photos in his hand. "I had the lab print up extra copies for you!" Tripp said. "These are the ones from out on his boat." He set the first photo on the desk and took his pen from his shirt pocket, then pointed it into the photo and directed the Detective to look closely. "You see this?" He began.

Carl looked intently at the tiny image in the photo and said, "Is that a candy dispenser?"

"No man!" Tripp declared. "It's an inhaler! You know, people with asthma and lung problems use them to open up their airways so they can breathe."

Next, Tripp dropped a close-up of the same countertop onto the desk for Carl to inspect. In the picture was the red inhaler next to a set of keys, three guitar pics, some currency, some change, and an open brass padlock.

"What is this?" Carl asked.

Tripp offered his friend a rather startling concern. "I've been trying to figure out why this stuff was on his boat when Billy was DOA under the dinghy
dock. Then I checked the evidence list and saw that his pockets were empty."
He dropped another photo on the growing pile for the detective to view and
said, "See that guitar case? If it has the same guitar inside that Billy was playing Monday night at Schooner's Wharf, then something ain't adding up!"

Carl looked carefully through the rest of the photos and asked, "You
knew Billy pretty well, didn't you?"

"I did!" Tripp answered. "And I know that if his '88 Telecaster is in that
case, then we've got questions that need answering." Tripp moved to the
cushioned chair by the door to sit down, then added, "He always uses that
guitar when he plays with Devin and his band, so how the hell did it get
out there on the boat if Billy was still at the dinghy dock waiting on the fog
to lift?" The question beckoned for an answer! "Also, I've never seen Billy
on shore without Flow! I read the Marine Patrol's initial chronological notes
that said Flow was on his sailboat, not on the shore! Why would that be?"

Carl slid his chair back against the wall and frowned as he considered
the evidence that was now coming to light. "Good questions!" he said, as he
grabbed the stack of pictures and began taking a closer look, then declared,
"Till now I would have bet this was just an explainable accident. Now I'm
going to have to rethink the whole case!" He picked up his phone and called
the Marine Division chief. "Carry, this is Carl Dixon," he stated. "I need to
get out in the mooring field, asap! Do you have anybody available that could
make that happen right now?"

"As a matter of fact," Carry answered, "Omar just pulled up to the dock
to refuel. I can have him hang out till you get down there."

"Sounds great!" Carl said. "I'm on my way!" He grabbed his notebook
and pulled his gun from his drawer. "You wanna go for a boat ride?" he said,
as he took his first step toward the door.

"I was hoping you'd ask," Tripp replied, as he jumped to his feet and followed the detective out the door. It was a short walk from the main office to
the Marine Division building at the back of the property. Two patrol boats
were tied up at the dock. Omar was standing in the hot sun, next to the gas
pump, waiting for Carl.

"Well!" Omar called out to the approaching officers. "It's good to see you guys on the outside for a change." He stepped into the boat and turned the key as Carl and Tripp climbed onboard and took their stand on each side of the console.

"I don't know about Tripp, but I was born without sweat glands!" Carl joked.

Omar spun the boat around and steered toward the open waters of the Gulf, then gently pushed the throttle forward until the boat was fully on plane. They motored past Dredger's Key and the Sigsbee Naval Base, then turned toward the North point of Fleming Key. As they rounded the point, Omar asked loudly, "Am I correct in assuming we're headed to the *Ghillie Dhu?*"

Carl asked, "What's a *Ghillie Dhu?*"

Tripp called out the answer, "That's the name of Billy's boat!"

Carl shook his head, "Oh! That's clever!"

"Yeah!" Trip responded. "Everything about Billy was clever! He was a real clever guy, till Tuesday morning, anyway!"

Omar slowed the craft as they pulled into the mooring field, then idled past the *Psyched Out* and made way toward the stern of the *Ghillie Dhu*. Tripp moved to the bow of the boat and readied himself to tie off the line. Omar killed the engines and asked, "You gonna leave me out here to cook in the sun?"

Carl turned and said, "It may not be any cooler up there, but you're welcome to join us." The three officers climbed onboard, then, after Tripp opened the hatch, they climbed into the cabin.

"Geeeezzzz! This is one beautiful boat!" Omar exclaimed. "Look at all that teak!"

Tripp had been on board Billy's boat a few times over the years and was familiar with its design. "Yeah!" he said. "Morgan makes great boats! They're really popular with the charter operations down in Saint John and Antigua. I think this one's fifty feet or more.

Carl looked at everything carefully as he slowly moved from one area of the boat to the next. He paid particular attention to the items he had seen earlier in the photos in his office. "Hey Tripp!" He called out to his partner.

"See anything missing here?" He pointed to the items that were on the shelf above the navigation station.

"Well, the money's gone!" Tripp answered, then reached for the guitar case that was leaning against the forward bulkhead and said, "Let's see what's in here." He lifted the case and set it on top of the table, then popped open the latches. Carl used the corner of his notebook to lift open the case.

"There she is!" Tripp exclaimed. "I think you've got your hands on a mystery, Detective Dixon!" He pulled a pair of gloves from his pocket and carefully lifted the guitar out of its case.

"Wait! What's that?" Omar pointed to the back of the guitar, and Tripp turned it around for him and Carl to see.

"Tripp immediately knew the answer and began to share it with his comrades. "Those, my friend, are what make this guitar one of the most sought-after instruments this side of Texas!"

"Ok, but what are they?" Tripp tilted the guitar toward the light streaming in through a small porthole and adjusted its position till the beams illuminated the backside of the beautifully stained guitar. Three ink signatures became fully visible, and the men strained their eyes to identify their signers.

After a few seconds, Carl admitted, "I can't make any of them out!"

Omar cast his best guess and said, "I think I see this first name as maybe Ambert, and that last name on the third one is definitely Lee, but that's all I can make out".

Under the body of the guitar was a plain white, unsealed envelope. Carl lifted it carefully with the edge of his notebook while Tripp lowered the guitar back into its case.

"This looks rather interesting!" he said, as Tripp gently took it from its precarious pedestal and held it up in the dusty stream of light for inspection. "Nothing seems to be out of the ordinary, yet!"

Next, Carl directed Tripp to open it carefully. Nothing seemed particularly suspicious about the 8 1/2" x 11", twice-folded piece of standard white paper that Tripp slid out of the envelope.

Omar's imagination was in freefall! He turned it loose and said, "That's got to be some kind of clue!

Carl and Tripp were both seasoned crime investigators. Every piece of evidence in any case, whether criminal or civil, holds the potential of becoming a clue! They ignored Omar's exuberant naivety as they studied the paper.

"I think it might be a letter of provenance!" Tripp exclaimed. "It's either that or some record of an event that the guitar may have been involved in!"

Carl said, "Let's quit guessing at what it is and read it!" He then directed Tripp to read it aloud.

He began, "Fender Telecaster (1988) Serial # E-812219 Standard Telecaster Factory Setup (graphite nut and string trees – aftermarket) Signatures on back: Albert Lee, Leo Kottke, and Lee Ritenour.

The following narrative is provided for the purpose of establishing the authenticity of signatures only. I, William Blain Chapman III, do testify and acknowledge that on Friday, May 22, 1992, I personally performed on the above-identified Fender Telecaster at the Virginia Beach Convention Center. This performance was the final recital before receiving my Master's of Music Performance Certification from Old Dominion University (1000 19th St., Virginia Beach, VA 23451). My recital was a juried performance and officiated by the four judges listed as follows: Mr. Chet (Chester) Atkins-Guitarist, Mr. Albert William Lee-Guitarist, Mr. Leo Kottke-Guitarist, Mr. Lee Ritenour-Guitarist. I testify that all signatures were exacted in my presence upon the completion of said recital, and that Mr. Chet Atkins, the presiding judge, had excused himself from the room when the signatures were obtained. Damn it! This description and testament is accurate and verifiable through substantial media reporting material. Thank You! William Blain Chapman III. Signed, this date: October 6, 2003."

"Well, that may not be considered evidence in my case, but it sure was interesting!" Carl remarked as Tripp reinserted the document into its envelope and placed it back in the case, under the guitar, then suggested, "I think we should lock this place up when we leave. We already know somebody came in and took Billy's money.

Carl agreed, then asked Tripp, "Did you bring your ALS?"

Tripp reached into his pocket and pulled out his keychain. On one end was his trusted UV mini-flashlight. "Right here!" he answered, as he held it up for viewing.

"Give this place a hit and let's see what shows up." Tripp pushed the on switch and pointed the light at the floor. The response was instantaneous! There was blood, but not much. Just a few drips near the footing of the companionway ladder and a little more on the rungs. Carl was pissed. "God damn, did the evidence team even check for blood?"

Tripp and Odie stood silently as the detective took the flashlight and conducted a closer inspection. "Well," he finally announced. "I suppose they were convinced by what they saw at the dinghy dock that it was an accident. I'm going to have to haul this thing out of the water so we can shake her down." He handed the light back to Tripp and turned to exit the cabin. "Try not to step in the center of these rungs. We've got to preserve what we can!"

Trip suggested, "I'll grab Billy's keys and see if one fits this lock. We can secure the hatch while we get set up to tow her to the yard. Hopefully, we can beat the rain." As they gathered on deck, Carl turned around and looked slowly out at the mooring field and the boats that were tied there, then said, "I think we've got until dark before we get drenched!"

He grabbed his phone and spoke his command, "Siri, call Mark at Tow Boats U.S.".

On the other end of the call was a familiar voice, "Tow Boats, this is Mark!"

Carl could tell by the background noise that Mark was running hot somewhere on the water. He called into his phone and plugged his ear with his finger. "Mark, this is Carl!" he said. "Carl Dixon! Can you hear me?"

Mark's voice was loud and insistent. "Hang on," he said. "I got a trawler in tow! Did you say Carl Dixon?"

Carl responded and Mark told him, "Give me ten minutes and I'll call you back. Is that ok?"

Carl answered, "Great!" then shoved his phone back in his pocket.

Tripp asked, "What's next, boss?"

Carl put his hands on his hips as he slowly scanned the neighboring boats and asked, "You wouldn't know whose boat that is, would you?" He was pointing his finger at the beautifully trimmed out 1978 Swan 43' Sloop they had motored past earlier.

Omar and Tripp both laughed as they answered in unison, "The *Psyched Out*?"

Tripp leaned over to lock the hatch and explained, "It's owned by a foundation that supports a lot of the indigent and homeless people that live on the boats out here. See that flag on the back, hanging from the halyard? It has the psychiatric symbol on it. When it's up, the people in the mooring field know that the psychiatrist is onboard and they can see him for counseling."

Carl was thrilled to have finally laid his eyes on the boat that he had been hearing about for so many years. "Would the doctor be onboard now?" He asked.

"Oh, yeah!" Tripp answered.

Carl grabbed his phone and called out his order, "Siri, call Walter!"

One ring, "Dr. Colburn!"

Carl stepped to the port gunnel and cordially asked, "What's for dinner?" He always started his calls with friends that way. He says he likes to hear them laugh before he hits them with bad news. They all know it about him. It was just something to be expected and laughed about.

"Well, unless your wife is doing the cooking tonight, I'm dining with Marie Callender again! What's up?" Walter asked.

"Are you with a client right now?" Carl asked.

"Not right now!" the doctor answered. "Witt was just about to call over the next one on his list. Why? What's up?"

"I'd like to talk with you about something that's come up regarding Billy. Would it be alright if I come over for a few minutes?" Carl asked.

"Well, that would be fine, but I'm about a mile and a half offshore right now, and I don't recall ever seeing you walking on water."

There was a tapping on the hull of the *Psyched Out.*

"Permission requested to come aboard!" Carl asked in a deepened voice.

Witt pulled himself up through the hatch and onto the deck, as Carl, Tripp, and Omar climbed over the railing.

"Ok! You found me!" Witt surrendered, as he clenched his fists and held out both arms for cuffing.

"I think we'll let you off with a warning this time." Carl reached his hand out and the two old friends shook a manly greeting. They were well matched gladiators of Gold's Gym.

"What's going on?" Witt asked.

Walt called through the hatch, "Come on inside! The A/C's on!"

The space was cramped for the five men, sweltering in the belly of the Swan. It took several minutes for them to get comfortably situated.

After the hatch had been tightly secured, Witt stood in the galley and announced, "We got beer, wine, and water! Choose yer poison, pirates!"

Water was the choice of all, and after the bottles were passed around and introductions were made, Dr. C. asked, "How can I help you guys?"

Carl looked over at Tripp and motioned for him to explain what he had found. "This morning," he began, "our lab delivered the last of the photos from the initial workup in Billy's case. I started going over them and couldn't figure out how Billy's dog, his guitar, his inhaler, his keys, and his money would have been out on his boat if he had never left the dinghy dock on Tuesday morning. Carl decided we should come out to verify what we saw in the photos, and we noticed someone had been on the boat. We wondered if you, maybe, have seen someone over there."

Carl added, "Maybe someone that you might talk to out here would have seen someone, and we just wanted to check with you."

Walt looked at Witt! Both were struck with an immediate answer. "Cairo!" Walt said, while the captain nodded in agreement.

"We pulled into the mooring field today a little after 8 am, and Cairo paddled over here from Billy's boat," the doctor explained. "He had a run-in with another guy about it, but it was Cai who later admitted he went over there. He said he went to look for some food."

Carl asked, "Do you know if he went back to his boat when he left here?"

Dr. Colburn shrugged his shoulders, then said, "I can't really say. We watched him when he was halfway there, but he didn't look like he knew if he was going back or going to Key West. He doesn't have a motor, so I couldn't imagine he's gone far."

Carl made a note in his notebook, then said, "I'm sure we'll catch up with him." He took a long sip from his water bottle, then asked, "Is there anyone else you can think of that might have been around Billy's boat on Monday night, or early Tuesday morning? Maybe someone that might have heard something?"

Witt looked over at Dr. C. and suggested, "Maybe CC or Manny! They might have heard something!"

Tripp spoke up! "I've got CC's number in my phone." He turned toward the detective and asked, "You want me to see if she's available?"

"That might be a good idea. Maybe she knows something that could broaden our perspective." Carl directed Tripp, "Give her a call." Then turned to Omar and asked, "Are you ok to work with us for a little while?"

Omar answered, "My boss is your boss!"

The three officers bid farewell to their hosts and proceeded to disembark the *Psyched Out*. As he climbed into the police boat, Tripp's phone made its connection. "CC, this is Tripp Hughes." He announced. "Are you on your boat?" When the call was over, he turned to Omar, pointed toward the North West, then commanded, "That way!"

16. THE TURTLE MUSEUM

Omar idled up to the Starboard side of CC's boat, *Afternoon Delight*, and hit the engine's kill-switch. Carl reached for the sailboat's side rail, and wrapped his hand tightly around it, to hold their boat in place.

Tripp slapped the palm of his hand twice against the hull and called out, "Sheriff's Office! Come out with your hands up!"

One of the Morgan's brass port-lights popped open and a voice called out from inside, "You want war? We'll show you war! Load the cannon, Manny!"

"Hey CC! I better warn you, I've got backup out here." Tripp and CC were close friends! Their banter was mutually endearing! Manny helped CC get situated, so she could see their visitors through the tiny window. Once adequately positioned, she saw the men's faces and called out, "Hey Carl! Is that Omar chauffeuring you guys around today?"

Omar and Carl shared their hellos, then Carl explained, "We just needed to ask you if you had any knowledge of somebody being on Billy's boat after we put up the tape on Tuesday."

CC replied, "Give me a minute! I'm gonna come outside."

After several minutes, Manny had her situated on deck, and she began to share what she knew. "Manny told me that he saw Cairo leaving Billy's boat this morning when he went over to the *Psyched Out* to get me scheduled to see the doctor.

Manny was standing behind her and added, "I didn't actually see him getting off of the boat, it was still too foggy, but it was pretty clear that's where he was coming from. It was a straight shot from Billy's boat to where he was, when I saw him."

"Thanks!" Carl said. "By chance, did either of you happen to hear or see anything out of the usual, on Monday night or Tuesday, early morning?"

CC looked up at Manny, who shook his head, then back at Carl and answered, "Not that we remember! We hadn't seen or heard anything from Billy since Saturday afternoon, when he came over to get Flow."

"You saw him on Saturday?" Carl asked.

"Yes! He stayed over here for a couple of hours, talking about stuff and just visiting," she offered.

"Did you see anything unusual in Billy's behavior, or did he say anything that you might consider out of character for him?"

CC turned again to look into Manny's face, then turned toward the officers in the boat and answered, "Well, one thing that we both noticed was different, his voice. It was raspy, and he was constantly trying to clear his throat. I've never known him to have that kind of problem. I was concerned that he might have something contagious and asked him about it, but he said it was just a reaction to some kind of dust exposure and that we didn't need to be concerned." Her curiosity was heightened by their questions, and led her to ask, "Is something going on? It was just an accident, wasn't it?"

Tripp sought to quell her anxiety and assured her, "We've just got to tie up all the loose ends before we can come to a conclusion. I think we'll have it all together soon! Thanks, CC! You too, Manny! Great to see ya both!"

As Omar turned the key, Carl pushed against the Morgan's hull, then called up to the pair as he waived them farewell, "We'll let you know something real soon! Thanks!"

"Well, what do you think?" Tripp asked his friend, as Omar idled toward the main channel.

Carl's eyes were fixed on the *Ghillie Dhu* as they passed by. "Honestly, something's going on, and I'm gonna find out what!"

Omar put the boat back on plane, then, over the scream of the engines, asked, "Where to next?"

Carl leaned toward him and said, "Let's head home! I've got work to do."

At 1530 hours, Carl sat back down at his desk and placed his gun back in the drawer. He opened the Chapman case file and began reviewing the notes he had taken while inspecting the site where Billy had been found dead. He began to speculate on the many possibilities that might lead toward foul-play as an element in the case. He took his phone in his hand and placed a call to Coreen Waddell, the owner of Schooner's .

"This is Reen!" She announced as she answered the call. "Hey Reenie, this is Carl Dixon." He announced.

"Oh, hey Carl." She responded. "Nice to hear your voice! How's Barb?"

"Oh, you know! She still thinks she's the Queen of Fantasy Fest, even though that was twenty years ago." After the chuckling faded, he asked, "Reen, does your live cam system have history capabilities?"

Her response was his best hope! "Oh yes!" she said. "We upgraded it about four years ago, but anything before that is history."

Carl was encouraged, and then asked, "If I needed to review your stage cam for last Monday night, how could I do that?" Reen was quick to answer, "You can come over and see it anytime you like or I can have it downloaded to a flash drive and send it to you." He was already out the door and said, "Thanks! See you in fifteen!"

Coreen's office window provided a north-east panoramic view of the Key West Bight harbor, and the out-islands where the mooring field is located. It also provided her a bird's eye view of the Harbor Walk that leads to the water-side front entrance of her bar. She was standing in her window, sipping tea, when Carl first appeared on the Harbor Walk and looked up at her smiling face, then waved. She pointed her finger toward the back stairway. He flipped a thumbs-up and turned toward that approach. Seconds later, she greeted him at the second-floor rear entrance to her office.

"Hi Carl!" She greeted him with a friendly hug. "Has this visit got anything to do with Billy's accident?" she asked, as she stepped to her desk and sat down.

"I'm afraid so, Reenie!" He stood watching as she punched in her password and began to pull up the live-cam archive selection screens on her computer. "Unfortunately, I'm out here to thread a needle that somebody failed to cinch tight on Tuesday morning. Hopefully, it will only take a few minutes."

"I went ahead and ordered you an Arnold Palmer! It'll be here in a minute!" Then she asked, "Any particular time frame you need me to start this with?"

Carl peered into the screen and asked, "Can you get me a look at Billy, when he was performing?"

"No problem," she said, as she typed in a 9:36 pm time parameter, then triggered play. Carl saw immediately what he was after. Billy was sitting on a tall stool, on the right side of the stage. In his hands was his white Fender Telecaster guitar. "That's it!" he declared.

There was a soft tap at the front door. Reen stepped to open it and asked, "What did you find?" She took the tea from the waitress and handed it to Carl as the door closed.

"Billy's guitar!" He answered. "He had the Telecaster with him that night! It should have still been with him. In the dinghy, on Tuesday morning."

"That's the guitar he always plays when he's here!" she said.

Reen had no idea the significance of what Carl had found. She knew better than to try to pry anything more than what he was willing to offer. "Is there anything else you need to see?" she asked.

Carl thought for a moment, then had an idea, "Billy usually brings his dog with him when he comes ashore! Isn't that right?"

"That's right!" Reen said. "He and the band always take the corner table in the back, where they leave their drinks and personal things. Flow stays right there whenever Billy's playing. He keeps her back there with a bucket of ice water. There aren't any speakers back there, so the loud noise doesn't hurt her ears."

Carl asked, "Is there a cam that might show the dog over in the corner, while Billy was playing that night?"

"Sure!" she said, as she switched to the crowd-cam. "There, she's lying down! You can see her clearly."

Carl now had the needle threaded, and his case was calling for an upgrade. Reen asked, "Is there anything else I can get you?"

He was busy pouring his tea down his throat. When he finished, he started to ask her to burn the videos onto a flash drive, but by the time he had dried his lips, it was already done. "You're the greatest!" he said, as they walked to the exit door.

"Tell your Queen to call me sometime! We've got a lot more shopping to do!"

Minutes later, Carl was back on the Harbor Walk, headed for his cruiser that was parked in the Margaret Street parking lot. The dinghy dock was crowded with boats, and several people from the mooring field were gathering belongings, loading supplies, unloading gear, or just hanging around. The back door to the Turtle Cannery Museum was open, and he decided to do some reconnaissance.

"Excuse me!" he called to the attendant, who was sitting at the other end of the open-air museum. Pointing his finger at the chain that was strung across the doorframe, he asked, "May I?"

The man swiveled his chair around to see who had called, then responded, "Sure, come on in!" As Carl made his way past the artifacts and cannery displays, he began to take interest in what was being presented. He stopped to look into the glass case that housed several implements and tools that were commonly used in the harvesting and cooking of the famous Key West Turtle Soup.

"That's remarkable!" Carl exclaimed as he turned in amazement, and came face to face with the skull of a Green Turtle and a pile of bones that had been excavated out of the neighboring pens, where the turtles were corralled until being hoisted into the slaughterhouse and cooked.

He was reading the plaque that explained the harvest processes when the gentleman at the desk asked, "Is this your first time in?" Carl turned and casually approached the man as he answered. "When I was a kid, my uncle managed this place."

The man stood to his feet and exclaimed, "No kidding!" When they were face-to-face, he added, "I'd be willing to bet you ate a lot of turtle burgers when you were a kid!" Carl grinned, as he extended his hand toward the man. "Carl Dixon!" Their hands locked, and the man responded with a smile, Dr. Renaldo T. Shagnasty at your service, but you can call me Bo!"

There was something genuinely eclectic about the man. The detective sensed no reason to raise his guard and said, "As a matter of fact, I did!" and returned, again, to his viewing of the bones. The curator turned his back and returned to his seat at the desk. "Were they good?" he asked, as he shaved another layer of skin from the apple he had previously been peeling.

There was a cushioned desk chair against the wall. Carl took hold of its crown and slid it over to the front of the little desk, then took a seat and answered, "Tasted like chicken as I recall!". They toasted to their new friendship with laughter.

"There's a saying," the man said. "You never know when you're going to make a friend for life, so live a friendly life!"

"That can't be your real name!" The detective provoked him toward an honest admission of his lie.

The man leaned back in his chair and answered, "That depends!"

Carl responded, "On what?"

The man slapped his hands on the desk and answered, "If you came all the way out here to serve me papers or not!"

The detective grinned, "Naw! I'm just lookin' under stones and tryin' to figure out what happened to your friend two days ago.

The man straightened his shoulders and asked, "How can I help you, Detective?"

Carl asked, "Were you close friends?"

"Oh, yeah!" He answered. I met Billy three years ago, right here in the museum. I was a historical interpreter out at Fort Jefferson 'till 2007, when I retired. Six months later, my wife threatened to murder me if I didn't find something to do, and this job fell in my lap. One morning, Billy and Flow came through that back door, just like you did, and started looking around." He turned and pointed up at the two guitars and a mountain dulcimer hanging on the wall above his desk, and continued, "He saw that Taylor 600 and asked if the pick guard was real turtle shell. I told him it was, and he asked if he could play it. He sat right there in that same chair and played a beautiful piece that he had composed when he was studying music at Old Dominion, in Virginia. He was fantastic! That was how our friendship began. He used to drop Flow off here, and she'd stay with me while he ran errands. She'd chase the birds that come through the open windows and the pigeons that nest under the dock. Sometimes, the girls that work in Turtle Kraals Restaurant would bring buckets of ice over and pour it out on the floor for her to lie on. She loved it! Yeah, Billy and I were good friends." He took a sip of coffee, then said, "Oh, by the way, I'm Alex, but you can call me Bo! It's short for Alex!"

Carl laughed heartily and asked, "How did Bo become short for Alex?"

Bo sliced off a piece of apple and tossed it in his mouth, then said as he chewed, "My sister gave me that name when I was five. She said Dip Shit was already taken by my father."

Carl almost fell out of his chair laughing.

Bo tossed the apple core in the trash, then walked across the museum to the sliding door where the turtles were historically pulled up into the building, and pulled the heavy, wooden door closed. He dropped the latch into the locked position, then moved to the door in the back of the museum. As he proceeded, securing the building, he continued talking. "Billy filled in for me for ten days while I was in the hospital. Over the years, he had gotten to know as much about this Turtle stuff as I do. I used to tell him if I got too sick to work, he could slip right in and take over. My boss completely agreed, too." Bo had one doorway left to secure. The time was 4:29 pm, when he locked his register and turned off the lights. Carl followed him through the front door, and as he slid it shut, he pointed over his shoulder at a thirty-foot charter boat that was backed into the slip directly across the dock and said, "See those boats?"

Carl turned to look, and Bo continued, "They're all owned by Eric Campanello! When Billy was fillin' in for me here in the museum, Eric was having two of his bait monkeys sand the paint off of every part of that bigger one, and all the dust blew into the museum. It was illegal to do it out here on the docks, and he knew it. Billy got sicker than hell after the first two days from breathin' all that dust. They use Baybright paint on these boats, and it's full of poison. Very dangerous stuff! Billy got really sick, and started seeing a pulmonologist, who sent him to Miami for tests. Baybright exposure can kill you."

Bo kept talking as they walked toward the parking lot. When they reached Carl's cruiser, he asked, "Have you checked with the city to view the surveillance tapes of the docks?"

Carl was surprised and remarked, "I've always heard that they never activated that system! It's only good as a deterrent to the people who don't know that the cameras aren't on."

Bo leaned in and placed his hand to his cheek, and in a muffled voice said, "Yeah, well, here's the latest unofficial update. It got activated two weeks ago! They're trying it out for thirty days, to see if it's financially doable, before they announce to the shop owners and charter operators that it's work-ing. The only reason I know about it is because my eldest son is the guy who flipped the switch. Keep it under your hat! OK?"

The two shook hands and Bo left with an offer for Carl to stop by again, if he needed more information.

On his way back to his office, Carl began mentally sorting through the new evidence and information that had been uncovered throughout the day. He pulled into his parking space and slipped the shifter into neutral, then grabbed his phone. "Siri, call Barb!" He dreaded telling his Queen that her favorite Knight would be working late! Again!

17. JEANNIE'S BACK IN THE BOTTLE-

Captain Witt dialed the next number on his list. "Hellll-lllllo?" The voice on the other end seemed muddled and fractured! The syllables were separated by an unusually long slur. Witt knew immediately that trouble had perched its wicked talons, once again, upon the shoulders of the sweetest little waitress that ever served breakfast at Schooner's Wharf.

"Jeannie?" He called into his phone as he turned his eyes toward the doctor, in deep concern. "This is Captain Witt Lowery, on the *Psyched Out*! Are you OK?" He put his phone on speaker, then held it up for them both to listen. There was no answer! The sounds of a restaurant were clamoring in the background. They heard the repeated squawking of a seagull, an intermittent knocking, then a clamor that sounded like she had dropped her phone onto something wooden. "OOOOOP'S!" she said. Next, the sounds of her fumbling with the phone, then it went dead.

"Oh! Oh!" Witt was troubled by what they had heard. He hit redial and waited. His call went to her voicemail, "I'm sorry, but the person you are calling's mailbox is full. Please..."!

The recording was interrupted when his phone rang. It was Jeannie, she had called back. "Whoooo is thhhhisss?" Her voice was slurred and slow!

"Hi Jeannie, this is Captain Witt. I was just checking on you to see if you're feeling alright!" He put the phone back on speaker for Dr. C to listen in.

"Whhhhooo?" Her struggling to connect was a sure sign to the captain that she was in trouble.

He thought he might provoke her memory by engaging with her in a more familiar context, and placed his order. "Thanks, Jeannie! I think I'll have the eggs benedict with a side of cheese grits, and maybe some of your home fries."

Her response was slow but expected, "Arrrrr uuuuu fffffuuuckinnngg wiiith meee!" Then, "Whooo arrrr uuu, mooootherr fuuukkerrrr?"

As he continued engaging with her, he signaled for Walter to hand him his phone. Once he had it in hand, he dialed in the phone number of Schooner's Wharf bar and directed the person on the other end to connect him with the owner, Coreen.

"Coreen!" She answered.

"Reen, this is Witt Lowery! I think there's a problem with Jeannie! Do you know where she is right now?"

She could tell he was seriously anxious and answered quickly. "I saw her just ten minutes ago. She looked sick, so I had her clock out early. I just watched her from my window! She dropped her phone, then was stumbling to climb the stairs in front of the Fury office. I can't put my eyes on her, but she couldn't have made it very far." Then she added, "I think she's gone back to drinking again!"

Witt was relieved to know she had not yet reached her boat, and asked, "Any chance you could try to catch her before she leaves the dock?" He switched back to his phone and called out, "Hey, I think I'll have some blueberry pancakes with my eggs! Can you add them to my order?" There was no answer, just the sounds of something banging against her phone.

Coreen now understood the unspoken seriousness of the call and asked, "Wouldn't you rather I call 911 and get them to dispatch someone from the Sheriff's office?"

Witt had already considered that scenario and answered, "There's not enough time! She'll be on her boat before they could get from the parking lot to the dinghy dock. Reen, we're wasting precious time! Can you try to stop her from getting on her boat?"

"Ok, I've got to lock up my office first. I'll call you when I see her!"

It took her a mere six minutes to put her eyes on the girl. She hit Witt's number and reported what she was seeing, "Too late! She's just beyond the end of 'C' dock. She's not paying attention to where she's going either! I just watched her bounce off that big Bertram that's docked out on the end." She paced the dock as she talked. "You want me to call 911 now? They could get the Marine patrol out and pick her up?"

Witt's mind was working through every alternative. "No!" He advised. "We're out in the mooring field, and should be able to see her from up on deck. I'll launch the skiff if she looks like she needs help and give you a call when we get her on board. I'm with the new doc that's filling in for Markus. He'll do his assessment and I'll let you know, later, how she's doing."

Dr. Colburn had already exited the cabin and was standing on deck, watching for the girl through Witt's binoculars.

Witt slipped his phone into his back pocket, climbed the ladder, and slid the hatch door closed. He stepped to the doctor's side and said, "You've met this girl, I'm sure!"

The doctor responded, "Oh, yeah! She served me breakfast while the sheriff's crew was over at the dinghy dock on Tuesday morning, cleaning up after Billy's body was removed. She was a mess!"

Dr. C. passed the binoculars to the captain, and as he lifted them to his eyes, he said, "She moors her boat over on the free side of the channel! Hopefully, she'll turn and come toward us. If she does, we'll know she's remembered she's supposed to meet with you. If she doesn't, I'll launch the Whaler and go get her. We've got at least fifteen minutes till she gets here."

"Do you know how close she and Billy were?" the doctor asked.

Witt was still watching for Jeannie when he began, "When Billy first started playing with Devin, over at Schooner's, Jeannie was working the bar from six to closing. She made a lot more money back then, a lot more than she does now, but at least she's away from the booze and cocaine. It used to flow pretty freely around the docks at night. Anyway, Billy saw the dead-end that she was headed down and began leading her toward getting cleaned up. Eventually, he and Markus fixed her up with an apartment over at Samuel's House, and through the foundation, they paid for her to get treated at Crossroads on Antigua." He took a long sip of water, then returned to the story as Dr. Colburn stood listening in awe. "She stayed for the full sixty-day session, and when she graduated, Marcus and Billy sailed Billy's boat to Antigua to be there for her discharge. After that, they made arrangements to stay a couple of days over in Jolly Harbor so Billy could sit in with his friend, Carson Diggney, and his Reggae band *Junakanoo*. When they brought her back to Key West, they fixed her up with the boat she's now living on. Billy and Markus have helped her stay sober ever since." He dropped the binoculars from his eyes, then continued, "Coreen's Jeannie's boss! She loves her like her own daughter and keeps an eye on her. It's kind of a beautiful thing! She's deeply loved all over this little island town!"

Walter turned again and looked toward the Key West harbor, "I think I see her!"

Captain Witt held up the binoculars, "Good girl!" he said. "She's on her way here."

Dr. Colburn stood looking across the water at the tiny boat that was now on course for their rendezvous. "What a wonderful story!" He turned to look at the captain, then added, "I sure hope we can find a way to get her back on track!"

"Well," Witt said, as he pulled the rope ladder out of the storage box and secured it to the cleats on the starboard gunnel, "in just a few minutes we should be able to start getting an idea of just how far over the edge she's fallen." He stepped back and leaned against one of the forward stanchions that held up the hardtop, and asked, "Should we talk about how you want to handle this, if she's as bad off as she sounded on the phone?"

The doctor noted Witt's concern, then explained, "It's impossible to speculate on reasonable outcomes before I'm able to evaluate her capacity for rational associations. I'll put her through a simple battery of questions, much like the police do in sobriety checks. I want to determine, as quickly as possible, whether or not she's medically compromised. If she can't stand up, or if her eyes can't track, then she should in no way be out on the water, unsupervised. Let's try to get through all that while we're up here on deck, where I can better test her depth of field and cognitive abilities."

They both looked toward the approaching inflatable. Jeannie didn't seem to realize she was about to collide with the side of their boat. The two men jumped to the railing and began shouting and waving their arms to alert her of the rapidly approaching danger. Poor Jeannie was slumped forward, trying to pull a cigarette out of its pack, oblivious to the consequences of her apparent inebriation. The duo jumped back as her dinghy slammed into the fiberglass hull andthrew Jeannie into the water. Witt kicked his shoes from his feet and flew over the railing headfirst. In seconds, he had one arm around her motionless body. Her head had hit with a tremendous impact. Blood was everywhere. She began to cough and choke as Witt reached with his free hand and grabbed the first rung of the ladder.

"Get towels! They're in the head! Quick!" he shouted to the doctor.

Upon his return, Dr. Colburn helped the captain lay the girl flat on the deck, then proceeded to dry her wound with a towel. Witt grabbed a bottle of water and gently washed the blood from her face. She was breathing, shallow but breathing! "Jeannie! Jeannie dear! Open your eyes, sweetie! Look at me Jeannie!" The doctor called to her in a calm and gated tone. He motioned for the captain to manage the wound while he proceeded to assess her condition. He took both of her hands in his, then called to her again. "Jeannie, if you can hear me, I need you to try and squeeze my fingers." There was no detectable response.

"What do you think?" the captain asked. "Broken neck?"

The doctor had his fingers on her wrist, checking her radial pulse, and his eyes were on the second hand of his watch. He couldn't respond to the captain's intrusion. There was a life on the line. As he stood to his feet, he directed the captain, "Don't let her move! Whatever you do, just keep her from moving!"

He pulled his phone from his pocket and dialed 911. The voice on the receiving end answered, "911, What's the nature of your emergency?"

"I have a female victim of a head trauma in need of immediate emergency services. She is breathing effectively with a weak and thready pulse. She is unresponsive to commands. I am requesting immediate medical transport."

"What is the location of your victim?" the dispatcher asked.

"We are on board the sailboat *Psyched Out*, tethered to Key West Bight mooring ball #36. The coordinates are as follows: 24.34-644N, 081.47-221W."

"Please stay on the line!" The dispatcher's voice was cool and calm as she transferred the information to the Key West Coast Guard and the Key West Police, then directed the doctor to remain on the line until the rescue agents arrived. He put his phone on speaker and knelt on one knee next to the girl lying on the deck.

"Prety bad, huh?" Captain Witt's voice was peppered with concern over the girl's condition.

The doctor shrugged his shoulders and explained, "At this point, we need to avoid any stimulation that might evoke a response. If you can just stay still and hold her head until EMS can stabilize her on a backboard for transport, I think that's the best we can do." The doctor adjusted his legs and slid backwards, until he was against the float locker, then looked over at Witt and asked, "You ok for a little longer?"

"No problem!" the captain answered. Then, "Listen!"

They both turned their heads toward shore. The first siren was faint, coming from the Northern point of Fleming Key.

"That's got to be the Key West Police, Marine patrol!" Witt said. "They're coming from Garrison Bight!" Before he finished his sentence, they heard the Coast Guard medical response boat's siren, as it pulled out of the harbor, racing toward the mooring field. "Those are the guys we need! They've got the gear it will take to keep her stabilized. The police boat is only coming to evaluate, write an incident report, and secure the scene!"

Minutes later, three guardsmen were rushing over the railing. Two EMT's immediately proceeded to evaluate Jeannie's condition. She was unresponsive but breathing. The lead EMT shone his light into her eyes, one, then the other. Her pupil responses were uneven, and her left pupil was larger than the right. Dr. Colburn was watching their every move. After the eye inspection, the first EMT looked at his partner and gently shook his head. Dr. Colburn recognized the severity of Jeannie's condition and understood the possibilities that the young man's response inferred. None of them were good. After her vital signs were taken and her wound was field dressed, the EMTs fitted her with a rigid cervical collar to stabilize her neck, then the five men lifted her carefully onto the trauma board. They placed several foam blocks around her body to further restrict any jostling during transport, cinched her tightly to the board, then the three Coast Guardsmen moved her to their boat and raced away.

The police boat had been idling in wait for several minutes. When the Coast Guard pulled away, the officer maneuvered into position on the starboard side of the *Psyched Out*, and introduced himself. "I'm Sergeant Tanner with the Key West Police Department." He pointed to the hull and said, "From the looks of all that blood, I'd say somebody wasn't looking where they were going! Any chance this might be connected to that runaway inflatable I just saw headed into the mangroves, over on Fleming Key?" He pulled his camera from his vest pocket and snapped several pictures of the impact site, then returned it and zipped the pocket closed.

Captain Witt was quick with his answer, "Unfortunately, probably yes!" He followed with, "I'm Captain Witman Lowery! This is Dr Walter Colburn! If you'd like, we can tell you all about it below! I keep our A/C set at 72 and the water on ice!"

The officer tossed his line to Witt and killed his ignition switch, then grabbed the railing and pulled himself onto the boat. "Mind if I get a few shots of your deck first?" He pulled his phone again from the pouch on his vest and turned toward the bloody towels that were still on the spot where the girl had been lying. "Gotta preserve what I see, when I see it!"

"Please!" Dr. Colburn ardently exclaimed. "Witt and I can answer any questions you have when we're below." The three shook hands, then climbed through the cabin hatch. Once inside, Witt offered the officer a seat, as he handed him a cold bottle of water and said, "I thought I knew all the guys over at the marine division! When did you come on board?"

The officer downed the first half of the bottle, wiped his lips with the back of his hand, and answered, "I transferred in from the Charlotte County Sheriff's Marine Unit, in Punta Gorda, on May 3rd. It took six weeks to get my boat equipped! I just hit the water yesterday, and here I am." He took another swig of water, then asked, "So, what's with all the blood on your boat?"

Witt reached into the cabinet above the navigation station and grabbed the folder holding the vessel registration papers and the pertinent licenses and records that identify the foundation's authorization to be operating from mooring ball 36, and explained, "The victim's name is Jeannie Anne Lorimier! I can't tell you much about her, but she works at Schooner's Wharf Bar and Grill as a waitress, and she lives on an older 33-foot Neptunian ketch with a light blue hull just offshore from the Sigsbee Naval Air Base RV park. You can't miss it! It's got an inflatable recreation pad tied on its port side."

The officer grabbed his notepad and began to write. "Was this a fatality?" he asked.

"No!" The doctor exclaimed. "Not fatal! Life-threatening, but not a fatality!" The officer turned his full attention to the doctor as he continued. "She was on her way here for an appointment with me. She was distracted and unfortunately miscalculated her approach. She was ejected when her dinghy made contact with our boat, and she suffered a serious head trauma. I made the call to your dispatch as soon as we had her on board."

The officer asked, "What kind of doctor are you?"

Dr. Colburn reached for his wallet and pulled out a card. "I'm a psychiatrist!" he exclaimed. "I run the outreach clinic over at the Depoo Medical Building, on Kennedy Drive."

The officer finished studying the doctor's card, flipped it over, and asked, "Is there another number we can use to reach you for further questioning?" As Dr. C. called out the number, the officer wrote it on the back of the card, then asked, "So, if you don't mind, could you explain to me what kind of appointment this girl could have been expecting, after coming all the way out here, to the mooring field?"

Captain Witt raised his hand to block Dr. C. from answering, and said, "I think I can explain this!"

The officer stopped him and said, "Before you get started, tell me once again, who are you?"

Witt pulled his MMC card from his wallet and handed it to the officer. After inspecting the license, he copied the information into his notebook and as he handed it back to the captain, exclaimed, "So, you hold a Master's endorsement?"

Witt grinned, "Oh, yeah!"

The officer couldn't resist asking, "How big?"

The question was loaded! They both understood the connotation. Witt answered, "A hundred ton!"

"Well, you are one ambitious sailor, aren't you!" It was a rhetorical question, and considered inappropriate by both Witt and the doctor.

Witt leaned forward and spoke very clearly into the officer's face. "Seargent Tanner, a dear friend of ours is hanging precariously close to death right now, and, if I'm not mistaken, you will be expected to have an accurately completed incident report on Chief Becker's desk when he shows up for work at 0700 hours tomorrow morning. And if Charlie, excuse me, Chief Becker doesn't see that report, well, I can't imagine how furious he just might be. If you would like, I'll be more than happy to write you a completely acceptable report right here, right now, and I can assure you that Charlie, I'm sorry, Chief Becker will be thrilled when he sees my signature on that report right where yours should have been. How does that sound to you, Seargent Tanner? Shall I pull out my notebook and begin?"

Tanner had just had his nose wiped, and he knew it! He would have been a fool to allow his ego to continue running wild and unbridled in the presence of such an obviously well-trained and connected maritime master. He set his pen to his notebook and began. "By chance, can you pinpoint just what time the girl made contact with your boat?"

It took less than ten minutes to finish the interview! As Seargent tanner climbed the companionway ladder to exit the cabin, Captain Witt was already on his phone, placing a call to Chief Becker's private number. "Charlie, you and Becca still commin' over for dinner Sunday night?" As the police boat motors roared to life, Witt closed the hatch and fumed, "That little asshole's the reason I quit the force! There's a whole new generation of snotnosed Tanners movin' in, and I had my fill!"

Did you really call Chief Becker?" the doctor asked.

Witt walked to the forward cabin and pulled the bottle of Scotch out from the cabinet, and said, "Naw! Didn't need to!" He grabbed two cups from the galley shelf and set them on the table. "I'll tell 'em tha whole story when he and Becca come over for dinner on Sunday! They live two houses down the canal from us!"

Witt slid across the cushion behind the table and poured the Scotch, then handed the doctor a glass and held his high for a toast, "Here's to one tough little girl! May all the hope of life be with her!"

"Here! Here!" The doctor raised his glass to the captain's and took a sip, then sighed and said, "Very nice!"

Captain Witt picked up his phone and dialed the number to Schooner's. "Coreen, please!" The girl transferred the call.

"Coreen!" She answered.

"Corren, this is Witt. I'm afraid I've got some bad news about your girl Jeannie." He reported. Then, added, "She had a bad accident in her dinghy, and the Coast Guard had to take her to the hospital."

Coreen became frantic! "Oh, no! Is she going to be alright? What happened?" Witt put the phone on speaker and set it on the table. I've got you on speaker with Dr. Colburn. He is Markus' stand-in till his leg gets better. I'll let him tell you."

The doctor began, "Hi Coreen. I think the best way is to just tell you what happened."

Coreen agreed, and the doctor continued. "Witt and I were watching her with binoculars as she motored out of the harbor. We were waiting to see if she would remember her scheduled counseling session with me. She was fumbling with a pack of cigarettes and not paying attention! Unfortunately, she didn't hear our warnings and plowed into our hull at high speed. Witt was able to get her on board, and after we evaluated her condition, we called for an emergency transport to the hospital for treatment. I can't really comment on her condition, but I'll tell you this: she's hurt pretty badly."

Coreen was in tears, obviously in great concern for Jeannie. Her words were choked by anguish as she struggled to respond. "It's all my fault!" she cried. "It's my fault! I could have stopped her!"

Witt tried to break through her torment several times, without success.

Dr. C. interposed with, "Coreen, no one is at fault! Jeannie tripped over something she couldn't have foreseen! It was an accident! She grabbed for the closest thing she thought could help get her out of the pain. Unfortunately, like so many others, her choice was in a bottle! There's no one to blame here! We just need to be patient, stay calm, and try to learn from what happens."

Coreen gained strength from his words and seemed to regain control over her distress, and said, "I'm sorry! I know what you're saying is true! I just feel so stupid right now! If I had been watching more closely, well, maybe," she was fighting her tears, "maybe if I was spending more time out there, out on the floor!" She was struggling to stay coherent. "Oh God! Do you know where they took her?"

Witt spoke up, "She's probably already in route from the Coast Guard dock to the Lower Keys Trauma Center on Stock Island. They'll get her stabilized there, then likely fly her up to Jackson Memorial in Miami on Trauma Star. My guess, she could be up there within the next three hours. They'll know best what she needs."

Before Coreen could respond, Dr. C. added, "We'll keep on top of her progress and let you know as soon as we learn something!" She was still whimpering sadly, as they said their goodbyes.

Witt took a drink from his glass, then set it gently on the table.

Dr. C. waited. The captain stared at his glass and quietly considered the gravity of the event. After a minute, he polished off his Scotch and announced, "I think we ought to call it a day!"

18. A SLOW SAIL HOME

D r. Colburn leaned against the forward pulpit and waited for the sound of the engine turning over. He slowly scanned the mooring field, then locked his gaze on Billy's beautiful boat, The *Ghillie Dhu*. Overtaken with the solemnity presented by the events that had befallen him, he failed to notice the engine come to life.

Captain Witt called out to him, "Ready when you are!"

Jolted back into the mission at hand, he bent over the railing and pulled on the tethered rope, then untied it from mooring ball number 36, and the *Psyched Out* floated free. He made his way along the foredeck, then climbed back into the cockpit and took a seat. As the captain turned into the main channel, Dr. C. commented, "That's the quietest engine I think I've ever heard."

"No better way to push a boat this size than the Perkins 37!" The captain went on to brag, "I overhauled it myself, in 2006! There's not a more dependable diesel on any boat in the Keys! I'd stake my Captain's license on it!" They were halfway back to the Bight when Captain Witt looked up at the wind vane on the masthead and asked, "When's the last time you manned the helm on a class A ocean racer?"

The doctor had only one answer, "I think I'd have to say *never*!"

The captain spun the wheel till the *Psyched Out* was facing into the wind, then knocked the kill switch with his foot and climbed to the front of the cockpit and commanded, "Take the wheel, good doctor!"

Dr. Colburn seized the opportunity and replied with enthusiasm, "Aye aye, Captain!" Then moved behind the helm and stood ready at the wheel.

Witt pulled the mainsail cover off and stowed it away, then checked and aligned the main halyard, checked his reefing lines, then loosened the main sheet, climbed back into the cockpit, and barked out the command. "Hoist away!"

Dr. Colburn grabbed the halyard and began to pull. When the sail was fully raised, he tugged until all slack had disappeared, then locked the line into the cleat. Like a swan, lifted toward the sky on wide-spread wings, the ship gently embraced the evening breeze and kissed all cares goodbye.

"Can you feel that?" He heard her quiet whisper inside his brain! "It's where we always knew we were meant to be." She was beckoning for him to recognize the truth that they had always longed to discover, back when she was still alive."

He took a deep breath of the salty sea air and sighed in relief as he felt her taking control of his thoughts. The yearning for her presence, the dream of a future filled with her in his arms, the pleasure of her loving embrace and the touch of her lips on his cheek. These were his most private indulgences! His most cherished memories! They were always available for him to grasp! Always waiting for him to pull the curtains back, and immerse himself in the blissful echoes she had left him forever listening for.

"I do!" He imagined his answer! "I feel it!

Witt smiled and looked over at his newest friend. "That's the ride of your life, right there!"

"He's right, you know!" She was relentless in her enchantment.

"No argument here!" Walter called back.

The captain pulled out his phone and held it in the air, and called over to Walter, "I need to call the last couple of clients, and let them know we'll be back on the hook about 0900 hours tomorrow! That sound OK with you?"

The doctor nodded his head in agreement, then called back, "Don't forget, J.C.'s boat needs to get over to Lewis at some point!"

The captain responded, "I sent a text after our lunch break! Waiting on Lewis to tell me when!" While the first call was ringing, he added, "We need to call Markus with an update on Jeannie! We can make that one on our way back in!"

Dr. Colburn acknowledged with an approving nod of his head, then quietly began to take in the magnificence of the moment. The evening was unfolding into perfection as they sailed past the docks of Mallory Square. The carnies were setting up their equipment for the sunset celebration. A mod-

est number of tourists were making their way around the waterfront promenade, enjoying watching the entertainers warming up for their evening per-
formances. Walter glanced at the digital display, inset in the fiberglass, just
outside of the cabin hatch. Six knots, it read as they passed the Mole pier
where the Navy docked their submarines during the Cuban Missile Crisis.
J.F.K. himself had stood on that very pier, commending the submariners for
their efforts in the defense of their nation. "How far out you wanna take it?"
He called over to the captain, who had just finished his last call. "

"I'm thinking we should catch the sunset from the Sand Key Lighthouse!
No better view anywhere! Clear shot of the horizon! Maybe she'll go green
tonight!"

Walter understood that his friend was talking about the elusive green
flash phenomenon that is sometimes seen when the sun disappears over an
unobstructed horizon. You could watch for a thousand nights and never
catch it once, then for no reason known to man, BLAM!

They were merely fifteen minutes away. Several other boats were already
anchored in the shallow sands that surround the old, rusty structure. The
captain asked, "Have you been out here before?"

Dr. Colburn steered past the next channel marker, then answered, "Never! What's the best approach?"

"Well," the captain started to explain as he stood to his feet, "Probably,
the best approach would be for me to take the helm before we come up on
the ledge that's just off the starboard side."

Walter stepped around the pedestal and turned loose of the wheel as the
captain took command. In true maritime fashion, he called out, "The helm is
yours, Captain."

Minutes later, Witt pulled the halyard from the cleat, and the mainsail
went slack. The *Psyched Out* drifted to a stop against the current. He held the
ignition switch and listened to the starter kick the engine over, then pushed
the throttle forward and motored into the deep-water approach just east of
the lighthouse. "Get ready to set the anchor," he called out to the doctor.

Walt climbed to the bow and pulled the anchor from its storage compartment, then stood, ready to drop it into the water.

Seconds later, the captain shouted, "That's good!"

The doctor lowered the anchor slowly into the crystal-clear water 'till it rested on the sand just ten feet below, then gave the rope several jerks to assure a proper setting.

The captain hit the kill switch, then wrapped the sail for storage. "Alright," he said, "Sunset in ten minutes!"

The breeze was softly blowing out of the northeast as the sun began to slowly melt away. The molten, blistering white, plasmatic sphere slipped deeper and deeper behind the edge of the Earth. In the last millisecond, a tiny bubble of green light popped from its trailing edge, then followed into tomorrow. Celebratory cheers, from the tourist-laden party boats that had come out to the lighthouse in hope of seeing the flash, echoed across the waters, then quickly faded into joyous chatter and music.

Witt climbed into the dark cabin to retrieve the bottle of Scotch. "Here, doc!" he called out from below and held the bottle and glasses up for him to grab, then pulled himself through the open hatch. "It'll probably be a while before anybody at the hospital can give us an update on Jeannie's condition, don't you think?"

Walter sat back on the cockpit cushion, and Witt poured some whisky into his raised glass. "Are you familiar with the Golden Hour?"

The captain took his seat behind the helm and responded, "Sure! It says a trauma victim's best chance for survival is to be treated within the first hour. When I went through the Maritime Safety Academy in Orlando, they pounded it into our brains."

Well," the doctor began to explain, "With Jeannie, we face at least two unfortunate circumstances. First, it was approximately seven minutes before we got her on board and evaluated how badly she was hurt. By the time my 911 call got the Coast Guard boat to leave their dock, we were fifteen minutes in. They were, I'd guess, another fifteen or more minutes in route to get out to the mooring field. That would put us at a minimum of thirty minutes! They were on board, getting her stabilized for another ten minutes minimum. They got her loaded and back to the dock. I'd give that probably twenty more minutes! I think, realistically, that's on the outside edge of her Golden Hour!" He took a sip of whisky, then continued. "Assuming the EMS truck was waiting at the Coast Guard Station, my guess is it would've taken them another ten minutes to get her transferred into their truck, and with the five o'clock traffic being what it is over the Cow Key Bridge on any Thursday afternoon, well, the math just doesn't fall in her favor!"

Witt offered no argument to the doctor's assessment and asked, "What's the second circumstance?"

The doctor stood to his feet and leaned against the support stanchion and explained "HIPAA only allows them to share information about her condition with her immediate family and her doctor, and I've never formally seen her as a patient."

Witt was quick to ask, "But, isn't your clinic a branch of the same hospital system? The doctor responded, "It is, but I can't expect to have access to a patient's records unless I'm on record as their doctor!"

The captain was a bit perplexed by his answer. He took a sip of his drink, then picked up his phone and said, "I think we need to let Markus know what happened!"

"Hang on, Witt," came the voice on the other end of the phone. Twenty seconds later, Markus was anxious with concern! "Thanks for holding on. I just got off a call with Bob Larkin over at the hospital. He told me all about Jeannie's accident! They're preparing her for transport up to Jackson Memorial on Trauma Star! I can't tell you how grateful I am that you guys acted so quickly! You probably saved her life!"

Witt had put the call on speaker mode for them both to listen.

Dr. Colburn leaned in and asked, "Did he say whether or not she regained consciousness?"

"She did not!" Dr. Grant responded. "They took neck x-rays and inserted a central IV! He's going to review the films and call me back. I'll, of course, keep you up on anything I hear."

"We had enough for one day, so we sailed out to Sand Key to see if we might catch the green flash and unwind! I think your replacement got a pretty good taste of what you and I dealt with all those years."

Markus laughed. "Did he pass the audition?"

"Barely!" Witt grinned. "Let's hold that decision till we see how tomorrow goes."

"All right, gentlemen," Dr Grant said. "Safe sailing tonight and stay between the channel markers!"

The two new friends sat under the great celestial canopy, talking about their lives and the adventures that meant the most to them. Witt talked about his years of sailing and the many different types of vessels he had captained. Walt talked about his Chicago psychiatric practice and the decades that he spent working in Washington, D.C. with Dr. Grant. They drank Scotch and talked about the love they had for their wives and children. Walt told the story of his last days with his wife, on vacation in Key West, and her passing after a brain aneurysm. They motored back to the marina sometime after midnight, secured the boat, and bid an end to the long, tiring day.

19. TRIBUTE TO A TROUBADOUR

Carl was busy at his desk, sorting through the 62 photographs that were now downloaded to his laptop, and making notes when his phone rang. "Dixon!"

It was Tripp Hughes! "Hey! You still at the office?"

Carl answered, "Yeah! What's on your mind?"

Tripp was casual as he explained his reason for calling. "I just thought I'd let you know that Meg was at Harpoon Harry's for lunch today and ran into Devin and Marty. Devin told her they're going to do a tribute tonight, at Schooner's, for Billy. I was just thinkin', you might want to catch them when they go on break and see if they can give you anything about how Billy was doing on Monday night. Might be worth a little overtime!"

It didn't take long for Carl to realize the merit. "Ya know, that might be a really good idea!" He exclaimed. "Do you and Meg want to join us?" Tripp confirmed the plan, and they agreed to meet at Schooners at eight.

Carl placed his call to his wife.

She answered, "Hey sugar, what's up?" Barb was sitting on the couch with a bowl of popcorn and her famous homemade Tabasco and peanut butter dipping sauce, watching the Channel 7 Evening News, when he called.

"Oh, I'm sorting through some evidence that Tripp came up with on Billy's case, and thought maybe you'd like to go over to Schooner's to hear *Slack Tide's* tribute to Billy. Tripp and Meg are going to be there. We can have dinner, and maybe I can get with Devin for a couple of minutes when they break. Tripp came up with some questions we think he might be able to answer. What do you say?"

She screamed into the phone. "Awah!!!" He jerked his phone away from his ear in pain. "What was that for?" He asked.

157

"I can't believe they showed that!" she exclaimed.

"What are you talking about? Showed what?" He was holding his phone safely, five inches from his head.

"Some guy just got hit by a train in Fort Pierce, and the stupid reporter was standing on the railroad tracks telling the story while the guy's body was being photographed over in the bushes. That's just gross!"

Carl chuckled! She acted like such a kid sometimes! He loved that about her! If asked, he'd admit it keeps him feeling young. "Hey, there's this tiny little button on the top of that remote in your hand. It says 'off'!"

"Smart ass!" she quipped, then asked, "You need me to pick you up?" They're home was on Cudjo Key, Mile Marker 22. A beautiful stilted, cedar-sided home with a wraparound porch. It was situated second house from the bay, of a swimmable canal, and has a kidney-shaped pool with a built-in hot tub. Carl's office was on Stock Island, just four miles from Schooner's Wharf Bar, and it was not at all unusual for Barb to pick him up at the Sheriff's office, then drop him off later, to pick up his cruiser. She hated riding in that smelly piece of cop car memorabilia anyway. She didn't like seeing it in her gravel driveway either. Her excuse was always played to the max. Baby wants her top down! She would be referring to their beloved Golden Retriever, Baby Nacho Dixon! Barbie goes nowhere, if Baby can't come! His answer should have been assumed upon her asking.

"Yeah! That'll be great!" he answered. "Give me about forty-five minutes to finish up these notes." They would soon be enjoying the night air, the moonrise, and the palm-tree-lined drive along the bayfront boulevard in Barb's Saab convertible. Just Baby, Barb, and one very content detective named Carl Dixon, cruising through Key West, with the top fully retracted.

"Geez! I can't find a parking spot!" Barb voiced her concern, as she steered through the lot for the second time.

Carl pointed toward the pier at the end of Margaret Street and directed, "Just park at the front door of the Turtle Museum! If there's any problem, I'll tell them I was working on the Chapman case." Barb drove onto the causeway that leads to the old Turtle Cannery and the Dockmaster's shack, and pushed the button to raise the top on the Saab. Carl grabbed the leash for Baby, and the three prepared for their walk over the dock to Schooner's Wharf. The summer night air was still and muggy! The breeze of the earlier evening had died, and the moon had risen high enough to cast a shimmer across the tidal waters that flowed in and out of the historic bight. The sailboats bounced gently to the rhythms of the tide.

Several young homeless men and women were gathered on the dinghy dock, seeking free rides with the mooring field residents out to Christmas Tree Island, where they camp illegally, and avoid the authorities that seek their capture. Carl stopped for a second and contemplated the possibilities that perhaps one of them had seen Billy in his dinghy, on that foggy, fatal Tuesday morning. He handed Baby's leash to Barb and directed her to keep walking along the dock. He entered the Turtle Kraal's Restaurant and walked through the dining area, then exited the other door in the hope that his stealthy approach might catch the group off guard. He walked down the gangway to the floating dinghy dock and stood at its foot, blocking the group from leaving the area. Holding his badge in his hand, he pointed it in their direction and said "Hey!" Once they were all looking, he said, "By chance, were any of you out here on the dinghy dock Monday night?" They were confused and apprehensive! He read their body language and knew how to gain their confidence. "I'm not lookin' to give you any trouble. I really don't care what you're doing. I just need to ask you if you saw anything suspicious Monday night or early Tuesday morning."

He waited while the ragged bunch looked at each other, then one young man offered, "You mean something dealing with Billy?"

"Maybe!" Carl answered. "Anything you can tell me?"

The young man set his backpack on the dock and started rifling through it in search of something yet unknown to the detective.

"Stop!" Carl commanded. "Take your hands out of the bag, slowly!"

The young man froze, then carefully pulled a harmonica out and held it in the air, and said, "He gave me this! Monday night. Mine was broken, and Billy gave me this one before he and Flow left to go home."

A second young man with a guitar case added, "We were sittin' right here, jammin'! We were all here, except Tonya!"

They were shaking their heads in unison as the young man went on to say, "Billy walked up the dock from Schooners and could probably hear how bad Cliff's harp sounded. As soon as he got in his boat and stowed his stuff, he climbed back up and handed him a little blue box with an old antique Hohner Marine Band blues harp inside. That's it, right there!"

Cliff opened the box and removed the harmonica, then held it up for the detective to see. Next, he beat it against his hand and put it to his lips, then belted out a purely magical blues riff.

Carl was delighted! Not as much in the beauty of the tune, as in the evidence and testimony that had just befallen him. "Listen, you guys are great!" he told them. "I guess you all know that Billy was found right here, under the dock, on Tuesday morning, right?"

The group acknowledged that they were aware of the incident, then the man with the guitar case commented, "Yeah, but I couldn't figure out how that could have happened, seein' as we saw Billy load his gear in his boat and head out. Something's pretty fucked up about that!"

Carl took that as an opportunity to invite them into his investigation, and after answering a few of their questions, he had them tripping over each other to give him their names and contact information.

"What was that all about?" Barb had been waiting for him at the top of the stairs that bridge the lower dock, where the charter boats tie up. It gave her a full, unobstructed view of the Turtle Cannery and the dinghy dock. Baby was sitting next to her, patiently waiting for him to rejoin them.

"They were here when Billy headed back to his boat on Monday night. He was apparently fine! He had his dog with him and his guitar. Now, I've got to find out why he ended up back here, under the dock, dead."

She tightened her grip around his goliath arm and leaned her head against his shoulder as they began to walk toward Schooner's, then mumbled, "You'll figure it out! You always do!"

The *Western Union* had just backed into her slip after their sunset excursion and was offloading the evening's cargo of tourists onto the dock area adjacent to the old icehouse building, now repurposed as a dining area for Schooner's Wharf Bar and Grill. Carl and his two girls pushed their way through the crowd and emerged on the final approach to the waterfront entrance. Coreen, the owner of the landmark bar, was standing at the entrance, as she does on special occasions, greeting guests and fraternizing with close friends.

"Hey Barb!" Reen threw her arms around her and hugged tightly, then held both her hands in hers as they shared their greetings. Carl and Baby pushed through the doorway and into the crowd of people that had come to celebrate the life of one of the island's favorite musicians. Carl spotted Tripp and Meg at a table just off to the left of the stage, and motioned to Barb where he was going to be. She was locked in conversation with Coreen and nodded, then waved him off with her hand.

He had almost reached the table when someone grabbed his arm. "Hey, bud!" Carl recognized the voice immediately.

"Oh, hey Paul! Haven't seen you since last year's Wrecker's Cup Race. How's everything?"

"Well," Paul began, "We've been doing a little traveling this year. Went up to the Upper Peninsula on Lake Superior, then over to Red Rocks for Jimmy's *I Don't Know* tour. How's Barb?"

"She's great!" he said. "You'll probably see her in a few minutes! She's over talking to Reen by the door." Then he asked, "Are you gonna be playing tonight?"

Well, I'm supposed to do a number or two later on, after Devin and the boys do some of Billy's numbers. I've been working on two that I've never performed before. You've probably heard *My Remedy*."

"Oh yeah! Beautiful piece! Nice choice!" Carl said.

"The other one's *I'm Goin Fishin'*. Either one would be fine with me."

Paul's wife interrupted him, and the two friends bid their goodbyes, then Carl and Baby continued toward their waiting seats. As he slid back into his chair, his eye caught a couple in the back corner, waving for his attention. Mallory Stockton and her husband Gene were sitting with Billy's wolf-dog, Flow, at the table in the corner where Billy had always kept her when he was on stage. Carl smiled and returned a wave, then seated himself next to Tripp.

"Paul Cotton!" Tripp was grinning ear to ear. "How did you two get to be so buddy-buddy?"

After Carl placed an order for a Bahama Mama for Barb, a Michelob Ultra for him, and one shrimp and oyster platter, he leaned back in his chair and explained, "I raced against him for four years straight with Billy. The first year, we lost to him in the *Psyched Out*! He took third and we took fourth!

We started using Billy's boat and won the next three races. He got second place last year! Good guy! Good captain, too!"

Tripp held a brochure in his hand for Carl to see and said, "Paul's on the program tonight, right after George Victory!"

"Let me see that," Carl said, as he took the brochure and began looking it over. On the first page was a picture of Billy standing on the aft deck of his boat, The *Ghilley Dhu*, waving. Below the picture of Billy were the dates of his life span. (October 12, 1955 – July 26, 2011) Then the following:

A Tribute to a Troubadour

Thursday, July 28, 2011

7 pm to sunrise

Join us at Schooner's Wharf Bar and Grill for a celebration of the life of Captain William Blain Chapman III, USN Retired. AKA, Three I'd BILLY

Carl opened the flyer and continued looking over the program details:

With sorrowful heart and mournful soul, we will be gathering together to lift up the memory of our dear brother, Bill Chapman. For the past decade, he has been a major contributor to Schooner's Wharf's musical platform. Bill has performed with all of your favorite Key West musical groups and has regularly been booked as a solo artist, performing his original works here at Schooner's Wharf. Thank you for joining us for:

A Tribute to Three I'd Billy

A philanthropist,

a sailor,

a mentor,

crusader,

a pilot,

defender,

a heart so tender,

a giver unmatched,

regrettably snatched,

from loved ones who knew,

this renaissance of a man,

gone in peace, oh one of a kind,

entombed in us all,

Your love we recall,

Happily haunted,
as we grow to be old,
in hope that we find,
those songs that remind,
always our troubadour of truth.
Poem by Dedra Zannatelli (July 27, 2011)
Schooner's Wharf Waitress 12 years

Carl looked up from the brochure as Devin, Marty, and one of the busboys set a stool, a small folding table, and a microphone on the right side of the stage. Next, Devin stood in front of the stage and directed the busboy to adjust one of the stage lights to illuminate the stool. When Devin and Marty were satisfied, Devin signaled the bartender to turn down the lights and the music.

Dedra began her walk from the bar. Slowly! Very slowly! One slow step at a time. The music faded to silence, and within seconds, everyone became quiet. It was unnervingly solemn as Dedra crossed the sand-laden patio. Across her left arm, a carefully draped blue towel! Held in her outstretched hand was an Arnold Palmer, light ice, unsweetened tea, with an unwrapped paper straw. She had been presenting him with that same drink and that same towel for ten years. Tonight, with all the pageantry due a legend, she would make her delivery, in tribute to how much good he had brought to the island, and had given to the people who call it their home. She set his drink on the little table and draped his towel over the back of the stool, then began to cry. She dropped to her knees and bellowed in grief. Marty and one of the other waitresses scurried to her side in support. They were immediately overcome and swallowed into her anguish. One by one, waitresses, musicians, busing staff, and bartenders, long-time customers and even some of the kitchen help were making their way to the swarm that kept building and spreading.

Devin stepped to the microphone on the other side of the stage and grabbed his guitar, then directed Tommy Too Low to join him and plug in his bass. Tommy was suffering from an inguinal hernia, but pushed through the pain. The two of them began to play one of Billy's most popular songs, *My Remedy*. Devin was playing the intro when George Victory stepped onto the stage and carefully removed the microphone from its clip, then began to sing the song in his beautiful, low Trinidadian voice.

"When my soul has left this earth, for what it's worth, I believe." George stretched his arm across Devin's shoulders and held the microphone for them both to sing,

"That in the hearts of the ones I loved, forever held in memory!"

Devin and Tommy stopped playing their instruments, and the entire throng began to sing along.

"I climbed mountains, sailed these seas, painted sunsets, from all of these..."

Coreen signaled to Warren, the bartender, to cut the lights completely off, and Schooner's Wharf Bar became lit by the fire of love for their departed troubadour.

When the song was over, George stepped to the middle of the stage and told this story. "When I was a likkle boy, me granny lived on de side of a hill dat look out to de sey. She haddda papaya fruity tree behind she house and de great big breadfruit tree in she side yard. She hadad nah mangos at all eh! We was livin way down de hill and there were plenty nice mangos in Mr. Filburn's yard na, and I used to steal de mangos and carry dem up the hill to give to me granny. I think Mr. Filburn knew, yuh know, it was me dat was stealing him fruity, but he must have known, too, I was sharing dem with me granny and never one time did him spoke wit me bout it. Me granny give to im all the breadfruit he want." He turned his face to the sky and placed his hand over his heart, then finished his story. "She say it aint tha climb dat goin' make yuh weak, it's de life yuh livin' an' de peoples yuh meet." He turned toward the audience and added, "When I was a sad likkle boy, or scarredie of somtin, this song she would sing ta me. It's called, *All Meh Pickney Face De Sea*". The only lights in the club were the candles on the tables, the tiki torches that lit the sides of the stage, and one spotlight, directed at Billy's stool. It was the perfect ambiance for a Trinidadian tune. George began to sing in his deeply resonant voice,

"All my children, face the sea, and learn a lesson, taught to me,

Alone and weary, you may be, but trust unto the journey,

Follow always to the light, through the sand, in dark of night,

The moon she smile to lead you right, the ocean holds no worry.

Steady go, me boy, oh me boy,

Steady go, be on tha sea,

Steady go, me boy, oh me boy.

Beyond the moon is free!

Wise and welcome be tha boy who tarries not in sorrow,

Sad and happy both agree, can greet him on the morrow.

Tide will rise and fall again, to free him from his trouble,

Take a breath and blow again, then climb inside the bubble.

Steady go, me boy, oh me boy,

Steady go, till tide she turn.

Steady go, me boy, oh me boy.

Steady go, from life we learn.

Steady go, forever!"

When he finished singing the song, he turned to the audience and bowed his head, "Peace ta all yuh nice peopl!" Then he turned to the lone chair and prayed on behalf of his departed friend, "Me Broser Me Friend, may yuh Love never end, as we go to our way, leave us Love all da day!

Cheers and jubilation rang through the air as he stepped off of the stage. One might have thought the Green Bay Packers had just won another National Championship, but, no, it was just a Key West Caribbean celebration of a good man's life, well lived.

Tripp leaned over to Carl and asked, "You still think you're gonna be able to ask Devin any questions tonight?" They sat back in their chairs and each grabbed a shrimp from the platter that had finally been delivered, then Carl answered, "Not a chance! Besides, the questions have already been answered!" Tripp was still chewing as Carl picked up an oyster shell and held it an inch from his lips, then added, "We are now, 100% in tha who done it mode!"

Tripp choked on his shrimp! Meg patted, hard, on his back while he choked and coughed himself back into reasonable communicability. "What?" His voice was strained from the torture the shrimp had enacted upon him. "He was murdered, wasn't he?"

Carl turned to check on Barb, but she was nowhere in sight! "Don't eat all the oysters!" he commanded as he stood to his feet. Baby was, attentively, at his side as he navigated through the crowd, searching for his beautiful blonde wife. He made his way over to the bar and called out to Warren, who was busy pouring a set-up of beer, "You seen my wife?"

Warren had only one hand free at that moment and pointed to the stairway that leads to Creen's office. Carl thanked him and proceeded toward the stairs. Baby stopped as they passed by the ice machine and looked hopefully up at Carl. "Ok, girl!" He told her! She immediately buried her face into the ice-cold bucket of water that the staff always kept ready to quench. When she had satisfied her thirst, Carl pointed toward the stairs and commanded her, "Up!" She bounded up the stairs with him close behind, then sat on the landing, waiting for him to knock.

"Come on in!" Coreen called out. Carl and Baby entered to find his wife Barb, Coreen and three other ladies, apparently enjoying a "GIRLS ONLY" party.

"OOOH! Look at this bodacious specimen of a caveman!" Reen stepped boldly toward him and slipped her arm around his waist, as his wife laughed and remarked, "Let me warn you, sister, he's more trouble than he's worth! Trust me!"

Carl grinned, embarrassingly, turned back toward the still open door, looked down at Baby, and said, "Stay if you want, but don't blame me if they boil you alive and eat ya! They look pretty hungry ta me!" He slipped out the door by the skin of his teeth, and left the dog to fend for herself.

Once he had returned to the table, Tripp asked, "New developments?"

"I'll brief you first thing tomorrow, but, yeah, new developments and a lot more questions yet to answer." He dripped some red sauce onto another oyster and sucked it into his mouth. After a generous flush from his bottle of beer, he added, "Somethin' ain't right!"

Devin and his band *Slack Tide* entertained the crowd with three of Billy's songs. Tray did his best to stay true to the lead work that had previously been performed by Billy, but his chops fell noticeably short in style and lacked Billy's finesse. When they finished the song, *Livin' in Paradise,* Devin introduced the next performer. "Let's put our hands together for the legendary Paul Cotton." Then he and his bandmates cleared the stage.

Paul stepped to the microphone and, as he adjusted his guitar strap, spoke to the audience, "Thank you, Devin! I feel so very honored to have been invited to join in this tribute for Billy, tonight. He meant so very much to us all. If, by chance, you knew Three I'd Billy, you would have known that you had been honored! I would describe our first meeting as amazingly serendipitous, and if not for a missed flight at the Norfolk International Airport in 1992, I might never have enjoyed the past eighteen years of inspiration and friendship he shared with me. I am humbled and grateful and forever indebted to the man we all came to love, respect, admire, and will now, forever, miss," he choked on his words and pulled away from the microphone. Turning to face the empty stool on the side of the stage, he pressed his tightened fist against his mouth and gathered composure. When he returned to the microphone, he whispered the words, "See you on the beach." Then he lifted his hand to the neck of his signature Gretsch White Falcon guitar and began to play for Three I'd Billy.

"I am an old woman, sittin' on my front porch swing,

ain't thinkin' bout nothin', not a gal-darn thing,

everybody that I ever knew, dun up and passed away,

every flower that I ever grew, laid 'em up on somebody's grave,

So I cried me an ocean, and I sailed me away.

I saw me a river, one night in a dream,

my life was slippin' away, torn apart at the seam,

no sign of an angel, no voice from above,

no bright light shinin' down ta carry me away in love,

So I cried me an ocean, and I sailed me away.

Don't get tha wrong idea, I ain't checkin' out of here,

I got a long, long way left to go!

I've got two books to write, before I lose my site

and another row left to hoe,

Then I'll cry me an ocean, and I'll sail me away!

I had me a lover, and we lived a life of strife!

Caught his leg in a hard-rock plow, and it cost 'em his life.

Left me three mouths to feed, they grew up like weeds,

left home and then they never came back,

So I cried me an ocean, and I sailed me away!

I am an old woman, sittin' on my front porch swing!

When he finished the song, everyone stood to their feet, and the place erupted into applause. It echoed across the bay and as far out, into the Gulf of Mexico, as any ears could hear. Raven Cooper played *Billy Be Gone* and *The App Song*. Jeff Clark played a spectacular rendition of Billy's song, *I'm*

Goin' Fishin', then closed the evening with *Jaws of Life.* The next day, the residents of the mooring field were all talking about how they enjoyed sitting on their boats and listening to Billy's songs under the moonlit sky. The celebration lasted into the early morning hours, and breakfast was provided, on the house, for anyone who wanted. It was a wondrously soulful celebration. A tribute to a troubadour!

20. SOUTHBOUND to MIAMI

She's a relentless and vindictive torturess! She burrows under your skin then gorges on you from the inside out. She eats away the fiber of who you are, then turns to feast on who you think you are. She's a parasite on your soul! She's a shipworm, ravenously devouring your rudder, leaving you haplessly adrift. She celebrates in your feckless efforts to thwart her intentions, and she will swallow you gone! She is your maniacal mistress! You have christened her with the name, Depression!

It was merely fourteen hours earlier that Cairo had stopped paddling his half-deflated little boat and surrendered to the currents that fought against his every stroke. He wasn't a strong boy! Not physically, and not psychologically. He had exhausted his last resource and now, he sat precariously in the place where destiny tempts fate.

His tortured childhood was laddered with abuse, abandonment, loneliness, fear and insecurity. He had barely made it to the twenty-second rung of his life, and now, he was sitting in a sinking dinghy, one long mile from Paradise and grasping for a dream that might save him. Behind him was a sailboat filled with the memories of solitude and despair, before him lay one last thread of hope. He yielded his will to the flow of the tide and tossed his ring in the air, hoping to find a ready hook.

Cai took his wallet from his wet, baggy pants pocket and pulled on the raggedy business card that had been given to him, one night by a drunken tourist. Like a fair weather wind captured by a slack sail, he heard the snap, then the thrust of hope, billowing into his life. With a fresh burst of enthusiasm, he stood to his feet and began to steer the derelict little dinghy toward the dock behind the turtle museum.

"Hey Cai, you got anything ta smoke?" A couple of rainbow kids were sitting in the shade behind the turtle cannery. Cai offered no acknowledgement to their inquiry and pressed passed them like a man on a mission. Once he reached the bike rack by the entrance to the *Half Shell Raw Bar*, he pulled the envelope that Dr. Colburn had given to him out of his pocket and counted the money. Ten, twenty-dollar bills! He punched in the combination, then dragged his bike from the crowded rack and pointed it toward the street. He soon realized that both tires were completely flat and shoved it into the bushes, then cussed his way across Margaret Street and over to Harpoon Harry's. Cai was not known, typically, to patronize the quirky little place on the corner! He projected an image more of a street kid, panhandler, dumpster diving kind of persona. He didn't bathe regularly, didn't make any attempt to brush his hair or his teeth, his blue jeans were always grubby, raggedy and hanging down to his crotch. His tennis shoes were begging to be mercifully thrown away! It was a huge surprise to Kelsey when she saw him slide back a chair and sit down at one of the little tables outside on the sidewalk.

She headed out the door, fully expecting to remind him that the tables were there for paying customers only. Imagine her surprise when he looked up at her with a big smile and asked, "Is it too early for me to order some meatloaf?"

She shook her head in total surprise, then answered, "We don't start serving lunch till eleven, but I can fix you anything you want off of the breakfast menu."

Cai asked, "What about pancakes and maybe some fruit?"

Kelsey was astounded when he pulled the envelope from his pocket and set it on the table, and suggested, "How about a stack of blueberry pancakes with blueberry syrup?"

Cai felt like he'd hit the jackpot at Vegas!

"Oh, yeah! What about bacon? Can I get some bacon?"

"You betcha!" She said. "Anything to drink?"

He was like a six-year-old kid, celebrating his birthday. "What about a glass of orange juice?"

She didn't have the heart to warn him about the potential stomach ache he might be facing on the other side of the mountain of sugar he was about to climb. "Sure!" She answered. "Anything else?"

He couldn't resist, and asked, "Can I get some strawberry ice cream to put on top of my pancakes?"

My God, she thought to herself! This guy's over the top! "You bet!" She decided to be the adult in the room, and cut him off with, "I'll go get it started, right now!" She turned and reentered the restaurant through the open front door.

Conrad, the owner, was loading a roll of printer paper into the cash register when Kelsey stepped around the counter heading toward the kitchen and asked, "Hey, Kelsey. Isn't that guy one of Billy's projects?"

She hooked the order on the wire at the kitchen window and answered, "Yeah! They call him Cairo!" She moved to Conrad's side and began wrapping silverware in napkins. "I've never known him to have any money," She added, "but today, he's got a stack of twenties!"

Conrad closed the lid on the paper feed and commented, "Huh! Kinda makes you wonder where he might have gotten it."

"Yeah!" She said. "I'd assume Billy's boat's been locked up since Tuesday. I hope he didn't break in and steal it!"

Conrad turned and leaned against the counter and looked directly into her eyes, then suggested, "When you go back out, see if you can't get him to open up to you. I've got a hunch he might be looking for someone to talk to. Maybe he'll spill some beans."

"You bet, boss!" She said, then proceeded to take Cairo his glass of orange juice. "Now," She said as she set the glass on his table, "I'm testing my memory, it's Cairo, right?"

He had finished half the glass of juice, before she finished. After wiping his lips on the back of his hand, he answered, "Yeah, or Cai! Most times it's just Cai!"

"I think I remember that you and Billy were close friends. I'm really sorry we lost him. He was one of our favorite regulars, ya know." She truly did feel sorry that Billy would never walk through her door again. Everyone at Harpoon Harry's would miss seeing him! Sitting in the corner booth, reading his paper, talking with staff and other locals as he waited on his breakfast to be served, his more than generous tipping, standing with Conrad at the front door talking about the issues in the day's news that they shared concerns over, and his fabulous contributions at their Friday night open mic jams, yes, everyone would miss Billy! "I'll go check on your cakes! They should be up by now!"

She left Cai to ponder over his future without Billy's generosity to rely on. She hoped that if he had stolen the money from Billy's boat, maybe something she had said would reach into his conscience and he'd come clean. She did not know just how wrong she was.

"Here you go!" She announced as she set his feast on the table. "I put your ice cream in a bowl so it wouldn't make your pancakes mushy, OK?"

He was ravenously engaged with dowsing the stack of cakes in syrup and far too lost in fantasy to hear her question. He plunged his overloaded fork into his gaping mouth and began to chew. She watched in amazement! He dug his spoon into the bowl of rapidly melting ice cream and drove it into his mouth.

Kelsey was aghast at his hideous display of poor etiquette, but found the strength to choke out, "Gee Cai, you have got the most beautiful teeth I think I've ever seen!"

Cai was in the midst of flushing down a mouthful of pancakes with orange juice, but pushed his eye balls hard left in their sockets, in confused surprise. Could she be flirting with me? He thought! His imagination was always ready to overrespond to even the least of attention aimed his way. "There not real!" He said as he closed them together, turned his head toward her, and opened his lips as far as humanly possible, then continued, "Billy took me up to the dental school in Bradenton and had them fix me up. We stayed two nights in a Holiday Inn Express and on the way back, he drove through the Everglades on the Tamiami Trail and I saw a huge alligator that got hit, on the side of the road." He returned to his feasting as if he had said it to a seagull. He had no expectation that a full-blown conversation with another human being had begun.

Kelsey stood, silently, by the table, watching him eat and looking for her next opportunity to coax him toward more disclosures. "Aren't the pancakes great here?" He didn't respond. "Any idea what they'll do with Billy's boat?" Again, he wasn't connecting!

He shoveled the last of the ice cream into his mouth, then leaned back in the chair and asked, "You know where I can catch a bus to the mainland?"

"The Greyhound station is right beside the Key West airport!" She answered. "You can buy a ticket there and catch the bus right out front!"

Cai reached into the envelope and pulled out a twenty-dollar bill and asked, "How much for the food?"

Kelsey grabbed his bill from her apron and set it on the table in front of him. He slapped the twenty on top of the bill and said, "Covered!" Then stood up and awkwardly pushed past her and into the building through the front door.

Conrad looked up from his paperwork and watched the gaunt and lanky young derelict of a man walk through the dining room and down the hall to the men's room.

Kelsey stepped to the register and recorded the sale. Upon closing the drawer, she put her hands on her hips and reported her discoveries. "I don't know where he got the money, but I did find out, he's leaving town!"

She and Conrad were both concerned that if Cai had stolen the money and was about to leave the island, someone might need to alert the police. As they were contemplating the ramifications, Cai exited the bathroom and approached the counter. He took a toothpick from the little brass dispenser and asked, "You know how I can get a ride to the airport?"

Conrad offered, "You could take an Uber!"

Cai asked, "What's that?"

Kelsey answered, "It's like a taxi cab, but it's really just a private driver in their own car. You pay 'em to take you wherever you want to go. I use 'em all the time."

Cai asked, "Does it cost much?"

"No!" Kelsey said. "It's only about twelve dollars to get to the airport!" Then she suggested, "I can call one for you and he'll pick you up out front!"

"Yeah!" Cai replied. "That'll be great! Thanks!" Then he walked back out front and sat down in the chair to wait. Conrad picked up his phone and as it was ringing, he walked to the back of the dinning room where Cai would not overhear him on the phone.

"This is Carl." The voice answered.

"Carl, it's Conrad, over at Harpoon Harry's!"

"Hey Bud!" Carl knew him well! They had been friends since Conrad first purchased the building and opened for business.

"What's up?" Carl asked.

Conrad began, "Well, I might be way out of line here, but are your people still involved in what happened to Billy on Tuesday over on the dinghy dock?"

"Oh yeah!" Carl answered. "We're taking a look at everything we can find. Why? You have something you can tell us?"

"Maybe, or maybe not!" Conrad explained. "There's this kid that Billy had been working with for the last couple of years. You know, one of his projects. Well, this morning, this kid was in for breakfast and had a wad of money. His name is Cairo! After he ate, he said he was headed over to the Greyhound station to catch a bus. We were thinking that he seemed pretty suspicious and I just thought I'd let you know he was leaving town." Carl listened intently and asked, "How long ago was this?"

The Uber car had just pulled away from the restaurant and turned onto Margaret Street! Conrad watched it pass by and conveyed what he saw as it happened. "There it goes now!"

Carl had just left his office and was headed toward Key West. The timing was perfect for an intercept at the airport. "Thanks!" He exclaimed. "I'll let you know what I find out!" He turned at the light and drove to the entrance of the airport complex, and backed into a parking place in front of the Fed Ex building, where he could watch for the Uber to arrive.

Minutes later, he watched as Cairo climbed out of the car and sauntered into the Greyhound office. The young man took no notice of the monstrous figure, with the gun on his belt, that had entered behind him. He stood at the counter and fumbled through his droopy pants pockets till his lanky fingers connected with the business card and pulled it out. "How much is a ticket to," he read the name of the town off the card, "Fort Pierce?" He asked the lady behind the counter.

She entered the data for his inquiry and reported her findings, "That price is eighty-nine dollars and fifty-seven cents."

While he struggled to pull the envelope of money out of his pocket, she suggested, "If you're wanting to go today, we have a ten o'clock departure pulling out in about fifteen minutes." She looked up into the detective's face and he winked his eye, affirming his approval. Cairo unfolded five of his twenties and paid the fare, then took his ticket and change. As he turned, he found himself blocked by the detective and stepped to the side, then started toward the row of chairs against the wall.

Carl waited till Cai was seated, then turned and walked across the room and stood with his huge arms folded across his roadblock of a chest, then asked, "Cairo, isn't it?"

The young man was indignant as he looked up and defiantly answered, "Yeah!" Followed by, "I didn't do anything!" Carl felt sure he could persuade the boy to cooperate. His next question would be the breaker. "That money you just paid for that ticket with, where'd you get it?"

Cai was confused but knew he could justify his stash and held the envelope up for the detective to inspect. *THE ONE FAMILY FOUNDATION*, Carl read. It was a name he was intimately familiar with. "Stay right here!" he commanded the raggedy young man, then stepped over to the glass doors to place a call. "Markus," He called out, "Easy question!"

Markus answered, "Come on, what's up?"

The detective leaned against the panic bar and stared out at the parking lot as he asked, "Is there any reason that a young man named Cairo would be walking around town with a bunch of twenty-dollar bills in one of the foundation's envelopes today?"

It was an easy answer for Dr. Grant. "Yeah!" He said. "Cairo was probably out on the *Psyched Out* earlier this morning. I can call Walt for verification, or, just ask Cai! He won't lie about it. Walter gives out those envelopes if he thinks the client needs some money. I'm sure that's what this is. Just ask him!"

"OK, no problem! I think I've got the answers I need." Carl completed the call and thanked his friend, then returned to Cai as the bus began to load. "Alright Mr. Cairo, I cleared it up with Dr. Grant. Now tell me why are you catching a bus to Fort Pierce?"

The boy was anxious to get on the bus and handed the business card with the hand written address on the back, and explained. "I've got a friend up there. He's got a place fixed up in his garage for me to live in, and I'm gonna help him with some carpentry work."

Carl inspected the card and determined there was no reason to detain the boy any longer. He handed back the card and said, "Have a nice trip!" then pushed through the heavy, glass double doors and climbed back in his cruiser. He called into his phone, "Siri, call Conrad... "Hey Conrad, I just wanted to give you an update on that kid, Cairo. It's all good! That money came from Dr. Grant's client services fund. They use it to help some of the indigents with food and clothes and stuff. Thanks for the heads up!" There was no further reason for the detective to waste another thought on Cairo. He would be off of the island in another ten minutes and as far as Carl was concerned, a million times better off than if he stayed.

Cai casually waddled down the aisle, surveying the vacant seating options as he made his way toward the back of the bus. There were only eight other passengers on board when the swish of the brake release signaled his journey had begun. He fell into the last seat on the right side, directly in front of the bathroom. Only someone with Cairo's lacking refinement would select a seat so close to the privy on a Greyhound bus. He pushed his greasy nose against the window and watched the jet skis racing across the Atlantic waters, one behind the next, behind the next, behind the next. "It couldn't be much fun being forced to follow each other, like school children on a fire drill. But that's how they get rich. Take em on a fast ride around the island and pick tha hundred-dollar bill out of their pocket. Shit," he thought. "I could a been one of those guys. Billy would have helped me set it up, too! I'd bet just ten thousand, could a got me in big money! God damn it!" The more he fantasized, the deeper he drifted away from reality. There was nothing tethered to the other end of his rope. He drifted from one unachievable dream to another, like a lost dinghy with no anchor, dragging its rope across the shallows, leaving nothing but a soon-to-fade-away impression in the silt and sand. What hope could there be for a soul like him?

Before the bus had crossed the bridge to Sugarloaf Key, Cairo had fallen over the edge. He was so deep in sleep that nothing could bring him back to the surface. Probably, the roar of the diesel engine, the spin of the huge double wheels, the pleasantry of the sixty-nine degree filtered air and the load in his belly could all share in the causation of his depth of slumber.

"Hey, fella!" The driver stood over him, pushing on his bent knee, trying to roust him out of his sleep. "Hey, come on, yer holdin up tha bus!"

Cairo stretched his arms and reached to pull himself up from his cramped and contorted burrow, then followed the driver to the front of the bus. As the huge man slipped into the seat he pointed through the open door and said, "That address on your card is three blocks that way. You turn left when you get to the water."

Cairo slung himself off of the bus and stood in the gravel staring down the road like a lost and bewildered refugee taking his first look at the promised land. The door closed and the Greyhound pulled back onto U.S. One, blowing a gust of exhaust on him as if to say, "good riddance!" He stood with his feet soaked in hope, and his belly full of blueberry pancakes marinated in orange juice. Within seconds, he realized he had a third-degree fire in his belly and in desperate need of a place to put it out before it took control of his future. On the far side of the four-lane highway, there was a building with the word REACH THRIFT boldly painted above the door. Cai pulled his droopy pants up and climbed the sandy embankment, then waited for the last car to pass and began dragging himself across the road.

"Can I help you?" There was a man sitting on a stool behind the counter, and a woman was leaning against a display case. Cairo was precariously close to detonation and, through his gritted teeth, said, "Men's room?" The man pointed to the back wall, and Cai shuffled quickly toward his fate. The man turned to the woman and made a face as he pinched his nose. She walked out the door and stood in the breeze. Seconds later, the man joined her on the sidewalk.

"This guy looks like he needs help!" The man remarked.

Several minutes later, Cai exited the building and stood looking across the road. He pointed toward the next right turn and asked, "Is that where I turn to get to Indian River Drive?"

The woman answered, "That's right! It's at the very end of Chamberlin Blvd. It runs parallel to the river. You can't miss it."

Cai was already on his way before she had finished talking. She called out to him, "We'll be having fellowship out back at seven o'clock. You can come if you like."

"Something ain't right with that kid!" The man commented.

The woman began to pray, "Jesus, we ask that your holy spirit go with this young lost soul and protect him and guide him with your holy spirit! Amen"

The man lifted his head and watched Cai as he crossed into the median strip, then waited for the next break in traffic and added, "Amen!"

It was about one mile from the thrift shop to the big yellow house on the hill that overlooks the Indian River. It was a masterpiece of waterfront architecture, with a sweeping veranda and X-crossed railing along the porch, a long driveway breaking into a circle at the approach, and a wide extension that leads to a two-car garage with an apartment on the second story. The main structure was a two-story Coastal Style design with wide panoramic windows flanking a magnificent etched glass double-doorway. Directly across the road was a grassy null, then a stone seawall to hold the river at bay. A long wooden dock led to a covered pavilion with an electric boat lift. It could have been a contender for house of the year in any architectural magazine.

Kenneth Sr. and his wife of twenty-nine years, Valerie, were halfway through their evening meal when their two German Shepards, Diablo and Puma, jumped to their feet and ran to the front window, barking excitedly. Kenneth finished chewing his last bite of crab and tossed his napkin on his plate, then slid his chair back and asked, "Best bet, Amazon or UPS?" Val was still enjoying her meal and quipped, "I didn't order anything!"

As he approached the front door he called to the dogs and pointed his finger toward the floor, "Uma, ruhig, platz!" Then to Diablo, "Ablo, ruhig, platz!"

The two dogs immediately stopped their barking and dropped to the floor. Kenneth had his hand on the doorknob and squinted at the figure standing in his driveway. He turned the knob and stepped into the half-opened door. "May I help you?" He called to the stranger.

The young man called back, "It's me, Cai!" Then took a step forward.

The dogs were on alert, and Puma began to growl. "Don't come any closer!" Kenneth ordered to the boy. "My dogs will eat you!"

Cai stepped back to the spot where he had first stood and waited.

"Am I supposed to know you?" The man called out.

Cai stood with his long lanky arms hanging down at his sides and flipped his right hand awkwardly as he talked, "I'm Cairo! You said you needed me to help you fix your garage up so I could live here and we could fish, and watch the rockets and stuff."

Val had joined her husband at the front door and asked, "What's going on? Who is it?"

He leaned his head toward her and said, "It's that homeless kid we met on the dock in Key West. Remember? We had dinner at Turtle Kraals and headed to Schooners when he stopped us. He was trying to hit us up for a handout. You remember!"

She did remember. "Oh yeah! What's he doing here?" Ken nudged her back inside and said, "I'll get rid of him," then closed the door behind him.

Both dogs jumped to their feet and watched intently as their owner gave the boy an ultimatum, "Listen up, I want you to turn around and get off my property, now! If I ever see you here again, I will use your bones as crab bait! Am I making myself clear?"

Cai stood looking at the man with his mouth wide open. "But you said we were friends!" The man opened the door and called to his dogs, "Uma, Ablo, komm!" The two dogs snapped to his side. "Zet-zen, Uma, Ablo!" They sat in obedience to his command.

"Now," he said firmly, "Get off my property and never come anywhere near my family again, you got that?"

Cai hung his head and walked over to the river, a shattered man. His last hope had turned out to be a bust! He stood at the seawall and gazed into the water.

"I said, get the fuck out of here, you little bastard! Go on! NOW!" The man could not have known how deeply he had crushed the poor kid. Maybe he wouldn't have cared if he had known. Some people are more afraid of what they could lose than what they could gain from allowing empathy into their life. All you can do at a time like that is walk away! That's what poor Cairo did on that Thursday evening. He turned and walked away.

He walked back through the neighborhood and came to the railroad tracks that he had crossed earlier. He stopped between the rails and looked South, then turned and looked North. Perhaps he was waiting for a new dream to land on his shoulder and direct him one way or the other. Alas, no dream appeared! No voice from an angel! No bright light shining down to guide him toward his next fantasy. He finally turned back toward the highway and started to walk.

"Hey, look who's back!" They were rolling the sales bins into the building when the pastor of The REACH THRIFT STORE ministry noticed their motley visitor making his way across the highway. His helper turned just in time to see a brodozer pickup truck swerve toward him, then blow their dual-tone train horn to scare him.

"Looks like your prayer got heard!" The pastor shoved the last bin through the door, then turned to greet Cai as he stepped onto the ramp that would lead him up to the front door. "Well, friend, did you find what you were looking for on Indian River Drive?"

Cai stopped at the entrance and looked into the store, then turned to the man and asked, "Do you have a table and two chairs? Something light that I can carry?"

The pastor thought for a second, then remembered that there was a picnic set in the children's area and offered, "I've got a bamboo table with two chairs, but they're kind of small. I think they're designed for kids. Let's go see if they'll do what you need." He led the way through to the back corner of the shop and cleared some games off the set. "There! Is that what you're looking for?

Cai picked up the first chair and studied it carefully. He set it up in the aisle, then sat down.

"Yeah! This is good!" They folded the items and carried them to the front of the store. As they passed a rack of glassware, Cai saw a pair of wine glasses with little pink flamingos painted on them and stopped to take a closer look. "Are these plastic?" He asked.

The Pastor set the table on the counter and walked to the shelf that held the goblets. "They're glass!" He answered. "You need some glasses to go with your picnic table?"

Cai did not respond. He grabbed them from the shelf and placed them next to the little table. "Can I buy some wine here?"

The pastor was becoming concerned for the young man's mental health and asked, "Do you have a problem that you think wine can solve?"

Cai had no idea what the man was talking about. He had a plan, not a problem! "No, I'm going to be meeting with my friend, and he likes to have a glass of wine sometimes."

"Oh!" the pastor exclaimed. "We don't carry any, but there's Guy's Meats on the other side of U.S. 1, and they sell wine. You can buy any kind you want over there."

Cai pulled the envelope from his pocket and paid for the items. The pastor wrapped the glasses and tied a cord around his new picnic set, then suggested, "Ya know, if you want to, we'll be starting our evening fellowship in just a few minutes. You might enjoy hanging around and meeting some of the brothers and sisters that live in the area."

Cai was already out the door and on his way to Guy's.

Fifteen minutes later, he was walking along the side of the highway with a bamboo table, two chairs, two flamingo goblets, a bottle of Beringer Chardonnay, and a plan. Not necessarily a good plan, but it was his! The road sign lit by a street light said Chamberlin Boulevard. He took a right and started walking into the darkness of the next block. Ten minutes later, he was back at the railroad crossing.

The Old Dixie Highway is a two-way road that runs parallel to the immediate west side of the railway. From the tracks, you can see the Indian River at the end of Chamberlin. Only two houses are on the approach to the intersection, and they are set back from the road substantially. Cai stood below the streetlight and melted under the weight of the day's events. He had no will toward the conjuring of courage that might lend strength to his intent. He was no warrior! The only honor he could claim was from standing in the shadow of a hero named Billy Chapman. He was a sidekick, a happenstance, stumbling from unfortunate circumstance to untimely coincidence. He was a product of failure, and over his twenty-two years of breathing in and breathing out, there was nothing to point to that could substantiate his existence. He was a shattered young man.

He crossed Old Dixie Highway, then climbed the embankment and walked along the edge of the track, till he was out of the streetlight's illumination. He spread the legs of the little table and pushed the locking mechanism into place, then set it between the tracks on the southbound rail. One chair facing north for Billy, the other facing south. He reached for the two goblets and unwrapped them from the paper. Realizing he had failed to buy a cork screw, he leaned to his right and slapped the neck of the bottle on the iron rail, then poured the golden ale into the challises and listened through the silence of the evening for a southbound train.

21. AFTER MATH

"Hello!" She always tried to answer the phone on the first ring. She felt it was the best way for her to protect the doctor from being distracted or annoyed by calls that he didn't need to take. She was a master at screening, but this call didn't fit the usual profile of a nine-thirty pm caller. This one came in on their landline, and the ID came up as "St. Lucie County Sheriff's Office. "Yes, I'll put him on the line!" She called downstairs, "Markus, it's a detective in Fort Pierce. Pick up the phone."

She covered the mouthpiece with her hand and listened in as he answered, "This is Markus Grant. May I help you?"

The voice on the other end identified himself. "Dr. Grant, this is Detective Robin Aldridge with the St. Lucie Sheriff's office in Fort Pierce. Are you the Chief Executive Officer of a foundation known as *The One Family Foundation*?"

"I am the Executive Officer, yes. How can I help you, Detective?" The doctor asked.

"Sir, I'm sorry to be calling so late, but there's been an incident up here, and one of your foundation's envelopes was found at the scene. I was just hoping that you might be able to help us tie up a few loose ends."

"By all means! Please, ask anything you like." Markus offered.

"Well," the detective began, "The incident in question involved a young man approximately six feet tall with long curly brown hair. By chance, would anything about that be something you might be able to help us with?"

Markus had one person in mind! "Everything you're telling me connects with a call I received this morning from Detective Carl Dixon at the Monroe County Sheriff's office involving a young man that I've been working with for the past three years, here in Key West. I'm not sure if this is a valid name, but he goes by Cairo Katsaros. Did he have dark skin and green eyes?"

The detective was limited in how much he could share over the phone and said, "Well, sir, I'm not sure we'll be able to tell what color his eyes were till the coroner performs his inspection, but yes, his skin does appear to be dark. I wouldn't say he looked particularly black, though! Maybe Eastern European?"

"Yes!" The doctor confirmed. "That sounds like the boy I'm referring to, Cairo. He was born in Egypt. I would assume from your reference to a coroner's inspection that we're talking about a fatality?"

The detective's freedom to divulge such information could be considered discretionary, and he answered accordingly. "Yes, sir, that would be a correct assumption."

Dr. Grant suggested, "This young man, Cairo, was at the Key West bus station this morning and was stopped by Detective Carl Dixon on an issue of suspicion that he can discuss with you later. Would it be alright for me to pass your number to him in the morning and have him give you a call?"

The detective called out his contact info, and Janet broke into the call from the upstairs phone, "I'll take the info, Markus!"

When the call was over, Janet joined her husband downstairs, and he brought her up to speed with what he knew about Cairo.

"This is just horrible!" She began to unleash her thoughts on what she had heard. "How could anyone find themself so beaten down that they'd think the best way out of their pain was to die?" She sat down on the couch next to the doctor's recliner and reached to hold his hand. "I know this must be tearing you up inside!" She gently massaged his hand with her thumb as they sat together, grieving over the event. "I remember hearing you mention his name a few times over the past couple of years. Did you work closely with him?"

The old doctor leaned his head back and stared at the ceiling, then slowly lowered it and sighed deeply, in sorrow, then said, "Billy took particular interest in Cairo. He was trying to keep him from falling back into the pit he climbed out of. The poor kid had a horrific childhood and never seemed to have anyone in his life who could teach him how to positively cope with his problems. He was deeply attached to Billy. We talked about it many times.

Billy worried about what would happen if, for some reason or another, he wasn't able to continue being Cairo's only support. Tonight, just proves the validity of his worries." He climbed out of his recliner and bent over to give his wife a kiss on her forehead, then crossed the room to the sliding glass doors and pushed them open. He stepped outside and leaned against the balcony railing, and turned his face toward the starlit sky.

Janet followed, then, from behind, wrapped her arms around him, buried her chin in his shoulder, and said, "No one really ever knows how easily one loss can lead to another, do they?"

He responded, "They never do!" His thoughts fell immediately to the depth of love she had always held for him. Sixty-one glorious years with her in his life completely grounded him. She was his lightning rod, safely protecting him from his innate compulsion to hero his way into battles he couldn't hope to win. Some were his, most were not! She knew his history! She understood his drive, and she shared his compassion! She moved to his side, and he wrapped his arm around her waist and, together, they gazed into the expanse of the universe.

"It's an amazing thing, how the ripples of one's life affect the ripples of so many others!" She was a woman of great compassion. Her art was in the understanding of the deeper realities of human nature and was often on the lookout for new rabbit holes to explore. That was probably why, in her younger years, she had developed an interest in the study of genealogy. "I wonder if we could have understood this boy any better if we knew his family history?"

Markus always appreciated her points of view. She never stopped looking for creative perspectives that might broaden his life experience. "Why do I get the feeling you're referring to my Uncle Charles?"

Sargent Charles Grant was an expert swordsman and became a legend for his heroic efforts at the Battle of Waterloo in 1815. He had charged into battle on his steed and captured Napoleon's prized Golden Eagle staff and flag. With it held high overhead, he parleyed his way back to the coalition's commanding officers, and his bravery was rewarded with an advancement to Ensign.

"Well," She smiled, "If you watch for the ripples, sometimes, you can avoid the waves!"

She was right! From his knowledge of how deeply seated traits of behavior get translated from one generation to the next, he understood that the point she was making was absolutely applicable to Cairo's short life.

"Unfortunate as it is, any lesson we could learn from his history wouldn't help him now! He's been swallowed up by his own wave!"

She pulled him closer and added, "Yeah! Tidal wave!"

They moved back into the living room, and while Jan worked cleaning in the kitchen, Markus sat at the table with a pad of paper, making notes and formulating a plan for how to move through the aftermath of Cairo's death.

He picked up his phone. "Carl? It's Markus! Sorry to have to call you so late, but I thought you might want to know that kid, Cairo, that you called me about from the bus station this morning..."

Carl stopped him in mid-sentence, "I just saw it on the eleven o'clock news. I recognized the business card and the envelope the officer had in his hand."

The doctor asked, "Any chance we could meet for breakfast tomorrow?"

Carl recognized immediately how Markus might lend insight to his investigation and answered enthusiastically, "You bet! That's a great idea. I've got some things that you could probably shine some light on."

Markus explained, "I'm going to see if Walt and Captain Witt can join us. They need to be up to date on any new developments that might impact anyone who heard about Cairo's death. How's seven at Harry's sound?"

The detective had the answer ready, "See ya there!"

Markus put a check mark on his notepad next to the name Carl, then dialed Walt's number. After his field crew was on board with his idea, he began making notes of topics that he thought would need to be discussed at the breakfast meeting. Several concerns weighed upon his mind as he contemplated how he might best capitalize on the opportunity at hand. So many developments were calling for resolution. One seemed equally as important as the other. Cairo's unfortunate end, how Billy's death might have been a murder, but more pressing that all other concerns, how to help a broken little girl named Jeannie. -

22. RIDIN' WITH THA KING

"**H**ey! You can't park that way!"

"I'm sorry, who are you?" The fog was as thick as a Louisiana ascent when Markus hit the curb and bounced his little yellow Icon Botero halfway onto the sidewalk and started to climb out. He reached for his cane, then turned toward the open door of Harpoon Harry's. With cane in hand, he asked again, "Really, I'd like to know! Who are you?"

The frivolous old woman jerked on the leash that hung from her hand, then she and her little schnauzer ran for their lives.

Nancy was sitting on a stool at the front door of the restaurant, writing the day's specials on the chalkboard. She laughed like a kid on her visit to the monkey farm when the woman turned and ran.

"Jesus, Doc, I think you made her wet her panties!"

He dragged his left foot toward the door and grit his teeth to the pain, and said laughingly, "I think her kids must have gone back to New Jersey and forgot to take her with them."

"Apparently, she didn't know she was dealing with, tha KING!" Nancy quipped as she picked up another color of chalk and began rubbing it into the flowers she had outlined as embellishment for her blackboard "daily specials" masterpiece.

The old doctor stepped through the doorway and surveyed the morning crowd of patrons, some sitting at tables, others feasting at the long counter under the whirling ceiling fans that kept the fog from sauntering through the open doors. It was mystic and wildly surreal, like a scene in a Twilight Zone episode. He half expected to find Rod Serling standing at the counter with his signature cigarette wedged between his fingers, but expectations are often trumped by disappointment, especially when fantasy collides head-on with reality,

"Hey, Dr. Grants here!" Conrad's smile could clear the sky of clouds on a gloomy day, and all his local patrons loved him for it. "Good morning! Good morning! Good morning!" he announced as he grabbed a menu and freshly wrapped silverware from under the counter and rushed to greet his old friend. "Carl and Captain Witt are already at your table, and they told me that Dr. Colburn will be joining you, too, so I've got you set up at the big table in the back," he explained as he led the doctor toward his friends.

As Markus greeted Carl and Witt, Bethanny slid a fresh cup of coffee onto his placemat, then silently slipped out of his way as he took his seat.

"Well, gentlemen, it's been quite a week, I'd say!" His remark drew no argument from his audience.

"Yeah! What a week!" Witt offered his agreement. "One shoe dropped, then the other!"

Walter made his way through the dining room and joined the group. "My God," he started, "this fog is absolutely brutal!"

Carl set his menu on the table and said, "Well, the good thing is, this time of year it starts burning off as soon as the sun pops over the horizon."

Bethanny returned to the table and opened her order pad. "Are you gentlemen ready to order?" A few minutes later, she placed the ticket on the wire at the kitchen window and began prepping their drinks for delivery.

"I guess the first issue we need to address is this incident up in Fort Pierce with Cairo and that southbound Amtrak train. It's almost too much for me to think about!" Dr. Grant removed his glasses and rubbed his eyes. "It shouldn't have been any surprise, I guess. He had become so dependent on Billy."

"Do we know if he had any next of kin we can call?" Walter asked.

"That'll be the responsibility of the Sheriff's office up there! They'll contact the Foundation for any more information they might need. I think you probably gave them the only name you know of, didn't you, Markus?"

"Oh yeah!" Markus offered. "I could have told them how he said his parents were extradited to Egypt, but that might have been all a lie. Same with the story about his brother and foster care. Maybe Billy had the truth on it, but I never saw any documentation that could verify the story."

Carl suggested, "Ya know, Tripp and his team are going through Billy's computer and phone data. I'll pass him a message to cull out anything related to the kid. Maybe we'll find answers to some of our questions and theirs, too!"

Bethanny returned to the table and quietly made rounds, topping off their coffees, then headed to the next table.

"One other thing I need to get out of the way is an update on Billy's investigation." The detective took a sip from his cup and, as he set it back down, explained, "Our director of forensics, Tripp Hughes, has uncovered some suspicious circumstances that, to be honest with you, I missed in my initial processing of the crime scene."

"Wait a minute," Witt spoke up. "Crime scene? I thought his death was an accident?"

"We're no longer looking at it that way!" the detective answered. "There are suggestions leading us to consider that some degree of nefarious activity may have been at play. I'm headed up to Miami, as soon as we finish here, to try to get some answers to some questions. Hopefully, before the end of the day, I'll be able to give you a full report.

"Bethanny arrived with their plates, and after each was delivered, she withdrew to attend to some of her other duties.

Carl continued, "For now, I'm designating each of you as key resources in the investigation. I'm asking that you consider all future communications regarding Billy's death as completely confidential. At some point, we may be seeking your professional opinions and perhaps your testimony. In turn, you will each have some degree of access to many of the case details as we uncover and evaluate them. Are you in agreement?" They each confirmed their intent to comply with his request and proceeded to partake of their breakfasts.

"So, are we thinking that Cairo had something to do with Billy's death?" Witt was the first to ask the top question on all their minds.

Carl took his second bite of key-lime French toast and leaned back in ecstasy as he chewed, then swallowed and said, "I haven't seen anything yet to implicate him, but we haven't finished exploring the data held on Billy's phone or laptop. We want to keep all possibilities open and close the doors as we go through them. Cairo's death has all the hallmarks of a suicide, but like I'm finding with Billy's case, you can't jump to conclusions till all the evidence is in the bag." He took a sip of coffee and another bite from his plate, then, after another sip, he added, "I'm hoping this trip to Miami proves to close a couple of those open doors. I'll call Markus this afternoon with what I find, and he can bring you each up to speed. Does that work for you, Markus?" He returned to the mission at hand and didn't retreat till the last bite had disappeared.

"That would be fine!" Markus announced, then directed their attention to another issue, "I've had a few questions asked, regarding Billy's belongings. In particular, his guitars, his car, his van, and his boat. According to some of his musician friends, some of his guitars might be highly valuable. I talked with his friend Devin McCollum, who said that Billy kept a storage unit over at that self-storage building on Staples Avenue, where he kept his collection in a climate-controlled environment. I remember Billy had mentioned it to me once, but I had forgotten all about it. Do your people know anything about how his personal belongings will get surveyed?"

Carl replied, "That's called victimology! It's all part of my responsibility, so I appreciate your providing anything that might help me connect all the dots."

"Well, here's a related issue!" The senior doctor moved to his next note. "Do we know where Billy's son is?"

Carl grabbed his pen and field book from his top pocket and began to take notes. "Hadn't heard anything about any relatives yet! I sent a request for records to the National Missing and Unidentified Persons data center, but haven't had a chance to check the response yet. What do you know?"

"Not much!" Markus began, "But, a few years ago, Billy flew up to Sanford to meet Jan and me at the auto-train and drive my car back to Key West. On the way, he told me about his son. It was a painful issue in his life! They've been estranged ever since his wife died in the accident with the Coast Guard. The boy's name was Sherridan, and he blamed Billy for his mother's death. Apparently, they had fought over Billy's decision to sell their home in California and move onto a boat. That's all I know about it. I have no idea where he is now, but I think he's probably in his late thirties. I hope that's of some help!"

"I'm sure it will be! Thanks!" Carl made some notes, then asked, "Anything else?"

Witt was curious and asked, "Can you talk about the reason you think this might have been a homicide?"

Carl explained, "Well, we've established several gaps in the timeline that need to be explored. One is how Billy's dog, Flow, could have gotten out to his boat after he left Schooner's for the night, if he was asleep on his dinghy, under the dock. That, plus finding the guitar he was playing on stage, his keys, and other items out on his boat instead of with him in the dinghy, points to one big question: why would he go back to the dock in those early morning hours, when the visibility was almost nonexistent due to the fog? That's the evidence we do have, but while Trip and his team are going over videos and hard-drive searches, I'll be interviewing a pulmonologist, up at Jackson Memorial, and a maritime attorney that Billy met with last week. Maybe they'll be able to provide some information that will tie up some of our loose ends."

"By chance, did you hear about what happened to Jeannie yesterday? The waitress over at Schooner's?" Walter asked.

"I did! I overheard the calls that went out over my radio. It caught my attention, so I did some follow-up later with the Chief over at KWPD. Pretty sad, but I don't think it had any tie to Billy's death."

Markus asked, "What's the chance that, while you're up at Jackson Memorial, you might check on her condition and let us know how she's coming along?"

"I had already planned on it! I'll call you as soon as I know more." The four men finished their breakfasts, stood to their feet, and tossed cash into a pile on the table as Bethanny approached from the front of the room.

"Any coffee to go?" She asked, as she slid one of the chairs to the side to allow an unobstructed access to her well-appreciated gratuities.

"I think that'll cover our bill," Markus smiled as he told her. He followed with, "Maybe a car payment too!"

She blew him a kiss as he headed toward the front counter, where Conrad was busy with another customer. When they left, Markus moved to the front of the counter and reached to shake Conrad's hand. "Beautiful job, my friend! Just perfect!"

After a warm and friendly exchange, Markus hobbled back to his electric cart and clumsily climbed into the driver's seat. Dr. Colburn and Captain Witt were waiting for him and stepped to the sides of the cart.

"Well, by the time you make it over to the other side of the bight, the visibility might be clear enough to shove off." Markus turned the key and directed them, "Hop on! No sense walking when you could be ridin' with the King!"

23. PRIMAL OOPS

"Tripp Hughes!" he answered.

"Hey, bud! Last we talked, you said something about running into a snag with accessing those dock surveillance videos. What did you come up with?" Carl made the call while driving across Big Pine Key on his way to the mainland. He hadn't had time, the day before, to tell Tripp he wouldn't be at the office.

Tripp updated the detective with an explanation of the previous day's events. "You know that girl with the red hair who works upstairs at the city's Dock Management office? I think her name is Sherrill?" Carl acknowledged his familiarity with her, then Tripp continued, "Well, yesterday afternoon, I went up there to take a look at how their system was set up, and she gave me a ration of shit!"

Carl wasn't surprised and laughed. "Did she know who you were?"

Tripp answered, "She does now! I showed her my badge, and she still insisted their system wasn't up and running. I stood right by her desk and called the mayor's office! They finally hooked me through to Bobbie, and I put her on speaker so she could ream her out. Anyway, I was able to pull all of Monday night's footage from sunset through 0700 hours Tuesday, on all three cameras at that end of the dock, and two more that cover the area from the old ice house building at Schooner's, to beyond where the Western Union's docked. I had just plugged in the first flash drive when you called. Are you in your office?"

"No! I'm on my way to Miami! The Chief signed two administrative requests, one for the pulmonologist who saw Billy last week at Jackson Memorial, and the other is for the Maritime Attorney who reviewed the file you found in the back seat of Billy's car. I hope to be back by 1400 hours. I've got a lot of paperwork to catch up on." Carl was on the approach to the Bahia Honda Bridge and finished the call with, "Listen, keep an eye out for anything connected to that kid, Cairo, that Billy was working with. It looks like he's the guy who caught that southbound train last night in Fort Pierce."

Tripp offered, "Oh yeah! I saw that on the news."

Carl continued, "I don't have anything yet that might implicate him in Billy's death, but you might come across something, so keep your eye out!"

"You bet! Be safe!" Tripp encouraged his friend.

After the call, he set a notepad on his desk next to his keyboard, and opened the first file, then assigned a name to the first clip, "Ice House camera (1) Monday-sunset". After it loaded, he pushed play, took a hardy sip from his cup of coffee, and settled in for six hours or more of viewing video clips.

It was 0823 hours! The fog had lifted enough to see the outline of Christmas Tree Island from the deck of the *Psyched Out*. Witt loaded the last cart full of water bottles onboard, while Dr. Colburn stood next to the golf cart, talking over expectations for the day with his old friend.

The captain turned the key, and the engine rumbled into life. "Hey, give 'em a kiss and tell 'em goodbye. We got people waitin'!

Walt laughed, then slapped Markus on his shoulder and jogged down the dock to the stern cleat and untied the rope. He stood waiting for the captain to return to the helm and give the command to cast off.

"Damn it!" Walt looked up to see what the problem might be. The captain climbed back on deck, and when he appeared at the railing, called down, "You know that soft cooler that I carry the sandwiches in?"

Walt answered, "Yeah!"

"I left it on the floor where I was sittin' when we had breakfast!" The captain seemed perturbed!

Walt asked, "You want me to go back and get it?"

A horn was blowing in the parking lot! They turned to see Conrad jump from the front seat and grab the cooler from the back, then run to bring it to them. "I'm so glad you hadn't left yet! I called Markus, and he said you were over here." He bent to catch his breath, then continued, "I'm so glad I caught you!"

"Man, that is some delivery service!" the captain called out. "Tip 'em an extra dollar for me, Walt. He earned it!" A few minutes later, they motored the sailboat out of the harbor and turned into the deep channel.

"Another perfect day to be on the water!" Witt steered the vessel toward the mooring field, then stepped away from the helm. "Take tha wheel, doc. I gotta make a head call!" He disappeared into the cabin and shut the hatch behind him, while Dr. Colburn took control. There was a light breeze out of the south, and the sky was perfectly clear. He gazed across the Gulf expanse that lay ahead, and took his brain off its leash.

"UMMM!" She hummed with pleasure. "This should have been us!" He felt the pounding in his chest, the warmth of the blood rushing through his veins, then there was that familiar lightheadedness that always warned him she was near. That slow increase of pressure at the under edge of both eyes betrayed his hope of maintaining composure. The tears were milliseconds away! He longed to be sharing this moment with her! Turning his face toward the sky, he whispered her name into the great expanse of blue. "Amelia!" She was all around him! She was inside and outside of every thought he held. Her memory both intoxicated and tormented him beyond limit.

"Love is like this, ya know!" She shouted into the deepest abyss of his soul. "It's pleasure and pain wrapped up together! Sweet and bitter at the exact same time! It's life, and death ever after, forever and forever till you, *too*, depart!"

He was always in love! With or without her, it didn't make a difference. His capacity to love her was not limited by her being gone. That was Dr. Walter Arlin Colburn's most endearing quality! He knew love like he knew life! And he lived them both with unfettered passion!

"What do you think?" Witt called out through the open hatch as he slid the top back. "You gonna sign up for one of my sailing classes?" He turned and slid the hatch closed, then sat down and added, "We've got two seats available in the August class!"

The doctor chuckled, "Let's see if I survive July first!" He knocked the throttle forward to gain some speed and asked, "What's in store for us today?"

"Well," Captain Witt explained, "I called the last four people on yesterday's list and told them we would get to them this morning, if they're still available. Once we get out to the site, I'll see who's waiting on us and add their names to the list. We won't know who we'll be seeing till we get out there."

The doctor pointed toward mooring ball # 36 and said, "Looks like we've got a few out there now!" It was still one-half mile to the site. The fog had almost completely burned off, and the visibility was close to 100%.

As they approached the shallow water, Walter cut back on the throttle and turned into the mooring field, then handed the helm over to the captain. The sun was already blistering hot when they pulled up to the ball. There were two kayakers and one dinghy waiting for their arrival. Walter moved to the bow and lifted the coiled rope from the anchor locker, and tossed it to a man in a kayak to tie it off.

"Thanks!" he called out, as the young man turned and paddled to the back of the sailboat, where the others were waiting for instructions.

"Hey, Parker!" Witt knew all three of them! "How's yer dad doing? Haven't seen him goin' on two years now."

Parker lived with his dad on their trawler, about fifty yards behind Christmas Tree Island. His dad used to be one of the managers at the Waterfront Market, and Parker worked for Witt's wife, Kitty, in the deli. Parker's father, Donald, had become too sick to continue working and, in 2009, was forced to medically retire at the age of fifty-nine. Billy and he had become friends when Donald still worked at the market, and their friendship grew stronger after Donald retired. His neglect of his diabetes led to unbearable suffering from neuropathy. It had become so painful that he refused to leave the comfort of his bed, so Parker became his source for everything. Billy helped on occasion, but the weight of their survival fell on Parker.

Parker answered, "He's not doing so good, Witt! That's why I decided to come talk with you guys."

Donald was a 30% service-connected disabled veteran and had access to full medical benefits at the Veterans Administration's Clinic, over on the east side of the Island. Between the V.A. and Parker, most of Don's needs were met. Parker, unfortunately, had an insatiable craving for the pleasures of cannabis and was as lazy as a California harbor seal on a Saturday afternoon.

"We'll get to you as soon as we can!" Witt called down to Parker.

After taking their names and callback numbers, Witt introduced Dr. Colburn, then reminded everyone to stay close to their phones and wait for his call. After the party of three had pulled out of the area, he turned to Walter and suggested they move inside to talk. When they were situated below deck, Witt began to discuss his concern. "I don't know about you, but yesterday's incident with Jeannie has me pretty shaken up!"

He leaned against the navigation station and rubbed his forehead with his hand as he talked. "I've had to pull dead bodies out of cars, lifted bloated carcasses from sunken boats, I even assisted with a headless extrication on the seven-mile bridge once, but none of those bothered me as much as what happened to Jeannie yesterday!" He stretched his neck and cocked his head from left to right, then finished with, "I got, maybe, two hours sleep last night!"

Walter stood with his back to the galley, listening intently to his new friend's complaint. "May I ask you a question?" he proposed.

"Sure, please!" the captain answered.

"Out of all of the cases that you responded to over the years, the ones that were fatal, or that could be considered critical, out of all of those, how many involved people that you could say you had previously known personally, and had some positive association with?"

Witt crossed his arms over his chest and searched his memory for the answer, "There was one!" he recalled. "When I worked for the Marine Patrol, a KWPD officer's son had crashed his jet ski into a dock out at Government Pass and got slammed, headfirst, into a concrete cleaning station. I was first on the scene! He was DOA, but even though I knew him and his whole family, it didn't have this kind of effect on me. He was a jerk! We were always tryin' to get him to slow down. He kinda got what he was apparently after, but Jeannie, my God, she had so much goin' for her!"

"Let's explore a couple of issues that might seem obvious, but nonetheless, need to be cleared up, if we're going to get past what happened. First, explain to me any feelings of responsibility toward what happened to Jeannie that you've been having!" The doctor held his hand up to stop Witt from answering, and added, "Think about this before you answer! I'm talking about any personal responsibility here! Strictly, what you feel that you could be held accountable for in relation to what happened with Jeannie. Got it?"

Witt thought about the question, then answered, "Yeah! I think I do! I'm the one who made the call to remind her she was scheduled to come out to see you. On the phone, she didn't seem to remember she had an appointment, but my calling her triggered her memory. If I hadn't made that call, she would have gone to her own boat and, possibly, not be in the shape she's in now."

"That's probably a major reason why your subconscious keeps punishing you with reminders of your role in her tragedy," the doctor explained. "It's going on 24/7, under the surface! Whether you're asleep or awake! It's constantly trying to get your conscious mind to decide where the best place for you to survive Jeannie's event might lie. It's part of a defense mechanism that's trying to protect you from the potential damage caused by guilt! In its extreme, we find absolute denial. Knowing that your subconscious is constantly working toward a healthy balance should be comforting."

The doctor reached into the cooler and pulled out two bottles of water. He handed one to Captain Witt and continued, "The human brain is always seeking to validate causation. It's part of a complex survival instinct! If it can't reconcile causation, it moves toward one or more of the reasoning mechanisms, always trying to obtain a balance between what we think is our accountability and what our ego can accept as a reasonable, self-executed punishment. The more we understand what's going on below the stage, the better equipped we are when faced with emotionally difficult challenges."

Witt listened intently! He understood that Dr. Colburn's advice would make an indelible impact on how he would face tragedies for the rest of his life! "Please, go on!" he implored.

The doctor continued, "We're talking about one of the deepest, inherently human, primal characteristics that define us as unique in the animal world, empathetic association!"

He took a sip from his water bottle, then went on to explain, "Your lack of sleep is completely explainable, and exemplifies some of the conditions of your mental health." He hesitated for the thought to sink in, then explained, "If you were completely unable to empathize with Jeannie, her incident would not have kept you awake through the night. Without these processes of subconscious reconciliation, constantly evaluating and sorting through the emotional episodes of our lives, we would never be able to fully experience the necessary empathy and accountability it would take for us to function as civilized humans. In fact, without these underlying mechanisms effectively at work, we would be living in a narcissistically dominated and psychopathic world of crime and chaos. That said, our best hope of recovery after an emotional trauma like you faced with Jeannie's accident is to make sure you get enough sleep for your subconscious mind to do its work. I hope that makes sense!"

Captain Witt blew the air from his lungs and raised his eyebrows in amazement. "Geez!" he exclaimed. "That's clearer than anything I ever heard in my Crisis Intervention Training classes!"

Dr. Colburn explained, "I probably could have just offered you a prescription for something to help you get to sleep, but I thought you might find it interesting to know why you might be having the trouble in the first place. There's really a lot more to it! I've published several books on the evolution and origins of the social traits of modern man and psycho-primatology. You might enjoy reading them sometime."

Witt enthusiastically responded! "Kitty and I are both avid readers. I'm always looking for something that will expand my understanding of human nature. Markus got me interested in some works by his friend E. Fuller Torrey several years ago. I just finished his audiobook, *Evolving Brains, Emerging Gods*! I've never had a piece of literature affect me so deeply! It was remarkable! Have you read it?"

Dr Colburn grinned modestly and remarked, "If you ever get a chance to look through the bibliography, well, I think you'll recognize many of my works are listed as references. Fuller and I were both research psychiatrists at the National Institute of Mental Health when Markus was the Director! He's still one of my closest friends. My wife, Amelia, and I stayed with him at his house in Bethesda three years ago. Markus said he's planning to come down for a week-long visit this winter. I'm sure we can arrange for you to spend some time with him, if you'd like."

"That sounds great!" the captain exclaimed. "Maybe he'd be willing to autograph my copy of *American Psychosis*!"

"I'm quite sure he'd be happy to," the doctor said. "So, who's on our list for today?" the doctor asked.

Witt pulled his notebook from his satchel. "We've got four carryovers from yesterday and three from this morning. You ready to get started?"

The doctor pushed his shoulders back, twisted his torso from left to right to stretch his spine, then asked, "Is the flag up yet?"

Witt responded, "Oops! You can blame that on my subconscious, if you like!"

24. MIAMI VICE GRIP

"How may I help you?" The receptionist asked, as she hung up her phone and looked up from her desk at the monstrous figure of the detective from Key West. Her mouth was still open as she leaned back in her chair for a better view.

He was used to it! He had always had that effect on women! His wife loved to tease him about it, too.

"I'm not sure if I'm in the right department," he stated. "I've got an appointment to see Dr. Carmina Goldstein in the Pulmonary department."

"Yes, sir!" The girl fumbled with her directory while she explained. "We've recently moved the pulmonary facilities into the new wing, and the information desk is still sending people here by mistake. It's a real pain for everybody." She located the phone number and made a call while she held one finger up for the detective to wait. When she hung up, she stood to her feet and directed him to follow her. It was a short walk to the corridor that would lead him to where he needed to be. "If you'll walk to the end of this hallway, you'll be met by her secretary, Anna. She'll take you the rest of the way."

He thanked the girl for her assistance and proceeded down the corridor.

"Are you Detective Dixon?" Anna called to him from an open door.

"Yes, Ma'am!" he answered, as he reached to take her outstretched hand.

"I'm Dr. Goldstein's assistant, Anna!" She motioned for him to follow her through the huge double doors, then led him down another hallway. "I'm sorry if you had trouble finding us! Hopefully, they'll get all the directories updated and it'll be a lot easier for everybody." She pushed open a door and led him into a waiting room, then said, "Dr. Goldstein is running a little late, but she's on her way!" She sat down at the desk and asked, "Would you like me to get you a cup of coffee?"

He declined her offer and began to browse through a *Southern Living* magazine.

A few minutes passed, then the doctor entered the room and greeted him. "Good morning, detective. I hope you weren't waiting too long." Dr. Goldstein introduced herself as she shook his hand, then told her assistant, "Anna, give Dr. Tiedemann's office a call and let him know that Detective Dixon and I are ready for him, when he can break away."

Anna picked up her phone as the duo disappeared into the doctor's office.

"Thank you for e-mailing me the Administrative Request for Mr. Chapman's records. I've had our legal department review it, and they've advised me I'm cleared to answer any questions you might have." She was now seated behind her desk with Billy's file in front of her, and added, "How can I help you?"

Carl began to explain, "Thank you for taking time out to meet with me. As mentioned in the request, Mr. Chapman met with an unfortunate end on Tuesday morning in Key West, and at first, we thought his death might have been an accident. Our investigative team has uncovered evidence that suggests there may be good reason to reconsider that assumption. I'm just backtracking through the days that preceded his death, and I noticed he had an appointment in your department last Friday."

There was a tap at the door! "Come on in, Rodger!" Dr. Goldstein called out. A man wearing a lab coat stepped into the room and reached to shake Carl's hand. "Roger, this is the detective from Key West that's looking into William Chapman's case!" she announced.

"Rodger Tiedemann!" the man introduced himself.

"Carl, Carl Dixon! Monroe County Sheriff's Office!"

Dr. Tiedemann took a seat and turned his attention to his colleague, sitting behind the desk. He listened as she explained his role in Billy's medical review to the detective.

"Rodger's in his third year of fellowship with us and is specializing in industrial hazardous materials exposures. I had asked him to take a look at the findings of Mr. Chapman's bronchoscopy, which I had performed on

Thursday. The appointment you referenced took place the next day, after the lab completed their analysis. That's when Rodger and I met with Mr. Chapman to go over the findings. I'll have Rodger explain what we found in just a minute, but I think it might be important to go over with you how Mr. Chapman came to be a patient with us."

Carl took his notepad from his satchel and positioned himself in his chair to write. "Please!" he said. "If you don't mind, I'm going to take some notes as you talk. Go on!"

She opened the file on her desk and began, "We received a call from Dr. Dennis Breslin, a pulmonologist in Key West, on Wednesday morning, last week. He described a patient who was in need of immediate intervention after exposure to concentrations of dust from the sanding of a marine paint product. We arranged for Mr. Chapman to be seen the next morning, and I personally performed his exam. Upon auscultation, I heard rales and rhonchi with consolidation upon palpation, which gave me concern. These observations, combined with Mr. Chapman's severe shortness of breath, led me to immediately order a C.T. scan of his chest, which revealed pleural effusion, narrowing of bronchial lumens, and several areas of constriction. It was at that point that I called Dr. Tiedemann to see if Mr. Chapman's condition might be of interest in relation to his research on Reactive Airway Dysfunction Syndrome. We discussed the benefits of a bronchoscopy and agreed that it may provide us with a look at both the specific chemical makeup of the exposure and could help us identify any fungal, bacterial or parasitic activity that might be causing his inflammation. After we discussed the procedure with Mr. Chapman, the informed consent and a consent for anesthesia were signed. I personally performed the procedure that afternoon. After the patient recovered, Dr. Tiedemann and I went over our preliminary findings with Mr. Chapman, and scheduled a ten o'clock am appointment the next morning for a comprehensive review of our findings. Mr. Chapman arranged for overnight accommodations at the Spring Hill Suites Hotel, and was released from our care at four thirty-seven pm." She slid her notebook across the desk to Dr. Tiedemann, and said, "That's the treatment record for Mr. Chapman. Now, unless you have any questions, I'll have Dr. Tiedemann go over the diagnostic report and the lab reports."

Carl had been taking notes as she talked. "No!" he exclaimed. "What you're doing is perfect! Please, go ahead!"

Dr. Tiedemann began, "As Dr. Goldstein mentioned, the nature of Mr. Chapman's condition was, in fact, very interesting to me! According to his description, he had become exposed to concentrations of dust from the sanding of a very toxic and dangerous industrial marine paint product that employs cyanide isotopes as the antifouling agent."

"Would that be Baybright paint?" Carl asked.

"Yes!" Dr. Tiedemann answered. "It's one of the most popular marine paints on the market today! The handling of it is highly regulated, though! They offer several formulas, but the most dangerous is the formula used to retard the growth of barnacles, muscles, ascidians, algae, and other microorganisms on the bottoms of boats. Boat owners can buy it at any marine supply provider, but if they don't read the material safety data sheet, they can suffer irreparable damage to their health. Mr. Chapman was, apparently, an innocent bystander when he became exposed to the dust."

Carl asked, "If the boat was sanded while it was tied up at the dock and still in the water, wouldn't the dust that he was exposed to be the less dangerous of the two formulas? The one without the antifouling agents?"

Dr. Tiedemann offered the following explanation: "That's a reasonable assumption, but boat owners sometimes apply the antifouling paint all the way up to the boat railing. From the samples that Dr. Goldstein provided, I can say, unequivocally, that the dust that was found in the deeper areas of Mr. Chapman's lungs can be attributed to paint that was infused with antifouling agents!"

Detective Dixon caught his breath and sat back in his seat, then asked, "What is in the formula that causes it to be so dangerous?"

The doctor looked across the desk at Dr. Goldstein. Then, after she nodded her approval, he offered, "Well, we've already mentioned cyanide isotopes, but they've been banned from being used in paint for decades. However, we regularly come across evidence that they're still finding their way into the lungs of shipyard workers. There's even a name attached to people who suffer from the effects of long-term exposure! They call them boatyard zombies! We inspected several of Mr. Chapman's specimens with our scanning electron microscope and were able to identify an extensive list of components that could be positively attributed to exposure to antifouling paint. Would you like me to read you the list of what we found?"

"Please!" Carl answered.

The doctor adjusted his eyeglasses and flipped through several pages of the file, then began, "We examined nine biopsy samples! Four bronchial and five transbronchial samples were subjected to general ultrastructure analysis utilizing both Scanning (SEM) and Transmission Electron Microscopy (TEM). Our analysis concluded with the identification of the following National Institute for Occupational Safety (NIOSH) recognized hazardous chemicals being present in Mr. Chapman's lungs: Ethyl benzene, Propylene glycol, monomethyl ether acetate, Diisobutylketone, Ethoxy ethyl Acetate, Xylenes, Monomeric and Polymeric Isocyanates, Methyl Isocyanate, Zinc Chromate, Propylene Glycol..."

Carl stopped the reading and offered his appreciation. "Thank you, I think I've got the picture. There seems to be no doubt of his exposure. Thank you for clarifying that for me!" He closed his notebook and added, "You've both been a tremendous help! I think I'll be able to pull together a comprehensive summary of what he was dealing with before he died. I really appreciate you taking the time to meet with me today!"

The two doctors walked him out to the reception area, then offered their further assistance if needed. Carl turned and walked down the corridor to the directory that was posted on the wall next to the elevators, and searched for directions to the Intensive Care unit. He stood looking confused and wondering if his offer to check on Jeannie's condition might have been a mistake, when a young gentleman in green hospital scrubs advised him, "If you're lost, don't feel alone! This place is more confusing than finding your way into somebody's brain through their left nostril!"

Carl laughed!

The young surgeon asked, "Where are you trying to go?"

"I'm looking for the Intensive Care Unit!" the detective remarked.

"Is this dealing with a trauma case?" the man asked.

"Yes!" Carl answered. "There was a young girl, suffering from a serious head trauma transported up here yesterday afternoon, from Key West! I was hoping to see how she's doing."

The doctor stepped into the down elevator and directed him, "Come on! She'd be over at the Ryder Trauma Center building. I'll show you how to get there." On the first floor, the doctor led Carl to a huge diorama of the Jackson Memorial Complex and pointed to the Ryder Trauma Building at the back of the complex. "You could walk it if you have the time, but then it's a long way back if your car is here at the Wellness Center! If you drive over, you'll need to come in on NW 19th Street from NW 12th. I hope that helps you!" The two shook hands, and Carl headed to the parking garage to find his car.

It was eleven fifteen when he walked up to the information desk of the Ryder Trauma Center. "Yes, sir, how can I help you?"

Carl loved his trips to Miami! No matter the reason! No matter how long the stay! He always enjoyed the hustle and bustle of its eclectic vibe. Her Latin accent was his invitation to practice his Spanish! "Buen dia! Me gustaria preguntar sobre la condicion de un paciente.." He explained.

The girl asked for the patient's name. "Jeannie A. Lorimier!" He replied. Then added, "Ella volo aqui en Trama Star anoche desde Key West!"

The girl offered, "Yes, sir!" She entered the name into her patient identification system and confirmed, "Miss Lorimier was admitted last evening and is currently registered as a patient at the trauma center. If you need any further information, I can refer you to our Director of Patient Information, if you would like."

"Please!" he answered.

The detective waited while the girl made the call. Seconds later, he was greeted by the director. "Good morning, I'm Lois Van Norton!" she introduced herself to him. "I understand you were asking about a patient from Key West. Is there something I might help you with?"

He knew very well the protective limits allowed under the HIPAA law. He was personally sworn to the enforcement of those limits! He expected her next question would be to ask him if he was related to the patient. He presented his badge and ID for her to inspect, and told her, "Miss Lorimier was an unfortunate collateral in a possible homicide case in Key West. I was hoping that I might be able to tell the team that affected her rescue how she might be doing."

Ms. Van Norton took a close look at his ID and suggested he follow her to her office. "I'm sure you understand that we are limited in how much we can tell you, but let me take a look and see if there's something I can give you that might be helpful." She sat down at her desk and entered the name. "Lorimier, yes! She arrived via medevac on our helipad at 1918 hours yesterday, in critical condition with a traumatic brain injury (TBI) and possible spinal trauma. Prior to arrival, our trauma team was activated and proceeded, immediately, to evaluate the extent of her injuries. Ms. Lorimier was stabilized, and a neurological assessment was performed by the trauma surgeon. CT scans were performed, and she was transferred into the care of our neurology team. She was in surgery for the next six hours. Then Ms. Lorimier was transported to the Surgical Trauma ICU, and per her most recent status update, her condition is reported to be critical, but stable. That's really all I'm able to tell you!"

Carl was surprised by her generosity and offered his appreciation. "Thank you for being so helpful," he said. "She is a deeply loved member of our little island community. She's a waitress at one of our popular restaurants. We are all pulling for her to have a strong recovery and get back to us as soon as she can! Thank you!"

As he talked, Ms. Van Norton was paging through the doctor's notes and chronological entries made by the ICU nurses. Carl had finished talking and sat watching her eyes as they scanned across her computer screen. Her silence, and the frown on her face as she read, was a clear call for him to remain silently patient.

A few moments passed! She pushed her chair back from her desk, placed her hand over her eyes, and took a deep breath, then reached into her desk drawer for a tissue and said, "I'm sorry, detective! I have a daughter! She's twenty-one years old! She's a waitress at a cute little place over in Coconut Grove, and I was a trauma nurse here at Ryder until about a year ago. They offered me this position as an alternative to my having a complete nervous breakdown. I know what this girl is facing! It does not look very hopeful!" She wiped her eyes, stood to her feet, and leaned her body against the wall, then turned her head toward the ceiling and continued, "I can't count the number of times I've found myself in the middle of cases like this. Your little girl's life is hanging by a thread!" She sat down in her chair and swiveled toward the detective, then asked, "Could we talk, you know, off the record for a minute?"

Carl felt like a bystander on the scene of an accident, with no options for leaving, and answered, "Of course! Whatever you say can stay right here!" Then he asked, "What's on your mind?"

She sighed deeply, "I'm going to go out on a limb and just tell you. This little girl, Jeannie," she paused, closed her eyes tightly, and lowered her head. After a few seconds, she faced the detective and returned to her narrative, "She's intubated and showing no signs of self-initiated respiration. She's on continuous IV sedation with anti-seizure meds, and she's on a high dose of Levophed to keep her blood pressure stable. They inserted a drain in her brain to control the pressure. She's unresponsive to stimulation, and her pupils are fixed and dilated." She looked directly into Carl's eyes and confessed, "I could lose my job and my license for telling you this, but, in my best judgment, this poor girl has little chance of a functional recovery."

On his way back to his car, he called Dr. Grant to share what he had learned. "Hey, Markus! I'm leaving the trauma center and wanted to give you an update on Jeannie." He stepped into the bright sun and turned toward the parking garage. The temperature was already in the mid-90s, and sweat was beginning to soak his shirt. "She's critical but stable, and still in ICU. She had surgery last night, but I can't get any more information related to a prognosis."

"Thanks, Carl! I'll pass that on to Witt immediately. He and Walter are out on the boat, seeing clients. I expect I'll be hearing from them when they break for lunch. Were you able to make any progress on your case with Billy?"

Carl answered, "As a matter of fact, yes. I'm learning a lot about what he was dealing with the week before he died." Then he asked, "Did he ever tell you about the trouble he was having from the dust in the turtle museum?"

"Yes! We talked on the phone a couple of times a few weeks ago. I had referred him to my pulmonologist, Dennis Breslin, and Billy said that he was headed up to Miami for some testing. That's the last time I talked with him."

"Well, I learned quite a lot about what he was breathing into his lungs while he was out there in the museum, and nothing about it was good. I've got an appointment with the maritime attorney that Billy met with on the

Friday before he died. Maybe he'll be able to fill me in on what was going on. I'll catch up with you later today!"

Carl's phone rang as he drove past the beautiful Art Deco Bacardi Building on Biscayne Boulevard. "Dixon!" he answered.

It was Tripp Hughes, calling from the Sheriff's office. "You got a minute to talk?" Tripp asked.

"Yeah! What's up?" Carl answered.

"There's a couple of things I need to give you a heads up on, regarding what I think I'm seeing in these video clips," Tripp explained.

"OK! What have you got?" Carl asked.

"Well," he began, "I think Billy was being stalked Monday night, when he left *Schooner's*. I was watching the city's camera video that covers the Western approach to the dinghy dock. I saw Billy with his guitar case in hand climb into his boat with Flow, then head out of the harbor. The fog was light, and visibility was still pretty good. Seven minutes later, two guys approached from the West and stopped at that kayak rental rack that's on the lower dock, in front of the Historic Seaport sign. One of them took a key out of his pocket and unlocked the cables, then they slipped two kayaks off the rack and pushed them into the water. After they locked the rack, they climbed into the kayaks and pushed away from the dock. You can see them paddling past the breakwater and into the channel. After that, it gets too dark to see where they were headed, but over the next two hours, the fog rolls in, and by 0300 hours, you can't see the kayak rack at all. At 0815 hours, the fog had cleared enough to see that those kayaks were back on the rack. I printed hard copies of the two guys so you can have them in your file when you get back."

Carl asked, "Any idea who they might be?"

Tripp was ready with his answer! "Oh yeah! I cross-referenced the time period over to the video footage you got from Coreen, and the stage cam scanned the audience several times during the last set that Billy and Devin played. Get this, I spotted the same two guys that took off in the kayaks sitting at the bar with that charter-boat captain, Eric Campanello. You know! He owns those three boats in the slips right out the front door of the Turtle Museum. The captain left the bar when Billy finished his set, then his two mates stayed until right after Billy headed to his boat. I think we've got our hands on some suspicious stuff here!"

Carl had pulled into a parking place on Brickell Avenue to listen to Tripp's review. As he pulled back onto the highway, he said, "That's great stuff! Run all three of them through the system for criminal history and any background stuff you can find, then work up a suspect report on each one. I should be back at the office by 1530 hours. Maybe you'd want to go with me down to the dock to catch them when they come ashore."

"You bet! I'll see ya in a couple of hours!" Trip answered.

Carl arrived at the Miami Tower building with fifteen minutes to spare before his scheduled appointment with Tolson, Tolson, Mahon, and Associates, Attorneys at Law, on the thirty-second floor. Jonathan Tolson, and his wife, Mina, had built their reputation as distinguished South Florida Maritime Attorneys, litigating cases against the cruise ship industries that operate in the waters of Florida. Maritime law is a very specialized discipline of litigation that the Tolson family had become deeply invested in after losing their daughter, son-in-law, and two grandchildren in the 1994 ferryboat, *MS Estonia,* sinking, while crossing the Baltic Sea on their way to Stockholm.

Carl stepped off the elevator and turned toward the tall, glass doors to suite number 3201. ***TOLSON, TOLSON, MAHON and ASSOCIATES*** was boldly printed in gold lettering across the door. He could see through to the reception desk and a girl sitting behind it. A wall of beautifully polished wood climbed to the ceiling behind the girl's desk. Carl stepped through the door and stood silently, staring up at the sculpture that hung from the wall of wood. A broken ship, lying on the bottom of a torrential sea of glass ribbons, spattered with hundreds of tiny bodies, drifting lifelessly down from above. Blown glass lettering in colors of red and blue proclaimed the alarm, "Mayday, mayday, our ship is leaning!"

Carl felt shaken deeply! Something about the sculpture called out to be explained to him before he could redirect his attention to the purpose of his appointment.

"May I help you?" The girl looked up from her desk and asked. Carl's eyes had focused on a brass plaque mounted off to the side of the wall. "Yes, thank you!" he said, as he made his way over to the plaque. "I'm Carl Dixon. I have an appointment to see Mr. Tolson."

"Yes, sir!" She exclaimed, "I'll let him know you've arrived.

As she placed the call, Carl read the plaque on the wall.

MAYDAY-MAYDAY-MAYDAY
SEPTEMBER 28, 1994

While crossing the Baltic Sea in route from Tallinn, Estonia, to Stockholm, Sweden,

852 good and courageous souls were taken to their death on the Ferryboat M.S. ESTONIA.

We dedicate our lives to the telling of their story and the memory of their love.

Thank You! Tolson, Tolson, Mahon and Associates Dedicated February 6, 2001.

Carl stepped back and took a moment in silent contemplation, then said, "I don't think I've ever seen a more touching piece of art!"

The girl turned her head toward him and smiled, then said, "They're really serious about what they do here! They don't care if your case is big or small, everybody gets treated with the best they can give." She turned back to her work as Carl took a seat.

Minutes later, Jonathan Tolson stepped into the lobby and reached to shake Carl's hand.

"J.T. Tolson!" he introduced himself.

Carl stood to his feet and reached to make the connection.

J. T. was a height-challenged man, with the grip of a 700 lb. goliath grouper. Carl was caught off guard by his strength and stood locked, hand in hand, for what seemed to be an unnecessarily awkward length of time.

"Call me J.T.!" he said. It seemed an appropriate time for him to release, but he didn't. He kept on shaking, and as it continued, he progressively tightened his grip. Carl had never experienced such an unusual introduction. He wanted the man to turn loose and explain his reason for hanging on so long. He was perplexed by the event, but made no effort to resist.

"Detective Carl Dixon, Monroe County Sheriff's Office!" He hoped that the man might turn loose if he emphasized that he held a significant degree of authority, but no, the little man held tight.

"It's my great honor to meet you, Detective. I hope I haven't made you uncomfortable, but I can assure you, someday you will remember this meeting, and it just might change your life!" With that, he released his grip and turned toward the sculpture on the wall. "Do you hear her?"

Carl had, over the years, entertained more than his fair share of crazy people! He thought of himself as well-skilled at navigating around their quirks and idiosyncratic behaviors, but this little man seemed to be the grand master of weird! He looked over at the girl at the desk and asked, "You mean your receptionist?"

The attorney laughed, turned, and then looked into Carl's confused face. "No, detective, the sculpture! Did you hear the screams, bleeding into your soul as you stood on the shoreline, listening to their calls for help and thinking that if only you were close enough to grab their hand, you might be the hero who pulls them from their peril?"

Carl shrugged his shoulders and answered, "I'm sorry! I'm caught up in one hell of a homicide, and the only screams I'm hearing are the ones coming from my stomach saying Shorty's Bar-B-Que, ASAP!"

The three of them laughed heartily! J.T. slapped the detective on his back and directed, "Come on in!" He led him around the back side of the wooden wall and through another pair of glass doors.

A long wooden table dominated the room. A white box, with two handles, sat at one end. J.T. pressed a button on the intercom that sat next to the box and called out, "Carrissa, have Tobias join us in the conference room, as soon as he can break away, please." He stepped over to the plate-glass window and motioned for Carl to join him. "See that cruise ship?" he asked as he pointed down at the boat docked at Cruise Terminal A in the Port of Miami. "That's the *Royal Caribbean* boat *Freedom of the Seas*! They launched her in 2006 and, for a while, she was the largest cruise ship in the world. She carries 4,500 passengers and 1,300 crew members, and every time she sets sail, every one of them throw their lives to the mercy of the sea." He turned to take a seat at the head of the table and motioned for Carl to join him, then said, "She's merciless even on a good day, ya know!"

Carl took his seat and remarked, "No argument there!"

A man pulled open the door and stepped into the conference room, then reached across the table to shake Carl's hand. "Tobias Maldanado!" he greeted.

"Carl Dixon! Pleased to meet you!" he answered.

As the man took his seat, J.T. began pulling documents from the box and talked as he arranged the papers. "I would imagine you understand that despite the administrative request your office faxed to us, we are still bound by certain ethical protections in regard to the confidentiality of Mr. Chapman's case."

"Of course!" Carl exclaimed. "But, I'm sure that in this matter, you can appreciate my appeal for discretion. There is a murderer walking the streets of our little Island, and you may hold the only key that I can use to lock him up. I'm hoping you might have something you can offer that could help."

J.T. turned toward Tobias and motioned for him to exit the room. He slid his chair back and, as he stood to his feet, said, "Excuse us for a moment!" then followed his colleague out of the room.

Carl sat waiting quietly for several minutes. He was losing hope, then the door opened, and Tobias took a seat at the head of the table and said, "We were very sad to hear of Mr. Chapman's passing. I had begun reviewing his case documents last Friday, while he was here, and was looking forward to representing him. It was a complex, but very interesting case. He left these documents and photos with us, and I spent several hours on Saturday going over them in detail. He deserved to have his case litigated, and when I completed my assessment, I sent a text to J.T. that it was a very strong and financially promising case against a charter boat company, the City of Key West, and the company that held the license for the museum. Mr. Chapman had researched every aspect of the case, and what you see here is everything he left with us to review. J.T. sent Mr. Chapman a text on Monday morning for him to call us back and discuss how he wanted us to move forward. J.T. has directed that I show you the return text he received from Mr. Chapman on Monday afternoon, and to wish you good fortune as you heed all calls for Mayday!"

Tobias picked up the box from the floor and loaded the papers and files into it, then slid the box to the edge of the table and waited for the detective to raise his hand and take hold of the handle. Carl stood and grabbed the other handle with his free hand as Tobias turned to exit the room, then disappeared down the hall. A folded piece of paper was on the table. Carl picked it up and read:

To J.T. Tolman, Attorney at Law. Thank you for your speedy attention to my case. I have decided to withdraw my interest in the pursuit of litigation against the defendants we had discussed on Friday. Upon my returning to Key West, I had a chance encounter with the captain of the sanded charter boat, who implored that I reconsider my intent of seeking remedy through court action. The man was sincere in his remorse over the damages that his actions had caused me, and in consideration of the impact that litigation might have on his business, I am closing this case. Thank you for your assistance in this matter. Sincerely, William B. Chapman III.

Carl turned toward the window and gazed across the Island of Miami Beach and into the great expanse of ocean that rolled toward the Eastern horizon, beyond the clouds that held the promise of a cooling rain, and listened for the screams of a million Maydays. Yes, he heard her! He heard them all!

25. CATCH OF THE DAY

C arl turned into the parking lot and pulled his car into the only shaded spot he could find. The smell of smoking meats, sweetened perfectly in a wash of tomato sauce, garlic, onions, vinegar, and brown sugar, embedded itself into the receptors of his nose like the scattershot from a discharged shotgun. He felt the kick, and he hadn't even pulled the trigger yet.

"Good afternoon!" the portly lady greeted, as she handed him a menu. "You can sit wherever you like!"

My God, he thought! If heaven had a smell, this would be it!!! The dining room was well packed with the usual midday Friday Miami lunch crowd. George Strait's song, *Give It Away*, was washing over the feasting patrons as they slathered their favorite sauce over their pick of charred chicken, beef, and pork. It's an eclectic mix of wholesome Americana infused with Latin panic. Carl's favorite choice for lunch on any day of the week he had reason to be in Miami. He took a seat near the window that faced his car and opened the menu. Seconds later, his waitress asked, "Can I get you something to drink?"

The detective leaned to one side, for a better look at her face, and said, "I'll have an Arnold Palmer with light ice and unsweetened tea."

A few seconds later, she slid the drink onto the table and asked if he was ready to order.

He was quick to decide, "I'll have the spare ribs and chicken platter with a side of corn on the cob and an order of onion rings." Before she left, he added, "And a side of onion rings to go, please!"

She smiled and headed toward the kitchen to place his order.

"Well, I'll be a cross-eyed monkey's uncle! Carl Dixon, getting him some Shorty's Bar-B-Que, right here in ol Myyy-Mammie!" Carl grinned and turned to look into the face of an old comrade, Delonese Webber, and as they shook hands, he greeted him with, "Dell, you ol' scoundrel, I haven't seen you in fifteen years. How've you been?"

Del had started his career in law enforcement as a Monroe County patrolman after graduating from The School of Justice, Public Safety and Law Academy at Miami Dade College. Carl was supervising the Key West Sheriff's traffic unit back then, and Del was assigned to work in his division after his probationary period finished. He had married a girl from Pompano Beach, and they later moved back up to the mainland to be closer to her family. Over the years, the two officers had lost touch. "I'm still fightin' the bad guys! Ya know, tryin' ta keep from landin' in tha morgue! I hear you made detective!"

"Yeah, that's right! It's been about two years now." The waitress pushed her way between the two men and placed Carl's lunch on the table, then disappeared. "I'd guess you and Kimmy have a house full of little Dells by now!"

"Well, no!" he answered, with a touch of remorse or shame in his voice. "We got divorced that first year after moving back up here. I'm not sure she was ready to deal with me being on that much night patrol."

Carl grinned! He wasn't surprised by the news. Years of fostering young officers into their careers had helped hone his skill at assessing their potential both on the job and off it. "Well, it takes a lot out of a woman to be married to a cop! Nobody can argue that!" Carl salted his feast, poured on some sauce, picked up the ear of corn, and said, "Good to see ya, Del! Stay safe!"

He wasn't interested in entertaining the young man any longer than he had to. He had noticed him, sitting with the two other officers, across the room. Carl knew how it goes. He'd return to his seat and start bragging about things he never did when he was working for Carl in the Keys. The guy was just chasin' after a dream that was always outside of his reach! Carl had seen it in hundreds of young men over the years. He flushed those thoughts away with a long draw from his straw and tha suck of a chicken bone.

Stepping outside, he was slapped in the face by a fiery wave of sunshine. As he walked through the parking lot, he heard the onion rings screaming for mercy. It was hot, and he regretted not leaving his windows cracked. Minutes later, he pulled onto Old Dixie Highway. Next stop, Stock Island.

"Siri, call Tripp Hughes!" he commanded.

"What's happening, Bud?" Tripp answered.

As Carl pulled away from the last stoplight in Florida City, he said, "I think we've got everything we need, now! I'm bringing back the box of evidence Billy compiled, and it totally implicates your charter boat Captain, Eric Campanello." He drove past the turn-off to Card Sound Road, set his cruise control at 62 mph, and added, "Billy apparently had a strong case against him, but on Monday, he decided not to pursue it. Unfortunately, the captain had no clue that Billy had notified the attorney that he didn't want to screw up this guy's life. If he had known, he wouldn't have had a reason to have him killed!"

Tripp's response couldn't be more succinct. "There's your motive!" Then, he suggested, "Now that we have the guys in the kayaks identified, do you want me to talk to the D.A. and get her to work up warrants on the three of them?"

Carl had a plan and explained, "Everything we've got, so far, is circumstantial! We need something solid before we can go after warrants. I'm thinking we might want to be on the dock when they pull in this afternoon, and see how they react to being asked some questions. You wanna join me?"

Tripp was always more than willing to help out when a case was about to be blown open. There was no more exciting time to be on the scene than when a suspect gets cornered. It was the element of unpredictability that made his hard work so rewarding. The time when all the pieces fall in place. Carl didn't need to ask! Tripp answered, "Can't wait!"

"Hi guys! You here for happy hour?"

Carl looked at Tripp, and they both laughed out loud! "I don't think so!" Carl told her. "Just bring me an Arnold Palmer, light ice, unsweetened tea!"

The waitress turned to Tripp as he ordered, "I'll have a regular Coke and a basket of Buffalo Shrimp!"

The girl turned toward the kitchen as Carl lifted a brown paper bag and set it on the table, then tore it open and revealed its golden content. Tripp's face lit up in delight as he reached for a deep-fried treasure. After forcing the first ring into his mouth and crunching it into submission, he proclaimed, "Man! Ain't nothin' better than Shorty's onion rings on a stake-out!"

Carl grinned and turned to look across the sun-drenched marina. The air was still, the water was as smooth as glass, not a cloud in the sky, and the

Pelicans waited, perched on the roof of the Turtle Museum and floating in the kraal behind the trim table where, soon, they hoped to be feasting on the scraps thrown high in the air by the skilled filleters of the day's catch. The waitress made her delivery, and the two officers of justice focused on the details of their intention.

"How do you want to approach this?" Tripp asked.

Carl finished off a shrimp, wiped his hands of the red sticky sauce, then laid out his plan. "I made a call to the Key West Marine Unit Chief, and he's got a patrol boat watching for them to approach the harbor. When we get their call, I'll need you standing over in the shade on the back side of the Turtle Museum, while they pull into their slip. I've put out word that we're just here to shake these guys up and see how they react. I'll hold back until Campanello kills his engine and finishes shaking down his clients for tip money, then I'll throw out a rope and see if he wants to tie it around his neck. I've had several run-ins with this guy over the years, and he'll probably realize he's in trouble when he sees me heading his way. If we're lucky, he'll have both his mates with him. Once everybody is off the boat, the captain will be cleaning up and putting away the gear. When the mates are working on the fish, you show up and keep them from getting back on the boat. They won't know who you are, so just play it cool till I get the captain cornered. If this thing doesn't go south, we should be fine, but just in case, take a look up there."

Carl pointed to the upper deck bar tower, on the roof of the *Turtle Kraal's Restaurant*. Tripp looked through the window and bent low to get a better view. Two police officers were sitting at the corner table, perched with a perfect view of the dock. "Check over there." Carl directed Tripp to look out the window on the other side of the room. Another officer offered a thumbs-up, from the back side of the Dockmaster's Office. Carl next pointed into the parking lot. Tripp slid his chair back to see two more officers standing strategically ready to assist, one on each side of the lot.

Tripp scooted his chair back to the table, grabbed another onion ring, and dipped it into the hot sauce on the shrimp tray. "Ya know, you are one cagey son of a bitch! These guys haven't got a chance!"

Carl picked up his phone to take an incoming call and winked his eye at his friend as he answered, "This is Dixon!" Three seconds later, "Thanks, Chief! We're all set! Appreciate it!" He pushed back from the table and stood up for a clearer view of the harbor, and said, "They just idled into the marina. Let's get ready."

Tripp dropped a twenty-dollar bill on the table, then headed out the front door and into the hot sunlight.

The waitress approached and asked, "Are you guys finished?" Carl dropped a second twenty on the table and smiled as he nodded his answer. He walked over to the window and stood, waiting for the *Sea Witch III* to come into view. He saw the outriggers and the top of the flying bridge above the roofing on the Dockmaster's office, slowly making way. She was an old Bertram 37 Convertible, built in 1987 and outfitted beautifully for any type of offshore angling. Powered by two 375-horsepower, CAT diesels, she was considered a reliable and comfortable prize and a perfect dreamboat for any charter boat captain.

His phone rang, "Dixon!"

"Here we go!" Tripp was watching as the *Sea Witch III* negotiated its way into position and began backing into her slip. "Looks like he's got 'em both on board!"

Carl was watching from the Oyster Bar window. "Just what we hoped for!" He admitted.

Tripp was startled when the open window to the Turtle Museum slammed shut over his right shoulder. Several more slams led him to realize that the museum was about to close. Carl watched from across the water, as Bo stepped through the huge sliding door and placed the lock into the hoop, then shoved it closed and walked away. He looked over his shoulder as he cleared the edge of the building and took note of Tripp, standing in the shade. The fumes of the two diesel engines billowed up from the transom of the *Sea Witch,* as it slowly backed closer and closer to the stone causeway wall. Tripp held his breath for as long as he could, then stepped further down the dock where the air was clearer. Bo waved to Captain Campanello and headed toward the parking lot, while the two mates secured the tie downs and readied their clients to be offloaded with their prized bounty of fish.

"All right, gentlemen, I hope we passed the audition!" Captain Campanello skillfully cornered the main bigshot against the back of the fighting chair and held his bloodied hand out, ready to receive an expected, yet probably unearned, gratuity that he may or may not share with his mates. It was a dirty industry! Built on tricks of the trade, protected by unscrupulous navigators of the weaknesses of ego-driven men with big fat purses of gold and the scruples of sewer-dwelling slime bugs. Carl watched the unfolding drama with disdain. He knew this captain's game! He was one of the ones that you could never trust, and now, he was the target! Carl was encouraged when the last of the three fat-cat suckers pulled himself from the boat and joined his friends at the blood-soaked catch table, to watch the murderous knives tearing through the flesh of the beautiful dorados that lay on the dock, gulping their last breaths of air into their dying bodies. The pelicans jumped and flurried feverishly to catch the throw off as the harvesting proceeded. Tarpon ravenously bit at the pieces of skin that the pelicans missed. Yes, it's a brutal industry of charter! They pay for the right to kill!

Tripp had moved into the crowd of tourists that had gathered by the table, hoping to catch that perfect picture of a yellow-head jumping into the air and catching a morsel of fresh-cut fish gut in its bellowed beak. The two mates were busy skillfully filleting the Mahi-Mahi and working the crowd for applause, like masters of a circus side show.

The captain didn't notice the detective standing on the dock behind his boat. He was busy washing the scales and fish blood through the flush ports around his newly painted deck. Carl stood, with the sunset over his shoulder, looking down into the deck of *The Sea Witch III*, and its clueless captain.

"That is one beautiful paint job!" he called out. "What kind of paint did you use to get that kind of shine?"

Captain Campanello turned and held his hand up high in the air to block the blinding glare from the sun. Unable to see who had asked, he volunteered, "That's Baybright paint! Best on tha market!" He remained locked upon the shadowed outline of the man. His curiosity beckoned him to follow his instinct and continue the engagement. "You lookin' to go fishin'?"

Carl stepped to his left, into the shadow cast by the high metal roof of the museum, and answered, "No thanks! I'm thinking about having my Shamrock hauled out and her bottom painted sometime next year. Just wondering how you got yours looking so good."

The captain was gripped by a silent fear. No words came to his rescue! After several seconds of staring up at the menacing specter from his past, he turned back to the hosing off of his boat and convinced himself he was dreaming.

"Campanello, isn't it?" Carl crouched down till his buttocks bounced off his ankles. He rested his elbows on his knees, crossed his fingers, right hand into left, and called out his request, "Permission ta come aboard, captain!"

He was toying with him like a kitten playing with a cockroach. Eric was too mad to speak.

"I'm sorry, Captain. Was that, 'Come aboard'? I don't hear as well as I used to." He set one foot on the gunnel and landed his other on the deck of the boat. "God damn!" he said. "She's a beauty!"

The captain moved to the back of the boat and kept flushing debris through the ports. He turned his back to the detective and glanced anxiously up at the cleaning station, where a crowd of people were watching the two mates bagging up the last of the filets.

"Boy, those guys are going to have one hell of a great dinner tonight. Don't you think so, Captain?" Carl knew everything anybody needed to know about fishing. Growing up in Key West, he had probably caught every kind of fish you could find. From the reefs at Sombrero to the flats of Islamorada, he'd fished in and around every body of water there was.

"Those looked like schoolies your boys threw on the dock. Is that what they were, Eric, schoolies?"

The captain turned off the water and tossed the hose back up on the dock. He made his way to the ladder and climbed to the upper level of the tower, where he began gathering gear and storing it in the compartment below the flying bridge controls. Then he climbed back down, turned toward Carl, and asked, "What do you want from me, detective? You're not out here to talk about fish! Now, what is it you want to say to me?"

Carl pulled a disingenuous smile out of his bag of cop tricks, and pasted it across his lips, then said, "Aw now, Captain, I'm just pickled tink ta be having a little chat with my ol' buddy, Eric Campanello! I was just passin' by and saw you pullin' in, and thought to myself, it sure would be nice ta spend a little quality time, catchin' up with ol' Eric. That ain't nothin ta get worked up about, now! Is it?"

The captain was boiling mad! He hit the backrest of the fighting chair, then turned toward the cabin door and grabbed the handle. Through clenched teeth, he muttered, "You can get tha fuck off my boat now!" Then he disappeared into the dark cabin and locked the door behind him.

Carl took a seat in the chair and watched as the crowd on the dock began to thin out. The last of the fish were bagged and handed to the three charter clients, then the tourists began wandering back toward the main dock.

Tripp stood facing the two mates who were hosing down the trim table with the hose that hung from its side. One of the mates turned and saw Tripp watching them from behind. He nudged his partner, and in unison, they turned and faced him. Tripp stood boldly with his arms crossed and his legs planted firmly.

"Man," he said, "You guys are really talented!"

He could see the panic in their eyes. One filet knife was still on the table, and the other had been sheathed on the younger man's belt.

"You need something?" asked the taller of the duo. Tripp's badge and gun were on full display. The young men had no doubt who he was, and no clue of what he was going to do.

"Naw, man!" Trip grinned as he spoke. "I'm just hanging out, enjoyin' tha show!"

The two officers in the tower were now standing at the junction of the main dock and the causeway to the museum. One stood on one side, one on the other. Two patrol cars were slowly approaching, through the Margaret Street parking lot, while the officer at the dockmasters building moved toward the entrance to the Turtle Museum, then stood, watching attentively. The young men were cornered, and they knew it. The taller one glanced over at the knife on the table, and Tripp advised him, "Not a chance in hell, buddy!" He grinned and added, "If you think you could get to that knife before I could put a bullet through your brain, go ahead! Give it a try!"

The younger thug raised his hands in the air and began to cry bitterly. "I knew we'd get caught!" He moaned in despair as he dropped to his knees. "I told you we shouldn't have done it!"

"Shut up, God damn it! Shut up!" The second young man was furious.

Captain Campanello pushed through the cabin door and yelled at him, "Shut up, you fucking bastard! They don't have anything on us, you idiot! If they did, they'd have arrested us already! Shut up!"

Carl was standing beside the fighting chair with his hand on the handle of his gun. "You really believe that, Eric? You think we're that stupid?"

The captain backed against the wheel and began to face the bitter reality. He was caught! The younger mate was throwing up on the dock and bellowing like a lovestruck mule. "He made us do it! I didn't want to! He told us we had to, but I didn't want to kill him! I didn't want to!"

Tripp grabbed the knife off the table and tossed it on the ground behind him, then ordered the taller mate to put his hands behind his back. The man complied, and Tripp pulled a set of cuffs from his belt, then said, "You have the right to remain silent. Anything you say can, and will, be used against you in a court of law..." As Tripp continued, the police officers approached the other mate and placed him in custody.

Carl's arms were crossed across his broad chest. His eyes were fixed on the sloppily dressed, blood-covered captain, and he said, "Man, I sure do wish I'd ordered those hearing aids I saw on TV last week! I can barely hear what's going on up there. It almost sounds like he's reading them their Miranda rights." The captain's eyes were shifting between the scene on the dock and the detective on his boat. His breathing betrayed his hope for control, and his heart was caught in a marathon. Realizing the fate of the situation, he turned slowly and put his wrists behind his back. Carl unsnapped the handcuff pouch on his belt and began reading the captain his rights. "You have the right to...".

Several police officers climbed into the boat to assist with the big man's extraction. Tripp stepped across the dock and stood, looking down at his friend. "I'd say that went pretty smooth!"

Carl chuckled, "To be honest, I feel like a blue marlin just jumped into my boat!" Tripp reached for his friend's hand and pulled him from the deck of the *Sea Witch III*.

As they walked the short stretch to the parking lot, they waved to the tourists who were holding their camera phones out through the open restaurant windows and on the sidewalks. The cheers and applause brought chills to the crusaders' spines. They stopped in the middle of the roadway and shook hands, then headed toward their respective vehicles.

"Siri!" Carl directed his mysterious minion, "Call Barb!" It was always the first call he made when he had successfully walked away from a risky situation. She was his selfish reward for crafting his way, unscathed, through the fires he had dedicated himself to extinguishing. Just the sound of her sweet voice melted his stress away.

"Hey, sweetie!" she answered. "Did you make it back from Miami ok?"

26. A FLASH of GREEN

Carl closed his laptop, stood to his feet, pulled his service weapon from the top drawer of his desk, then stepped into the hallway and turned toward the elevator. There was a deep feeling of satisfaction permeating through his conscience as he stepped through the doors and pushed the down button. He walked through the parking lot, tired and proud. His phone rang. "Dixon!" he answered.

"Well!" The voice brought an immediate smile to his face. "Am I the first to offer you congratulations for a job well done?"

"Depends!" he replied. "If you're referring to that score I made last week on the White Street Bocce court, naw! That one got loads of grats already!"

Markus chuckled, then asked, "Are you home yet?"

"Not yet. I'm just leaving the office. It's been a long day!" Carl answered.

"Well, I guess you wouldn't have heard it yet, but your afternoon take-down of that trio of killers just got played on the six o'clock news! Apparently, it was being recorded by a guy having dinner with his wife, who works for Channel Seven in Miami. He was shooting from one of the windows at Turtle Kraal's Restaurant. You look pretty damn good for an old guy!"

Carl slid into the front seat and turned the key. "I'm sure I'll hear all about it from Barb when I walk through the door. There wasn't much to it, ya know!" He sighed, then continued, "Sad thing is, Billy wasn't even a threat to that guy! It was one big misunderstanding, and that's all! Now, there are all these lives left in the aftermath. Sad!"

Markus felt sympathetic and offered, "Well, I wanted you to know that the word is out. No telling how it's going to play with the homies!" A somber silence was his cue to finish the call. "Anyway, have a good weekend! I'll talk to you later on!"

"You bet, doc! Thanks!" Carl turned onto U.S. One and headed home to his wonderful life, with his beautiful wife and a golden retriever named Nacho.

"You're not planning on sleeping all day, are you?" She was dripping wet, standing on the deck in her tiny bikini, looking through the open French doors at him lying in bed, twisted up in her favorite top sheet. "Hey, I'm talkin' to you, mister!" she yelled.

He heard a splash from the backyard pool, below the deck. "Leave me alone!" he moaned.

A minute passed, and she launched herself into the only space on the mattress not yet claimed by his sprawl. He was used to her abuse. He just hoped she wouldn't start... Oh! Oh! There she was! Licking his underarm! He jumped to his feet and bumped his head on the slow-spinning blade of the ceiling fan.

"You are such a disgusting animal!" he scolded. "Don't you ever do that to me again!" He was mad as hell! She was laughing like a deranged banshee. Nacho climbed the stairs and shook herself dry in the morning sunshine, then started barking wildly at them both. That was their Saturday routine! Not much different than the one they'd choose on Sunday. It was held, perfectly in place, by love!

"Breakfast in five!" she yelled from the kitchen.

He strutted through the bedroom door with a pink towel wrapped around his waist and shaving cream smeared over one-half of his face. "Any plans for what you want to do today?"

She stepped to the table and set a platter of pancakes next to his coffee cup. Looking up, she said, "Well, as a matter of fact, yes, I did! But," her voice dropped into her seductive, Barbie mode. "I could be persuaded to change them if you have something else in mind!" She turned back toward the kitchen, but kept her eyes locked on him. She stuck her finger in her mouth and slowly pulled downward on her lower lip. She was a sultry devil sometimes! His favorite tease! "I was thinking, maybe we could go chase hogfish out at Sambo Reef. The weather's perfect and tha visibility's probably over fifteen feet. We can throw the skid off the back, and you can pull me around for a while."

She loved to fish! It was one of her favorite ways to spend a Saturday, and one of the passions that made him fall in love with her over thirty years earlier. "Sound good?"

He returned to the bathroom sink and finished shaving, then stepped back into the doorway, ripped the towel from his waist, and wiped the last of the foam from his chin. Barb set his plate of eggs on the table, looked up at him, and joked, "I think that pole's a little light for hogfish, sweetie!"

They laughed as he pulled his shorts on and fastened his belt. His huge chest was her favorite nature walk. She wrapped her arms around him and began nuzzling through his wildly thick and manly forest of chest hair, gently planting kisses as she wandered between his pecks.

"Swack!" He landed a wake-up call on her bikini-clad backside, then demanded, "Let's eat!"

They had just gotten seated when his phone buzzed on the table to alert him of an incoming text. She shook her head and twisted her lip in disapproval as he tilted it and read the ID. "It's Tripp!" he said as he wiped his mouth and lifted the phone for viewing.

"What's it say?" she asked.

He finished reading the note, then slid it over for her to read while he shoveled a forkful of syrup-doused cakes into his mouth. She read the note, then pushed a couple of buttons, and set the phone back down on the table.

Tripp's voice greeted, "Hey!"

Barb swallowed her egg and washed the remnants out of her mouth with coffee, then asked, "Is Meg going?"

Carl stiffened his back and tighten his grip on his knife and fork, then threw a frown toward her.

Trip answered, "She's already got the boat loaded up with picnic stuff. I'm watchin' her, now, stowin' my drone and my fishin' gear on board."

"What time are they gonna get started?" Barb asked.

"Coreen said everything starts at 1400 hours. Meg wants to go fishin' out at Content Key before we head over. You guys wanna go?"

Barb ignored Carl's gestures of defiance and offered a confident response, "See ya on tha beach!" then pushed the phone back across the table toward him.

"What?" he exclaimed, while holding both hands in the air. "Am I just wallpaper?"

She ignored him completely. "Pass me the salt and pepper when you're finished with that whine, will ya?"

Tripp's text had addressed a plan for a celebration of Billy's life, to be held on Christmas Tree Island that afternoon. It had begun with the reports of Friday's arrest of Captain Campanello and his cohorts in crime. Devin had suggested the idea to Coreen, and she had spent all night designing posters to promote it. The Coconut Telegraph would be setting phones ablaze, as the friends and fans of Three I'd Billy passed the plan across and around the island.

Captain Witt's wife, Kitty, ramrodded a plan to have the whole thing catered by Conrad Gilmore's popular eatery, *Harpoon Harry's*, and Janeene and Rocco Brantley's place, *Blue Heaven*. Tom Hargrove, the guy who owns *Danger Cruises,* would move two of his schooners over to the dock at the end of Simonton Street to ferry any attendees who wanted to sail over, and Keenen Moyer of *The Southernmost Water Puppies Excursions, Inc.,* offered to provide a rack of kayaks for people who wanted to paddle over, all at no charge to the public.

In the plan's earliest hours, it was proving the promise of becoming a hugely successful celebration and was billed as the *See ya on the Beach Celebration of Life*. Billy always used that as his way of saying goodbye! He ended his phone calls with it, signed autographs with it, and always said it when he walked away from anyone. He used to say that it was his way of paying tribute to the soldiers who had died over on the beaches of Normandy in World War II. They were the last words that they heard before the ramps on the landing craft dropped open on the sand, and they charged, arm in arm, into the wall of German bullets that would deliver them into the hands of eternity. Billy was a Navy man! A champion for freedom! A world-class hero! And a friend to the downtrodden of his beloved little island!

Markus was about to slide into his recliner, expecting to enjoy his morning cup of coffee and a casual read of the news, when his phone rang.

"It's a great day to be alive at the Grant house! You have the Admiral's attention!" It was his favorite captain on the line.

"Good morning, Markus!" Witt greeted his friend. "I know it's Saturday, but I wanted to check and see if you might like to join Walt, Kitty, me, and a whole lot of other great people for a celebration, out on the island."

Markus tossed his paper on the couch and focused his attention on the call. "What's going on out there?"

Witt explained, "Well, with the recent discovery of Billy's murder and Carl's arrest of the guys who did it, Devin and some of Billy's music buddies have put together a kind of celebration of his life. It's starting to look like a big event. Walt and I were hoping you and Jan might join us, so we tossed a quarter to see who'd make the call. I won! Or lost, depending on how ya look at it. What do ya say? I can pick you up at one!"

Markus looked at his watch, then made his decision. He had three hours to get ready. "Sounds fabulous! I'll have Jan start packing up some snacks and chill a bottle of wine."

"Great!" Captain Witt exclaimed. "I'll ferry everybody over to the island in the dinghy, and we can stay until you've had enough. Sound good?"

"Thanks! It does! Real good! We'll meet you over on the dock. I'll drive my cart over, though! You can just be there to help me get up on the boat."

The captain finished with, "I am so glad you're going to join us! It'll be fun! I guarantee it!"

Later that day, he steered the *Psyched Out* through the marina, rounded the breakwater, then turned toward Christmas Tree Island.

"Holy Moly!" he called out in surprise. "Look at this!"

The deep waterway passage between Key West and Christmas Tree Island was crowded with power boats, paddleboards, kayaks, sailboats, jet skis, dinghies, and even a few kite surfers, all headed toward the little island and Three I'd Billy's, *Celebration of Life.*

Unfortunately, my health has been on the decline recently, and limited me from being able to join Markus and the others for the trip, but later on, I walked out to my favorite little spot behind the Dockmaster's office and pulled the old green chair from behind the ice machine and sat down, waiting for the sunset. I could hear the music and the crowd singing along to some of Billy's songs. The sky was absolutely brilliant! The sunset was a spectacular blaze of gold, yellow, and red! The stage was set, and with just the right amount of luck, a flash of green might seal the closing of the day. As she slowly dropped toward the horizon, the crowd of people made their way to the beach, on the back side of the island, and watched with fingers crossed.

I was startled by the unexpected movement of something to my right, and turned to look. It was Devin McCollum, at the controls of his fishing boat, pulling away from the dock with another fishing boat in tow. He was headed out of the marina. I waved to him as he idled past the dockmaster's office, then I read the boat's name, painted on the transom, *Sea Witch III*. When he cleared the breakwater, he gunned his engines and headed toward the western horizon.

A few minutes later, the crowd was counting down as the sun began to melt into its final descent. Their voices roared across the glassy waters. Five, four, three, two... The applause and celebratory cheers rolled like waves through the evening air, as the sun sank behind the thin line that holds tomorrow at bay, then, a kiss of green and the timeless keeper of light disappeared.

The jubilation was spine-tingling! Seconds passed! The cheers died back to a raucous rumble of booming music and exuberant celebration. I folded the green chair and pushed it back into its hiding place behind the ice machine, then turned to walk back to my little cottage on Eaton Street. I flipped the latch and pushed open the gate, then just as I placed my foot on the first step to climb to my beautifully decorated porch, I heard a loud explosion ricochet through the trees, followed by the roar of a crowd. Saphire was pacing from one side of the porch to the other, meowing sweetly, as she always did, announcing her joy to see my return. I sat down in my favorite wicker chair and Saphire leaped into my lap, then began her soulful purring. I love this ol' blue-eyed cat! I remember the day she followed me home from *Pepe's*! Changed my life!

Anyway, I didn't have a clue what could have caused that explosion till I was getting ready for bed, listening to the news.

"It was billed as *Three I'd Billy's Celebration of Life*, and drew crowds of residents and visitors to the little island at the end of the road. Cayo Hueso, more commonly known as Key West." Don Tarkenton began the next segment on Saturday's eleven o'clock news.

"That's right, Don!" Candice Ramerez picked up the story. "City officials estimate over four thousand revelers took their lives into their own hands and braved the crossing of the treacherous passage between Key West and Wisteria Island, more commonly known as Christmas Tree Island, to attend the celebration of life, held to honor a local musician, whose mysterious death was just upgraded from a possible accident to murder. For more on this story, we turn to our Key West affiliate at WCAY TV, Jennifer Landon James."

"Thank you, Candice! I'm here on the Key West out island, Christmas Tree Island, with Devin McCollum, the originator and Chief Director of Programs for the event held today to commemorate the life of local musician and songwriter Billy Chapman. Mr. McCollum, it appears this event is turning out to be a..."

The video stopped abruptly with a loud explosion! The camera shook wildly from the percussive blast. Then, as the cameraman recovered, he panned across the horizon and focused on a lone fishing boat consumed in flames, drifting slowly out to sea. I removed my glasses and set them on the nightstand, pushed the 'off' button on the TV's remote, pressed my head deeply into my pillow, then whispered into my iPhone, "Siri, play *I'm Not Supposed to Care*, by Gordon Lightfoot." Then I closed my eyes and fell, once again, into the waiting arms of innocence and bliss.

THE END

PS: May all your Maydays find a hero's ear!

27. Epilogue

It's been 2 weeks since the Monroe County Sheriff's Marine Patrol towed Eric Campanello's burned-out Sea Witch III to the impound dock on Stock Island. No one seems to know how it got out of the harbor, or who set it ablaze. That just may remain another one of those Key West mysteries that never gets solved, like whatever happened to Bum Farto. Anyway, I'll be picking up Dr. Grant in one hour and driving him up to Miami to check on Jeannie. Her father and brother are down from Vero Beach, and Markus wants to go over his plan for her long-term care, to be covered by the foundation. I'm always thrilled when he calls and asks me to drive him somewhere in his Land Cruiser. To Sanford, to catch the Auto Train up to Virginia, Miami for a meeting with his accountants, or just a shopping trip to the other side of the island, it never matters to me! Janet hasn't driven for ten years now, since being diagnosed with macular degeneration. And as for Markus, well, even on his good days, the gout just about cripples him. Anyway, I've been retired from social work for over a year now, and always looking for ways to occupy my time and challenge my thinking. I try to stay in a perpetual state of wonder! Humph, like what really did happen to Bum Farto?

See ya on the Beach!

Ian Ritchie Stewart

28. Photo Gallery

The *Psyched Out* in the Key West mooring field

Captain Witt at the helm of the *Psyched Out*

The *Psyched Out cabin, where the counseling was done*

Harpoon Harry's Restaurant

Billy's Booth at Harpoon Harry's

The Galleon and A&B Marina (see chapter 1)

Reach Thrift, where Cairo bought his table, chairs, and wine glasses, and
Guy's Meats, where Cairo bought wine, before catching the southbound to
Miami (see chapter 20)

The repainted boat that destroyed Billy's lungs (see chapter 24)

The fish cleaning station at Turtle Kraals (see chapter 25)

The Key West dinghy dock, just outside the Key West Turtle Museum

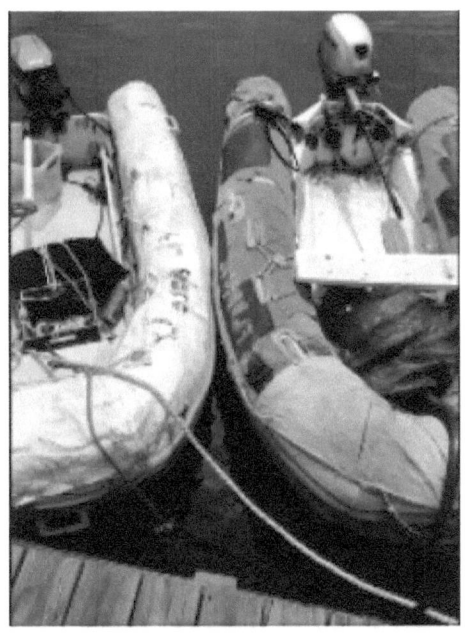

Key West Turtle Museum, next to the Key West dinghy dock. Billy's dinghy is on the right, before the "accident".

Inside the Key West Turtle Museum

Billy's autographed guitar (see Chapter 15)

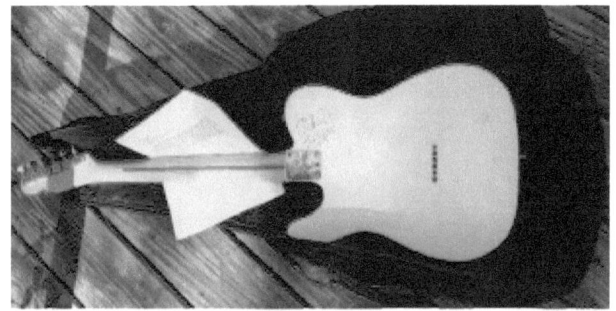

Billy's boat, The Ghillie Dhu

This book is dedicated to Rear Admiral Dr. Bertram S. Brown, for his support, inspiration and friendship. Dr. Brown, with the author.

Don't miss out!

Visit the website below and you can sign up to receive emails whenever Ian Ritchie Stewart publishes a new book. There's no charge and no obligation.

https://books2read.com/r/B-A-HHQCB-RJSDH

BOOKS 2 READ

Connecting independent readers to independent writers.

Did you love *The Legend of Three I'd Billy*? Then you should read *Lost Souls of Paradise*[1] by Ian Ritchie Stewart!

[2]

This compelling and compassionate mystery takes place in the quirky and intoxicating island town of Key West Florida where 21-year-old Jillian Dougherty, a newly graduated Boston nursing school student away from home for the first time, finds herself completely absorbed into the homeless population. Meet the island inhabitants who live under the bridges, behind the hedges, and on the edge of sanity in this tourist island mecca. Follow Jillian as she is swept away on the home-built sailboat 'Canadian Soul' to the Caribbean Island of St. John. Lost Souls of Paradise is a book for beachcombers. Those of us who glue our eyes to the sand with the highest expectation, in search of that hidden treasure that lies waiting to be discovered just beyond our next step. A shell, a shark's tooth, a pattern in the sand worth storing in memory, or a gold doubloon stolen by a pirate and lost to the sea; it really doesn't matter how big or small, how obscure or insignificant, it is the lost

1. https://books2read.com/u/merJxV

2. https://books2read.com/u/merJxV

time, as we indulge in our search, that causes us to value the experience. May you find yourself enjoyably lost for a little while, as you walk the beach with Ian, searching for the Lost Souls of Paradise. Approximately 330 pages

Read more at https://www.lostsoulsofparadise.com/.

Also by Ian Ritchie Stewart

Lost Souls of Paradise
The Legend of Three I'd Billy

Standalone
Lost Souls of Paradise

Watch for more at https://www.lostsoulsofparadise.com/.

About the Author

Florida native, Ian Ritchie Stewart delivers a unique perspective on living life at the "End of the Road". As a Community-Based Care Social Worker, Family Services Coordinator, and long-time resident of the Florida Keys, Mr. Stewart is profoundly familiar with the hidden pitfalls and challenges that lie in wait, ready to swallow the dreams of ill-prepared seekers of Paradise!

Read more at https://www.lostsoulsofparadise.com/.

www.ingramcontent.com/pod-product-compliance
Lightning Source LLC
Chambersburg PA
CBHW020749250626
47155CB00003B/994